Aristotle and Dante Discover the Secrets of the Universe

ALSO BY BENJAMIN ALIRE SÁENZ

POETRY

Calendar of Dust

Dark and Perfect Angels

Elegies in Blue

Que Linda la Brisa

Dreaming the End of War

The Book of What Remains

FICTION

Flowers for the Broken

Carry Me Like Water

The House of Forgetting

In Perfect Light

Names on a Map

YOUNG ADULT

Sammy and Juliana in Hollywood

He Forgot to Say Goodbye

Last Night I Sang to the Monster

CHILDREN'S BOOKS

A Gift from Papa Diego

Grandma Fina and Her Wonderful Umbrellas

A Perfect Season for Dreaming

The Dog Who Loved Tortillas

Aristotle and Dante Discover the Secrets of the Universe

BENJAMIN ALIRE SÁENZ

SIMON & SCHUSTER BFYR
NEW YORK   LONDON   TORONTO   SYDNEY   NEW DELHI

An imprint of Simon & Schuster Children's Publishing Division
1230 Avenue of the Americas, New York, New York 10020
This book is a work of fiction. Any references to historical events, real people, or real places are used fictitiously. Other names, characters, places, and events are products of the author's imagination, and any resemblance to actual events or places or persons, living or dead, is entirely coincidental.
Copyright © 2012 by Benjamin Alire Sáenz
All rights reserved, including the right of reproduction in whole or in part in any form.
SIMON & SCHUSTER BFYR is a trademark of Simon & Schuster, Inc.
For information about special discounts for bulk purchases, please contact Simon & Schuster Special Sales at 1-866-506-1949 or business@simonandschuster.com.
The Simon & Schuster Speakers Bureau can bring authors to your live event. For more information or to book an event, contact the Simon & Schuster Speakers Bureau at 1-866-248-3049 or visit our website at www.simonspeakers.com.
Also available in a SIMON & SCHUSTER BFYR hardcover edition
Book design by Chloë Foglia
The text for this book is set in Berling.
Manufactured in the United States of America
First SIMON & SCHUSTER BFYR paperback edition April 2014
22 24 26 28 30 29 27 25 23 21
The Library of Congress has cataloged the hardcover edition as follows:
Sáenz, Benjamin Alire.
Aristotle and Dante discover the secrets of the universe / Benjamin Alire Sáenz.
p. cm.
Summary: Fifteen-year-old Ari Mendoza is an angry loner with a brother in prison, but when he meets Dante and they become friends, Ari starts to ask questions about himself, his parents, and his family that he has never asked before.
ISBN 978-1-4424-0892-0 (hc)
[1. Coming of age—Fiction. 2. Families—Fiction. 3. Mexican-Americans—Fiction. 4. Friendship—Fiction. 5. Homosexuality—Fiction.] I. Title.
PZ7.S1273Ar 2012
[Fic]—dc22
2010033649
ISBN 978-1-4424-0893-7 (pbk)
ISBN 978-1-4424-0894-4 (eBook)

To all the boys who've had to learn

to play by different rules

Acknowledgments

I had second thoughts about writing this book. In fact, after I finished the first chapter or so, I had almost decided to abandon the project. But I'm lucky and blessed enough to be surrounded by committed, brave, talented, and intelligent people who inspired me to finish what I started. This book would not have been written without them. So here is my small and certainly incomplete list of people I'd like to thank: Patty Moosebrugger, great agent, great friend. Daniel and Sasha Chacon for their great affection and their belief that I needed to write this book. For Hector, Annie, Ginny, and Barbara, who have always been there. My editor, David Gale, who believed in his book and the whole team at Simon & Schuster, especially Navah Wolfe. My colleagues in the Creative Writing Department whose work and generosity continually challenge me to be a better writer and a better person. And finally, I would like to thank my students, past and present, who remind me that language and writing will always matter. My gratitude to all of you.

WHY DO WE SMILE? WHY DO WE LAUGH? WHY DO we feel alone? Why are we sad and confused? Why do we read poetry? Why do we cry when we see a painting? Why is there a riot in the heart when we love? Why do we feel shame? What is that thing in the pit of your stomach called desire?

The Different Rules of Summer

The problem with my life was that it was someone else's idea.

One

ONE SUMMER NIGHT I FELL ASLEEP, HOPING THE WORLD would be different when I woke. In the morning, when I opened my eyes, the world was the same. I threw off the sheets and lay there as the heat poured in through my open window.

My hand reached for the dial on the radio. "Alone" was playing. Crap, "Alone," a song by a group called Heart. Not my favorite song. Not my favorite group. Not my favorite topic. "You don't know how long . . ."

I was fifteen.

I was bored.

I was miserable.

As far as I was concerned, the sun could have melted the blue right off the sky. Then the sky could be as miserable as I was.

The DJ was saying annoying, obvious things like, "It's summer! It's hot out there!" And then he put on that retro Lone Ranger tune, something he liked to play every morning because he thought it was a hip way to wake up the world. "Hi-yo, Silver!" Who hired this guy? He was killing me. I think that as we listened to the William Tell Overture, we were supposed to be imagining the Lone Ranger and

Tonto riding their horses through the desert. Maybe someone should have told that guy that we all weren't ten-year-olds anymore. "Hi-yo, Silver!" Crap. The DJ's voice was on the airwaves again: "Wake up, El Paso! It's Monday, June fifteenth, 1987! 1987! Can you believe it? And a big 'Happy Birthday' goes out to Waylon Jennings, who's fifty years old today!" Waylon Jennings? This was a rock station, dammit! But then he said something that hinted at the fact that he might have a brain. He told the story about how Waylon Jennings had survived the 1959 plane crash that killed Buddy Holly and Richie Valens. On that note, he put on the remake of "La Bamba" by Los Lobos.

"La Bamba." I could cope with that.

I tapped my bare feet on the wood floor. As I nodded my head to the beat, I started wondering what had gone through Richie Valens's head before the plane crashed into the unforgiving ground. *Hey, Buddy! The music's over.*

For the music to be over so soon. For the music to be over when it had just begun. That was really sad.

Two

I WALKED INTO THE KITCHEN. MY MOM WAS PREPARING lunch for a meeting with her Catholic-Church-lady friends. I poured myself a glass of orange juice.

My mom smiled at me. "Are you going to say good morning?"

"I'm thinking about it," I said.

"Well, at least you dragged yourself out of bed."

"I had to think about it for a long time."

"What is it about boys and sleep?"

"We're good at it." That made her laugh. "Anyway, I wasn't sleeping. I was listening to 'La Bamba.'"

"Richie Valens," she said, almost whispering. "So sad."

"Just like your Patsy Cline."

She nodded. Sometimes I caught her singing that song, "Crazy," and I'd smile. And she'd smile. It was like we shared a secret. My mom, she had a nice voice. "Plane crashes," my mother whispered. I think she was talking more to herself than to me.

"Maybe Richie Valens died young—but he did something. I mean, *he really did something*. Me? What have I done?"

"You have time," she said. "There's plenty of time." The eternal optimist.

"Well, you have to become a person first," I said.

She gave me a funny look.

"I'm fifteen."

"I know how old you are."

"Fifteen-year-olds don't qualify as people."

My mom laughed. She was a high school teacher. I knew she half agreed with me.

"So what's the big meeting about?"

"We're reorganizing the food bank."

"Food bank?"

"Everyone should eat."

My mom had a thing for the poor. She'd been there. She knew things about hunger that I'd never know.

"Yeah," I said. "I guess so."

"Maybe you can help us out?"

"Sure," I said. I hated being volunteered. The problem with my life was that it was someone else's idea.

"What are you going to do today?" It sounded like a challenge.

"I'm going to join a gang."

"That's not funny."

"I'm Mexican. Isn't that what we do?"

"*Not* funny."

"Not funny," I said. Okay, not funny.

I had the urge to leave the house. Not that I had anywhere to go.

When my mom had her Catholic-Church-lady friends over, I felt like I was suffocating. It wasn't so much that all her friends were over fifty—that wasn't it. And it wasn't even all the comments about how I was turning into a man right before their eyes. I mean, I knew bullshit when I heard it. And as bullshit went, it was the nice, harmless, affectionate kind. I could handle them grabbing me by the shoulders and saying, "Let me look at you. *Dejame ver. Ay que muchacho tan guapo. Te pareces a tu papa.*" Not that there was anything to look at. It was just me. And yeah, yeah, I looked like my dad. I didn't think that was such a great thing.

But what really bugged the living crap out of me was that my mother had more friends than I did. How sad was that?

I decided to go swimming at the Memorial Park pool. It was a small idea. But at least the idea was mine.

As I was walking out the door, my mom took the old towel I'd slung over my shoulder and exchanged it for a better one. There were certain towel rules that existed in my mother's world that I just didn't get. But the rules didn't stop at towels.

She looked at my T-shirt.

I knew a look of disapproval when I saw one. Before she made me change, I gave her one of my own looks. "It's my favorite T-shirt," I said.

"Didn't you wear that yesterday?"

"Yes," I said. "It's Carlos Santana."

"I know who it is," she said.

"Dad gave it to me on my birthday."

"As I recall you didn't seem all that thrilled when you opened your father's gift."

"I was hoping for something else."

"Something else?"

"I don't know. Something else. A T-shirt for my birthday?" I looked at my Mom. "I guess I just don't understand him."

"He's not that complicated, Ari."

"He doesn't talk."

"Sometimes when people talk, they don't always tell the truth."

"Guess so," I said. "Anyway, I'm really into this T-shirt now."

"I can see that." She was smiling.

I was smiling too. "Dad got it at his first concert."

"I was there. I remember. It's old and ratty."

"I'm sentimental."

"Sure you are."

"Mom, it's summer."

"Yes," she said, "it *is* summer."

"Different rules," I said.

"Different rules," she repeated.

I loved the different rules of summer. My mother endured them.

She reached over and combed my hair with her fingers. "Promise me you won't wear it tomorrow."

"Okay," I said. "I promise. But only if you promise not to put it in the dryer."

"Maybe I'll let you wash it yourself." She smiled at me. "Don't drown."

I smiled back. "If I do, don't give my dog away."

The dog thing was a joke. We didn't have one.

Mom, she got my sense of humor. I got hers. We were good that way. Not that she wasn't something of a mystery. One thing that *I completely got*—I got why my father fell in love with her. Why she fell in love with my father was something I still couldn't wrap my head around. Once, when I was about six or seven, I was really mad at my father because I wanted him to play with me and he just seemed so far away. It was like I wasn't even there. I asked my mom with all my boyhood anger, "How could you have married that guy?"

She smiled and combed my hair with her fingers. That was always her thing. She looked straight into my eyes and said calmly, "Your father was beautiful." She didn't even hesitate.

I wanted to ask her what happened to all that beauty.

WHEN I WALKED INTO THE HEAT OF THE DAY, EVEN THE lizards knew better than to be crawling around. Even the birds were laying low. The tarred patches on the cracks of the street were melting. The blue of the sky was pale and it occurred to me that maybe everybody had fled the city and its heat. Or maybe everyone had died like in one of those sci-fi flicks, and I was the last boy on earth. But just as that thought ran through my head, a pack of guys who lived in the neighborhood passed me on their bikes, making me wish I *was* the last boy on earth. They were laughing and messing around and they seemed like they were having a good time. One of the guys yelled at me, "Hey, Mendoza! Hanging out with all your friends?"

I waved, pretending to be a good sport, *ha ha ha*. And then I flipped them the bird.

One of the guys stopped, turned around and started circling me on his bike. "You want to do that again?" he said.

I gave him the bird again.

He stopped his bike right in front of me and tried to stare me down. It wasn't working. I knew who he was. His brother, Javier, had tried to mess with me once. I'd punched the guy. Enemies for life. I wasn't sorry. Yeah, well, I had a temper. I admit it.

He put on his mean voice. Like it scared me. "Don't screw with me, Mendoza."

I gave him the bird again and pointed it at his face just like it was a gun. He just took off on his bike. There were a lot of things I was afraid of—but not guys like him.

Most guys didn't screw with me. Not even guys who ran around in packs. They all passed me on their bikes again, yelling stuff. They were all thirteen and fourteen and messing with guys like me was just a game for them. As their voices faded, I started feeling sorry for myself.

Feeling sorry for myself was an art. I think a part of me liked doing that. Maybe it had something to do with my birth order. You know, I think that was part of it. I didn't like the fact that I was a pseudo only child. I didn't know how else to think of myself. I was an only child without actually being one. That sucked.

My twin sisters were twelve years older. Twelve years was a lifetime. I swear it was. And they'd always made me feel like a baby or a toy or a project or a pet. I'm really into dogs, but sometimes I got the feeling I was nothing more than the family mascot. That's the Spanish word for a dog who's the family pet. *Mascoto*. Mascot. Great. Ari, the family mascot.

And my brother, he was eleven years older. He was even less accessible to me than my sisters. I couldn't even mention his name. Who the hell likes to talk about older brothers who are in prison? Not my mom and dad, that was for sure. Not my sisters either.

Maybe all that silence about my brother did something to me. I think it did. Not talking can make a guy pretty lonely.

My parents were young and struggling when my sisters and brother were born. "Struggling" is my parents' favorite word. Sometime after three children and trying to finish college, my father joined the Marines. Then he went off to war.

The war changed him.

I was born when he came home.

Sometimes I think my father has all these scars. On his heart. In his head. All over. It's not such an easy thing to be the son of a man who's been to war. When I was eight, I overheard my mother talking to my Aunt Ophelia on the phone. "I don't think that the war will ever be over for him." Later I asked my Aunt Ophelia if that was true. "Yes," she said, "it's true."

"But why won't the war leave my dad alone?"

"Because your father has a conscience," she said.

"What happened to him in the war?"

"No one knows."

"Why won't he tell?"

"Because he can't."

So that's the way it was. When I was eight, I didn't know anything about war. I didn't even know what a conscience was. All I knew is that sometimes my father was sad. I hated that he was sad. It made me sad too. I didn't like sad.

So I was the son of a man who had Vietnam living inside him. Yeah, I had all kinds of tragic reasons for feeling sorry for myself. Being fifteen didn't help. Sometimes I thought that being fifteen was the worst tragedy of all.

Four

WHEN I GOT TO THE POOL, I HAD TO TAKE A SHOWER.
That was one of the rules. Yeah, rules. I hated taking a shower with a
bunch of other guys. I don't know, I just didn't like that. You know,
some guys liked to talk a lot, like it was a normal thing to be in
the shower with a bunch of guys and talking about the teacher
you hated or the last movie you saw or the girl you wanted to do
something with. Not me, I didn't have anything to say. Guys in the
shower. Not my thing.

I walked to the pool and sat on the shallow side and put my feet
in the water.

What do you do in a pool when you don't know how to swim?
Learn. I guess that was the answer. I *had* managed to teach my body
to stay afloat on water. Somehow, I'd stumbled on some principal of
physics. And the best part of the whole thing was that I'd made the
discovery all on my own.

All on my own. I was in love with that phrase. I wasn't very good
at asking for help, a bad habit I inherited from my father. And anyway, the swimming instructors who called themselves lifeguards
sucked. They weren't all that interested in teaching a skinny fifteen-
year-old punk how to swim. They were pretty much interested in

girls that had suddenly sprouted breasts. They were obsessed with breasts. That's the truth. I heard one of the lifeguards talking to one of the other lifeguards as he was supposed to be watching a group of little kids. "A girl is like a tree covered with leaves. You just want to climb up and tear all those leaves off."

The other guy laughed. "You're an asshole," he said.

"Nah, I'm a poet," he said. "A poet of the body."

And then they both busted out laughing.

Yeah, sure, they were budding Walt Whitmans, the two of them. See, the thing about guys is that I didn't really care to be around them. I mean, guys really made me uncomfortable. I don't know why, not exactly. I just, I don't know, I just didn't belong. I think it embarrassed the hell out of me that I was a guy. And it really depressed me that there was the distinct possibility that I was going to grow up and be like one of those assholes. *A girl is like a tree?* Yeah, and a guy is about as smart as a piece of dead wood infested with termites. My mom would have said that they were just going through a phase. Pretty soon they would get their brains back. Sure they would.

Maybe life *was* just a series of phases—one phase after another after another. Maybe, in a couple of years, I'd be going through the same phase as the eighteen-year-old lifeguards. Not that I really believed in my mom's phase theory. It didn't sound like an explanation—it sounded like an excuse. I don't think my mom got the whole guy thing. I didn't get the guy thing either. And I was a guy.

I had a feeling there was something wrong with me. I guess I was a mystery even to myself. That sucked. I had serious problems.

One thing was for sure: there was no way I was going to ask one of those idiots to help me out with my swimming. It was better to be alone and miserable. It was better to drown.

So I just kept to myself and sort of floated along. Not that I was having fun.

That's when I heard his voice, kind of squeaky. "I can teach you how to swim."

I moved over to the side of the pool and stood up in the water, squinting into the sunlight. He sat down on the edge of the pool. I looked at him suspiciously. If a guy was offering to teach me how to swim, then for sure he didn't have a life. Two guys without a life? How much fun could that be?

I had a rule that it was better to be bored by yourself than to be bored with someone else. I pretty much lived by that rule. Maybe that's why I didn't have any friends.

He looked at me. Waiting. And then he asked again. "I can teach you how to swim, if you want."

I kind of liked his voice. He sounded like he had a cold, you know, like he was about to lose his voice. "You talk funny," I said.

"Allergies," he said.

"What are you allergic to?"

"The air," he said.

That made me laugh.

"My name's Dante," he said.

That made me laugh harder. "Sorry," I said.

"It's okay. People laugh at my name."

"No, no," I said. "See, it's just that my name's Aristotle."

17

His eyes lit up. I mean, the guy was ready to listen to every word I said.

"Aristotle," I repeated.

Then we both kind of went a little crazy. Laughing.

"My father's an English professor," he said.

"At least you have an excuse. My father's a mailman. Aristotle is the English version of my grandfather's name." And then I pronounced my grandfather's name with this really formal Mexican accent, "*Aristotiles*. And my real first name is Angel." And then I said it in Spanish, "*Angel*."

"Your name is Angel Aristotle?"

"Yeah. That's my real name."

We laughed again. We couldn't stop. I wondered what it was we were laughing about. Was it just our names? Were we laughing because we were relieved? Were we happy? Laughter was another one of life's mysteries.

"I used to tell people my name was Dan. I mean, you know, I just dropped two letters. But I stopped doing that. It wasn't honest. And anyway, I always got found out. And I felt like a liar and an idiot. I was ashamed of myself for being ashamed of myself. I didn't like feeling like that." He shrugged his shoulders.

"Everyone calls me Ari," I said.

"Nice to meet you, Ari."

I liked the way he said *Nice to meet you, Ari*. Like he meant it.

"Okay," I said, "teach me how to swim." I guess I said it like I was doing him a favor. He either didn't notice or didn't care.

Dante was a very precise teacher. He was a real swimmer,

understood everything about the movements of arms and legs and breathing, understood how a body functioned while it was in the water. Water was something he loved, something he respected. He understood its beauty and its dangers. He talked about swimming as if it were a way of life. He was fifteen years old. Who was this guy? He looked a little fragile—but he wasn't. He was disciplined and tough and knowledgeable and he didn't pretend to be stupid and ordinary. He was neither of those things.

He was funny and focused and fierce. I mean the guy could be fierce. And there wasn't anything mean about him. I didn't understand how you could live in a mean world and not have any of that meanness rub off on you. How could a guy live without some meanness?

Dante became one more mystery in a universe full of mysteries.

All that summer, we swam and read comics and read books and argued about them. Dante had all his father's old *Superman* comics. He loved them. He also liked *Archie and Veronica*. I hated that shit. "It's not shit," he said.

Me, I liked Batman, Spider-Man, and the Incredible Hulk.

"Way too dark," Dante said.

"This from a guy who loves Conrad's *Heart of Darkness*."

"That's different," he said. "Conrad wrote literature."

I was always arguing that comic books were literature too. But literature was very serious business for a guy like Dante. I don't remember ever winning an argument with him. He was a better debater. He was also a better reader. I read Conrad's book because of him. When I finished reading it, I told him I hated it. "Except," I said, "it's true. The world is a dark place. Conrad's right about that."

"Maybe your world, Ari, but not mine."

"Yeah, yeah," I said.

"Yeah, yeah," he said.

The truth is, I'd lied to him. I loved the book. I thought it was the most beautiful thing I'd ever read. When my father noticed what I was reading, he told me it was one of his favorite books. I wanted to ask him if he'd read it *before* or *after* he'd fought in Vietnam. It was no good to ask my father questions. He never answered them.

I had this idea that Dante read because he liked to read. Me, I read because I didn't have anything else to do. He analyzed things. I just read them. I have a feeling I had to look up more words in the dictionary than he did.

I was darker than he was. And I'm not just talking about our skin coloring. He told me I had a tragic vision of life. "That's why you like Spider-Man."

"I'm just more Mexican," I said. "Mexicans are a tragic people."

"Maybe so," he said.

"You're the optimistic American."

"Is that an insult?"

"It might be," I said.

We laughed. We always laughed.

We weren't alike, Dante and I. But we did have a few things in common. For one thing, neither one of us was allowed to watch television during the day. Our parents didn't like what television did to a boy's mind. We'd both grown up with lectures that sounded more or less like this: *You're a boy! Get out there and do something! There's a whole world out there just waiting for you . . .*

Dante and I were the last two boys in America who grew up

without television. He asked me one day. "Do you think our parents are right—that there's a whole world out there waiting just for us?"

"I doubt it," I said.

He laughed.

Then I got this idea. "Let's ride the bus and see what's out there."

Dante smiled. We both fell in love with riding the bus. Sometimes we rode around on the bus all afternoon. I told Dante, "Rich people don't ride the bus."

"That's why we like it."

"Maybe so," I said. "Are we poor?"

"No." Then he smiled. "If we ran away from home, we'd both be poor."

I thought that was a very interesting thing to say.

"Would you ever?" I said. "Run away?"

"No."

"Why not?"

"You want me to tell you a secret?"

"Sure."

"I'm crazy about my mom and dad."

That really made me smile. I'd never heard anyone say that about their parents. I mean, no one was crazy about their parents. Except Dante.

And then he whispered in my ear. "That lady two seats in front of us. I think she's having an affair."

"How do you know?" I whispered.

"She took off her wedding band as she got on the bus."

I nodded and smiled.

We made up stories about the other bus riders.

For all we knew, *they* were writing stories about *us*.

I'd never really been very close to other people. I was pretty much a loner. I'd played basketball and baseball and done the Cub Scout thing, tried the Boy Scout thing—but I always kept my distance from the other boys. I never ever felt like I was a part of their world.

Boys. I watched them. Studied them.

In the end, I didn't find most of the guys that surrounded me very interesting. In fact, I was pretty disgusted.

Maybe I was a little superior. But I don't think I was superior. I just didn't understand how to talk to them, how to be myself around them. Being around other guys didn't make me feel smarter. Being around guys made me feel stupid and inadequate. It was like they were all a part of this club and I wasn't a member.

When I was old enough for Boy Scouts, I told my dad I wasn't going to do it. I couldn't stand it anymore.

"Give it a year," my dad said. My dad knew that I sometimes liked to fight. He was always giving me lectures about physical violence. He was trying to keep me away from the gangs at my school. He was trying to keep me from becoming like my brother who wound up in prison. So, because of my brother, whose existence was not even acknowledged, I had to be a good boy scout. That sucked. Why did I have to be a good boy just because I had a bad-boy brother? I hated the way my mom and dad did family math.

I humored my dad. I gave it a year. I hated it—except that I learned how to do CPR. I mean, I didn't like the bit about having to breathe into someone else's mouth. That sort of freaked me out. But for some reason the whole thing fascinated me, how you could get a heart to start again. I didn't quite understand the science of it. But after I got a patch for learning how to bring someone back to life, I quit. I came home and gave the patch to my dad.

"I think you're making a mistake." That's all my dad said.

I'm not going to wind up in the slammer. That's what I wanted to say. Instead, I just mouthed off. "If you make me go back, I swear I'll start smoking pot."

My father gave me a strange look. "It's your life," he said. Like that was really true. And another thing about my father: He didn't give lectures. Not real ones. Which pissed me off. He wasn't a mean guy. And he didn't have a bad temper. He spoke in short sentences: "It's your life." "Give it a try." "You sure you want to do that?" Why couldn't he just talk? How was I supposed to know him when he didn't let me? I hated that.

I got along okay. I had school friends. Sort of. I wasn't wildly popular. How could I be? In order to be wildly popular you had to make people believe that you were fun and interesting. I just wasn't that much of a con artist.

There were a couple of guys I used to hang around with, the Gomez brothers. But they moved away. And there were a couple of girls, Gina Navarro and Susie Byrd, who liked to torment me as a hobby. Girls. They were mysteries too. Everything was a mystery.

I guess I didn't have it so bad. Maybe everybody didn't love me, but I wasn't one of those kids that everyone hated, either.

I was good in a fight. So people left me alone.

I was mostly invisible. I think I liked it that way.

And then Dante came along.

Five

AFTER MY FOURTH SWIMMING LESSON, DANTE INVITED me to go over to his house. He lived less than a block from the swimming pool in a big old house across the street from the park.

He introduced me to his father, the English professor. I'd never met a Mexican-American man who was an English professor. I didn't know they existed. And really, he didn't look like a professor. He was young and handsome and easygoing and it seemed like a part of him was still a boy. He seemed like a man who was in love with being alive. So different from my father, who had always kept his distance from the world. There was a darkness in my father that I didn't understand. Dante's father didn't have any darkness in him. Even his black eyes seemed to be full of light.

That afternoon, when I met Dante's father, he was wearing jeans and a T-shirt and he was sitting on a leather chair in his office, reading a book. I'd never known anyone who actually had an office in his own house.

Dante walked up to his father and kissed him on the cheek. I would have never done that. Not ever.

"You didn't shave this morning, Dad."

"It's summer," his dad said.

"That means you don't have to work."

"That means I have to finish writing my book."

"Writing a book isn't work."

Dante's father laughed really hard when he said that. "You have a lot to learn about work."

"It's summer, Dad. I don't want to hear about work."

"You never want to hear about work."

Dante didn't like where the conversation was going so he tried to change the subject. "Are you going to grow a beard?"

"No." He laughed. "It's too hot. And besides, your mother won't kiss me if I go more than a day without shaving."

"Wow, she's strict."

"Yup."

"And what would you do without her kisses?"

He grinned, then looked up at me. "How do you put up with this guy? You must be Ari."

"Yes, sir." I was nervous. I wasn't used to meeting anybody's parents. Most of the parents I'd met in my life weren't all that interested in talking to me.

He got up from his chair and put his book down. He walked up to me and shook my hand. "I'm Sam," he said. "Sam Quintana."

"Nice to meet you, Mr. Quintana."

I'd heard that phrase, *nice to meet you*, a thousand times. When Dante had said it to me, he'd sounded real. But when I said it, I felt stupid and unoriginal. I wanted to hide somewhere.

"You can call me Sam," he said.

"I can't," I said. God, I wanted to hide.

He nodded. "That's sweet," he said. "And respectful."

The word "sweet" had never passed my father's lips.

He gave Dante a look. "The young man has some respect. Maybe you can learn something from him, Dante."

"You mean you want me to call you Mr. Quintana?"

They both kept themselves from laughing. He turned his attention back to me. "How's the swimming?"

"Dante's a good teacher," I said.

"Dante's good at a lot of things. But he's not very good at cleaning his room. Cleaning a room is too closely related to the word *work*."

Dante shot him a look. "Is that a hint?"

"You're quick, Dante. You must get that from your mother."

"Don't be a wiseass, Dad."

"What was that word you just used?"

"Does that word offend you?'

"It's not the word. Maybe it's the attitude."

Dante rolled his eyes and sat on his father's chair. He took off his tennis shoes.

"Don't get too comfortable." He pointed up. "There's a pig sty up there that has your name on it."

It made me smile, the way they got along, the easy and affectionate way they talked to each other as if love between a father and a son was simple and uncomplicated. My mom and I, sometimes the thing we had between us was easy and uncomplicated. Sometimes. But me and my dad, we didn't have that. I wondered what that would be like, to walk into a room and kiss my father.

We went upstairs and Dante showed me his room. It was a big room with a high ceiling and wood floors and lots of old windows to let in the light. There was stuff everywhere. Clothes spread all over the floor, a pile of old albums, books scattered around, legal pads with stuff written on them, Polaroid photographs, a couple of cameras, a guitar without any strings, sheet music, and a bulletin board cluttered with notes and pictures.

He put on some music. He had a record player. *A real record player from the sixties.* "It was my mom's," he said. "She was going to throw it away. Can you believe that?" He put on *Abbey Road*, his favorite album. "Vinyl," he said. "Real vinyl. None of this cassette crap."

"What's wrong with cassettes?"

"I don't trust them."

I thought that was a really weird thing to say. Funny and weird. "Records scratch easily."

"Not if you take care of them."

I looked around his messy room. "I can see that you really like to take care of things."

He didn't get mad. He laughed.

He handed me a book. "Here," he said. "You can read this while I clean my room."

"Maybe I should just, you know, leave you—" I stopped. My eyes searched the messy room. "It's a little scary in here."

He smiled. "Don't," he said. "Don't leave. I hate cleaning my room."

"Maybe if you didn't have so many things."

"It's just stuff," he said.

I didn't say anything. I didn't have stuff.

"If you stay, it won't be so bad."

Somehow, I felt out of place—but—"Okay," I said. "Should I help?"

"No. It's my job." He said that with a kind of resignation. "As my mom would say, 'It's your responsibility, Dante.' Responsibility is my mother's favorite word. She doesn't think my father pushes me hard enough. Of course he doesn't. I mean, what does she expect? Dad's not a pusher. She married the guy. Doesn't she know what kind of guy he is?"

"Do you always analyze your parents?"

"They analyze us, don't they?"

"That's their job, Dante."

"Tell me you don't analyze your mom and dad."

"Guess I do. Doesn't do me any good. I haven't figured them out yet."

"Well, me, I figured my dad out—not my mom. My mom is the biggest mystery in the world. I mean, she's predictable when it comes to parenting. But really, she's inscrutable."

"Inscrutable." I knew when I went home, I would have to look up the word.

Dante looked at me like it was my turn to say something.

"I figured my mom out, mostly," I said. "My dad. He's inscrutable too." I felt like such a fraud, using that word. Maybe that was the thing about me. I wasn't a real boy. I was a fraud.

He handed me a book of poetry. "Read this," he said. I'd never read a book of poems before and wasn't even sure I knew *how* to read a book of poems. I looked at him blankly.

"Poetry," he said. "It won't kill you."

"What if it does? Boy Dies of Boredom While Reading Poetry."

He tried not to laugh, but he wasn't good at controlling all the laughter that lived inside of him. He shook his head and started gathering all the clothes on the floor.

He pointed at his chair. "Just throw that stuff on the floor and have a seat."

I picked up a pile of art books and a sketch pad and set it on the floor. "What's this?"

"A sketch pad."

"Can I see?"

He shook his head. "I don't like to show it to anyone."

That was interesting—that he had secrets.

He pointed to the poetry book. "Really, it won't kill you."

All afternoon, Dante cleaned. And I read that book of poems by a poet named William Carlos Williams. I'd never heard of him, but I'd never heard of anybody. And I actually understood some of it. Not all of it—but some. And I didn't hate it. That surprised me. It was interesting, not stupid or silly or sappy or overly intellectual— not any of those things that I thought poetry was. Some poems were easier than others. Some were inscrutable. I was thinking that maybe I *did* know the meaning of that word.

I got to thinking that poems were like people. Some people you got right off the bat. Some people you just didn't get—and never would get.

I was impressed by the fact that Dante could be so systematic in the way he organized everything in his room. When we'd walked in, the place had been all chaos. But when he finished, everything was in its place.

Dante's world had order.

He'd organized all his books on a shelf and on his desk. "I keep the books I'm going to read next on my desk," he said. A desk. A real desk. When I had to write something, I used the kitchen table.

He grabbed the book of poems away from me and went looking for a poem. The poem was titled "Death." He was so perfect in his newly organized room, the western sun streaming in, his face in the light and the book in his hand as if it was meant to be there, in his hands, and *only* in his hands. I liked his voice as he read the poem as if he had written it:

He's dead
the dog won't have to
sleep on the potatoes
anymore to keep them
from freezing

he's dead
the old bastard—

When Dante read the word "bastard" he smiled. I knew he loved saying it because it was a word he was not allowed not use, a word that was banned. But here in his room, he could read that word and make it his.

All afternoon, I sat in that large comfortable chair in Dante's room and he lay down on his newly made bed. And he read poems.

I didn't worry about understanding them. I didn't care about what they meant. I didn't care because what mattered is that Dante's voice felt real. *And I felt real.* Until Dante, being with other people was the hardest thing in the world for me. But Dante made talking and living and feeling seem like all those things were perfectly natural. Not in my world, they weren't.

I went home and looked up the word "inscrutable." It meant something that could not easily be understood. I wrote down all the synonyms in my journal. "Obscure." "Unfathomable." "Enigmatic." "Mysterious."

That afternoon, I learned two new words. "Inscrutable." And "friend."

Words were different when they lived inside of you.

Six

ONE LATE AFTERNOON, DANTE CAME OVER TO MY house and introduced himself to my parents. Who did stuff like that?

"I'm Dante Quintana," he said.

"He taught me how to swim," I said. I don't know why, but I just needed to confess that fact to my parents. And then I looked at my mom. "You said don't drown—so I found someone to help me keep my promise."

My dad glanced at my mom. I think they were smiling at each other. *Yeah*, they were thinking, *he's finally found a friend*. I hated that.

Dante shook my dad's hand—then handed him a book. "I brought you a gift," he said.

I stood there and watched him. I'd seen the book on a coffee table in his house. It was an art book filled with the work of Mexican painters. He seemed so adult, not like a fifteen-year-old at all. Somehow, even his long hair that he didn't like to comb made him seem more adult.

My dad smiled as he studied the book—but then he said, "Dante, this is really very generous—but I don't know if I can accept this."

My dad held the book carefully, afraid to damage it. He and my mother exchanged glances. My mom and dad did a lot of that. They liked to talk without talking. I made up things about what they said to each other with those looks.

"It's about Mexican art," Dante said. "So you *have* to take it." I could almost see his mind working as he thought of a convincing argument. A convincing argument that was true. "My parents didn't want me to come over here empty-handed." He looked at my dad very seriously. "So you have to take it."

My mother took the book from my father's hands and looked at the cover. "It's a beautiful book. Thank you, Dante."

"You should thank my dad. It was his idea."

My father smiled. That was the second time in less than a minute that my father had smiled. This was not a common occurrence. Dad was not big on smiling.

"Thank your father for me, will you, Dante?"

My father took the book and sat down with it. As if it was some kind of treasure. See, I didn't get my dad. I could never guess how he would react to things. Not ever.

Seven

"THERE'S NOTHING IN YOUR ROOM."

"There's a bed, a clock radio, a rocking chair, a bookcase, some books. That's not nothing."

"Nothing on the walls."

"I took down my posters."

"Why?"

"Didn't like them."

"You're like a monk."

"Yeah. Aristotle the monk."

"Don't you have hobbies?"

"Sure. Staring at the blank walls."

"Maybe you'll be a priest."

"You have to believe in God to be a priest."

"You don't believe in God? Not even a little?"

"Maybe a little. But not a lot."

"So you're an agnostic?"

"Sure. A Catholic agnostic."

That really made Dante laugh.

"I didn't say it to be funny."

"I know. But it *is* funny."

"Do you think it's bad—to doubt?"

"No. I think it's smart."

"I don't think I'm so smart. Not like you, Dante."

"You are smart, Ari. Very smart. And anyway, being smart isn't everything. People just make fun of you. My dad says it's all right if people make fun of you. You know what he said to me? He said, 'Dante, you're an intellectual. That's who you are. Don't be ashamed of that.'"

I noticed his smile was a little sad. Maybe everyone was a little sad. Maybe so.

"Ari, I'm trying not to be ashamed."

I knew what it was like to be ashamed. Only, Dante knew why. And I didn't.

Dante. I really liked him. I really, really liked him.

Eight

I WATCHED MY FATHER THUMB THROUGH THE PAGES. It was obvious that he loved that book. And because of that book, I learned something new about my father. He'd studied art before he joined the Marines. That seemed not to fit with the picture I had of my father. But I liked the idea.

One evening, when he was looking through the book, he called me over. "Look at this," he said, "It's a mural by Orozco."

I stared at the reproduced mural in the book—but I was more interested in his finger as he tapped the book with approval. That finger had pulled a trigger in a war. That finger had touched my mother in tender ways I did not fully comprehend. I wanted to talk, to say something, to ask questions. But I couldn't. All the words were stuck in my throat. So I just nodded.

I'd never thought of my father as the kind of man who understood art. I guess I saw him as an ex-Marine who became a mailman after he came home from Vietnam. An ex-Marine mailman who didn't like to talk much.

An ex-Marine mailman who came home from a war and had one more son. Not that I thought that I was his idea. I always thought it was my mother who wanted to have me. Not that I really knew whose idea my life was. I made up too many things in my head.

I could have asked my father lots of questions. I could have. But there was something in his face and eyes and in his crooked smile that prevented me from asking. I guess I didn't believe he wanted me to know who he was. So I just collected clues. Watching my father read that book was another clue in my collection. Some day all the clues would come together. And I would solve the mystery of my father.

Nine

ONE DAY, AFTER SWIMMING, DANTE AND I WENT WALKING around. We stopped at the 7-Eleven. He bought a Coke and peanuts.

I bought a PayDay.

He offered me a drink from his Coke.

"Don't like Cokes," I said.

"That's weird."

"Why?'

"Everybody likes Cokes."

"I don't."

"What do you like?"

"Coffee and tea."

"That's weird.

"Okay, I'm weird. Shut up."

He laughed. We walked around. I guess we just didn't want to go home. We talked about stuff. Stupid stuff. And then he asked me, "Why do Mexicans like nicknames?"

"I don't know. Do we?"

"Yes. You know what my aunts call my mom? They call her Chole."

"Is her name Soledad?"

"See what I mean, Ari? You know. You know the nickname for Soledad. It's like in the air. What's that about? Why can't they just call her Soledad? What's this Chole business? Where do they get Chole from?"

"Why does it bother you so much?"

"I don't know. It's weird."

"Is that the word of the day?"

He laughed and downed some peanuts. "Does your mother have a nickname?"

"Lilly. Her name's Liliana."

"That's a nice name."

"So is Soledad."

"No, not really. How would you like to be named Solitude?"

"It can also mean lonely," I said.

"See? What a sad name."

"I don't think it's sad. I think it's a beautiful name. I think it fits your mom just right." I said.

"Maybe so. But Sam, Sam is perfect for my dad."

"Yeah."

"What's your Dad's name?"

"Jaime."

"I like that name."

"His real name's Santiago."

Dante smiled. "See what I mean about the nicknames?"

"It bothers you that you're Mexican, doesn't it?"

"No."

I looked at him.

"Yes, it bothers me."

I offered him some of my PayDay.

He took a bite. "I don't know," he said.

"Yeah," I said. "It bothers you."

"You know what I think, Ari? I think Mexicans don't like me."

"That's a weird thing to say," I said.

"Weird," he said.

"Weird," I said.

Ten

ONE NIGHT, WHEN THERE WAS NO MOON IN THE NIGHT
sky, Dante's mom and dad took us out into the desert so we could
use his new telescope. On the drive out, Dante and his dad sang
along with the Beatles—not that either of them had good singing
voices. Not that they cared.

They touched a lot. A family of touchers and kissers. Every time
Dante entered the house, he kissed his mom and dad on the cheek—
or they kissed him—as if all that kissing was perfectly normal.

I wondered what my father would do if I ever went up to him
and kissed him on the cheek. Not that he would yell at me. But—I
don't know.

It took us a while to drive out into the desert. Mr. Quintana
seemed to know a good place where we could watch the stars.

Somewhere away from the lights of the city.

Light pollution. That's what Dante called it. Dante seemed to
know a great deal about light pollution.

Mr. Quintana and Dante set up the telescope.

I watched them and listened to the radio.

Mrs. Quintana offered me a Coke. I took it, even though I didn't
like Cokes.

"Dante says you're very smart."

Compliments made me nervous. "I'm not as smart as Dante."

Then I heard Dante's voice interrupting our conversation. "I thought we talked about this, Ari."

"What?" his mother said.

"Nothing. It's just that most smart people are perfect shits."

"Dante!" his mother said.

"Yeah, Mom, I know, the language."

"Why is it you like to cuss so much, Dante?"

"It's fun," he said.

Mr. Quintana laughed. "It *is* fun," he said. But then he said, "That kind of fun needs to happen when your mother isn't around."

Mrs. Quintana didn't like Mr. Quintana's advice. "What kind of lesson are you teaching him, Sam?"

"Soledad, I think—" But the whole discussion was killed by Dante, who was looking into his telescope. "Wow, Dad! Look at that! Look!"

For a long time, no one said anything.

We all wanted to see what Dante was seeing.

We stood silently around Dante's telescope in the middle of the desert as we waited for our turn to see all the contents of the sky. When I looked through the telescope, Dante began explaining what I was looking at. I didn't hear a word. Something happened inside me as I looked out into the vast universe. Through that telescope, the world was closer and larger than I'd ever imagined. And it was all so beautiful and overwhelming and—I don't know—it made me aware that there was something inside of me that mattered.

As Dante was watching me search the sky through the lens of

a telescope, he whispered, "Someday, I'm going to discover all the secrets of the universe."

That made me smile. "What are you going to do with all those secrets, Dante?"

"I'll know what to do with them," he said. "Maybe change the world."

I believed him.

Dante Quintana was the only human being I'd ever known that could say a thing like that. I knew that he would never grow up and say stupid things like, "a girl is like a tree."

That night, we slept out in his backyard.

We could hear his parents talking in the kitchen because the window was open. His mother was talking in Spanish and his father was talking in English.

"They do that," he said.

"Mine too," I said.

We didn't talk much. We just lay there and looked up at the stars.

"Too much light pollution," he said.

"Too much light pollution," I answered.

Eleven

ONE IMPORTANT FACT ABOUT DANTE: HE DIDN'T LIKE wearing shoes.

We'd skateboard to the park, and he'd take his tennis shoes off and rub his feet on the grass like he was wiping something off of them. We'd go to the movies and he'd take off his tennis shoes. He left them there once, and we had to go back and get them.

We missed our bus. Dante took his shoes off on the bus, too.

One time, I sat with him at Mass. He untied his shoelaces and took off his shoes right there in the pew. I sort of gave him this look. He rolled his eyes and pointed at the crucifix and whispered, "Jesus isn't wearing shoes."

We both sat there and laughed.

When he came to my house, Dante would place his shoes on the front porch before he came inside. "The Japanese do that," he said. "They don't bring the dirt of the world into another person's house."

"Yeah," I said, "but we're not Japanese. We're Mexican."

"We're not really Mexicans. Do we live in Mexico?"

"But that's where our grandparents came from."

"Okay, okay. But do we actually know anything about Mexico?"

"We speak Spanish."

"Not that good."

"Speak for yourself, Dante. You're such a *pocho*."

"What's a *pocho*?"

"A half-assed Mexican."

"Okay, so maybe I'm a *pocho*. But the point I'm making here is that we can adopt other cultures."

I don't know why but I just started laughing. The truth is that I got to like the war Dante was having with shoes. One day, I just broke down and asked him. "So how come you have this thing with shoes?"

"I don't like them. That's it. That's all. There's no big secret here. I was born not liking them. There's nothing complicated about the whole thing. Well, except there's this thing called my mom. And she makes me wear them. She says there are laws. And then she talks about the diseases I could get. And then she says that people will think I'm just another poor Mexican. She says there are boys in Mexican villages who would die for a pair of shoes. 'You can afford shoes, Dante.' That's what she says. And you know what I always tell her? 'No, I can't afford shoes. Do I have a job? No. I can't afford anything.' That's usually the part of the conversation where she pulls her hair back. She hates that people might mistake me for another poor Mexican. And then she says: 'Being Mexican doesn't have to mean you're poor.' And I just want to tell her: 'Mom, this isn't about poor. And it isn't about being Mexican. I just don't like shoes.' But I know the whole thing about shoes has to do with the way she grew up. So I just wind up nodding when she repeats herself: 'Dante, we can afford shoes.' I know the whole thing has nothing to with the word 'afford.' But, you know, she always gives me this look. And then I give her the same look back—and that's how it goes. Look, me and my mom and shoes, it's not a good discussion." He stared out into the hot afternoon sky—a habit of his. It meant he was thinking. "You know, wearing shoes is an unnatural act. That's my basic premise."

"Your basic premise?" Sometimes he talked like a scientist or a philosopher.

"You know, the founding principle."

"The founding principle?"

"You're looking at me like you think I'm nuts."

"You *are* nuts, Dante."

"I'm not," he said. And then he repeated it, "*I'm not.*" He seemed almost upset.

"Okay," I said, "You're not. You're not nuts and you're not Japanese."

He reached over and unlaced my tennis shoes as he talked. "Take off your shoes, Ari. Live a little."

We went out into the street and played a game that Dante made up on the spot. It was a contest to see who could throw their tennis shoes the farthest. Dante was very systematic about the way he made up the game. Three rounds—which meant six throws. We both got a piece of chalk and we marked where the shoe landed. He borrowed his father's tape measure that could measure up to thirty feet. Not that it was long enough.

"Why do we have to measure the feet?" I asked, "Can't we just

46

throw the shoe and mark it with the piece of chalk? The farthest chalk mark is the winner. Simple."

"We have to know the exact distance," he said.

"Why?"

"Because when you do something, you have to know exactly what you're doing."

"No one knows exactly what they're doing," I said.

"That's because people are lazy and undisciplined."

"Did anybody ever tell you that sometimes you talk like a lunatic who speaks perfect English?"

"That's my father's fault," he said.

"The lunatic part or the perfect English part?" I shook my head. "It's a game, Dante."

"So? When you play a game, Ari, you have to know what you're doing."

"I *do* know what we're doing, Dante. We're making up a game. We're throwing our tennis shoes on the street to see which one of us can throw his shoe the farthest. That's what we're doing."

"It's a version of throwing the javelin, right?"

"Yeah, I guess so."

"They measure the distance when they throw the javelin, don't they?"

"Yeah, but that's a real sport, Dante. This isn't."

"It is *too* a real sport. I'm real. You're real. The tennis shoes are real. The street is real. And the rules we establish—they're real too. What more do you want?"

"But you're making this too much work. After every toss, we

47

have to measure. What fun is that? The fun is in the throwing."

"No," Dante said, "the fun is in the game. It's everywhere."

"I don't understand," I said. "Throwing a shoe is fun. I get that. But taking out your father's tape measure and rolling it out across the street seems like work. What's so fun about that? And not only that—what if a car comes along?"

"We move out of the way. And besides, we could play in the park."

"The street's more fun," I said.

"Yeah, the street's more fun." We agreed on something.

Dante looked at me.

I looked back at him. I knew I didn't have a chance. I knew we were going to play the game according to *his* rules. But the truth is, it mattered to Dante. And to me, it didn't matter so much. So we played the game with our tools: our tennis shoes, two pieces of chalk, and his father's tape measure. We made up the rules as we went along—and they kept changing. In the end, there were three sets—like tennis. There were six tosses per set. Eighteen tosses to make a game. Dante won two out of the three sets. But I had the longest toss. Forty-seven feet, three and a quarter inches.

Dante's father came out of the house and shook his head. "What are you guys doing?"

"We're playing a game."

"What did I tell you, Dante? About playing in the street? There's a park *right there*." He pointed his finger toward the park. "And what—" He stopped and studied the scene. "Are you throwing your tennis shoes around?"

48

Dante wasn't afraid of his father. Not that his father was scary. But still, his father was a father and he was standing there, challenging us. Dante didn't even flinch, certain that he could defend his position. "We're *not* throwing our tennis shoes around, Dad. We're playing a game. It's the common man's version of throwing the javelin. And we're seeing who can throw his shoe the farthest."

His father laughed. *I mean he laughed.* "You're the only kid in the entire universe who could come up with a game as an excuse to beat the holy crap out of his tennis shoes." He laughed again. "Your mother's going to love this."

"We don't have to tell her."

"Yes, we do."

"Why?"

"The no-secrets rule."

"We're playing in the middle of the street. How can that be a secret?"

"It's a secret if we don't tell her." He grinned at Dante, not mad— but like a father who was being a father. "Take it to the park, Dante."

We found a good spot to set up the game at the park. I studied Dante's face as he threw his tennis shoes with all his strength. His father was right. Dante *had* found a game as an excuse to beat the crap out of his tennis shoes.

Twelve

ONE AFTERNOON, AFTER WE'D FINISHED SWIMMING, we were hanging out on his front porch.

Dante was staring at his feet. That made me smile.

He wanted to know what I was smiling at. "I was just smiling," I said. "Can't a guy smile?"

"You're not telling me the truth," he said. He had this thing about telling the truth. He was as bad as my dad. Except my dad kept the truth to himself. And Dante believed you had to tell the truth in words. Out loud. Tell someone.

I wasn't like Dante. I was more like my dad.

"Okay," I said. "I was smiling because you were looking at your feet."

"That's a funny thing to smile about," he said.

"It's weird," I said. "Who does that—look at their feet? Except you?"

"It's not a bad thing to study your own body," he said.

"That's a really weird thing to say, too," I said. In our house, we just didn't talk about our own bodies. That's just not what we did in our house.

"Whatever," he said.

"Whatever," I said.

"Do you like dogs, Ari?"

"I love dogs."

"Me too. They don't have to wear shoes."

I laughed. I got to thinking that one of my jobs in the world was to laugh at Dante's jokes. Only Dante didn't really say things to be funny. He was just being himself.

"I'm going to ask my dad if he'll get me a dog." He had this look on his face—a kind of fire. And I wondered about that fire.

"What kind of dog do you want?"

"I don't know, Ari. One that comes from the shelter. You know, one of those dogs that someone's thrown away."

"Yeah," I said. "But how will you know which one to pick? There's a lot of dogs at the shelter. And they all want to be saved."

"It's because people are so mean. They throw dogs away like they're trash. I hate that."

As we sat there talking, we heard a noise, boys yelling across the street. Three of them, maybe a little younger than us. Two of them had BB guns and they were pointing at a bird they'd just shot. "We got one! We got one!" One of them was pointing his gun at a tree.

"Hey!" Dante yelled, "Stop that!" He was halfway across the street before I realized what was happening. I ran after him.

"Stop that! What the hell's wrong with you!" Dante's hand was out, signaling for them to stop. "Give me that gun."

"My ass if I'm gonna give you my BB gun."

"It's against the law," Dante said. He looked crazed. Really crazed.

"Second amendment," the guy said.

"Yeah, second amendment," the other guy said. He held on tight to his little rifle.

"The second amendment doesn't apply to BB guns, you jerk. And anyway, guns aren't allowed on city property."

"What are you planning on doing about it, you piece of shit?"

"I'm going to make you stop," he said.

"How?"

"By kicking your skinny little asses all the way to the Mexican border," I said. I guess I was just afraid these guys were going to hurt Dante. I just said what I felt I had to say. They weren't big guys and they weren't smart either. They were mean and stupid boys and I'd seen what mean and stupid boys could do. Maybe Dante wasn't mean enough for a fight. But I was. And I'd never felt bad for punching out a guy who needed punching out.

We stood there for a while, sizing each other up. I could tell Dante didn't know what he was going to do next.

One of the guys looked like he was about to point his BB gun at me.

"I wouldn't do that if I were you, you little piece of dog shit." And just like that, I reached over and took his gun away. It happened fast and he hadn't expected it. One thing I'd learned about getting into fights. Move fast, take the guy by surprise. It always worked. It was the first rule of fighting. And there I was with his BB gun in my hands. "You're lucky I don't shove this up your ass."

I threw the gun on the ground. I didn't even have to tell them to get the hell out of there. They just left, mumbling obscenities under their breaths.

Dante and I looked at each other.

"I didn't know you liked to fight," Dante said.

"I don't really. Not really," I said.

"Yeah," Dante said. "You like to fight."

"Maybe I do." I said. "And I didn't know you were a pacifist."

"Maybe I'm not a pacifist. Maybe I just think you need a good reason to go around killing birds." He searched my face. I wasn't sure what he was trying to find there. "You're good at tossing around bad words too."

"Yeah, well, Dante, let's not tell your mom."

"We won't tell yours either."

I looked at him. "I have a theory about why moms are so strict."

Dante almost smiled. "It's because they love us, Ari."

"That's part of it. The other part of it is that they want us to stay boys forever."

"Yeah, I think that would make my mom happy—if I was a boy forever." Dante looked down at the dead bird. A few minutes ago, he'd been mad as hell. Now, he looked like he was going to cry.

"I've never seen you that mad," I said.

"I've never seen you that mad, either."

We both knew that we were mad for different reasons.

For a moment, we just stood there looking down at the dead bird. "It's just a little sparrow," he said. And then he started to cry.

I didn't know what to do. I just stood there and watched him.

We walked back across the street and sat on his front porch. He tossed his tennis shoes across the street with all his might and anger. He wiped the tears from his face.

"Were you scared?" he asked.

"No."

"I was."

"So?"

And then we were quiet again. I hated the quiet. Finally I just asked a stupid question, "Why do birds exist, anyway?"

He looked at me. "You don't know?"

"I guess I don't."

"Birds exist to teach us things about the sky."

"You believe that?"

"Yes."

I wanted to tell him not to cry anymore, tell him that what those boys did to that bird didn't matter. But I knew it *did* matter. It mattered to Dante. And, anyway, it didn't do any good to tell him not to cry because he needed to cry. That's the way he was.

And then he finally stopped. He took a deep breath and looked at me. "Will you help me bury the bird?"

"Sure."

We got a shovel from his father's garage and walked to the park where the dead bird was lying on the grass. I picked up the bird with the shovel and carried it across the street, into Dante's backyard. I dug a hole underneath a big oleander.

We put the bird in the hole and buried it.

Neither of us said a word.

Dante was crying again. And I felt mean because I didn't feel like crying. I didn't really feel anything for the bird. It was a bird. Maybe the bird didn't deserve to get shot by some stupid kid whose idea of fun was shooting at things. But it was still just a bird.

I was harder than Dante. I think I'd tried to hide that hardness from him because I'd wanted him to like me. But now he knew. That I was hard. And maybe that was okay. Maybe he could like the fact that I was hard just as I liked the fact that he *wasn't* hard.

We both stared at the bird's grave. "Thanks," he said.

"Sure," I said.

I knew he wanted to be alone.

"Hey," I whispered, "I'll see you tomorrow."

"We'll go swimming," he said.

"Yeah, we'll go swimming."

There was a tear running down his cheek. It seemed like a river in the light of the setting sun.

I wondered what it was like, to be the kind of guy that cried over the death of a bird.

I waved bye. He waved bye back.

As I walked home, I thought about birds and the meaning of their existence. Dante had an answer. I didn't. I didn't have any idea as to why birds existed. I'd never even asked myself the question.

Dante's answer made sense to me. If we studied birds, maybe we could learn to be free. I think that's what he was saying. I had a philosopher's name. What was *my* answer? Why didn't I have an answer?

And why was it that some guys had tears in them and some had no tears at all? Different boys lived by different rules.

When I got home, I sat on my front porch.

I watched the sun set.

I felt alone, but not in a bad way. I really liked being alone. Maybe I liked it too much. Maybe my father was like that too.

I thought of Dante and wondered about him.

And it seemed to me that Dante's face was a map of the world. A world without any darkness.

Wow, a world without darkness. How beautiful was that?

Sparrows Falling from the Sky

*When I was a boy, I used to wake up thinking
that the world was ending.*

One

THE MORNING AFTER WE BURIED THE SPARROW, I woke up on fire with a fever.

My muscles ached, my throat hurt, my head throbbed almost like a heart. I kept staring at my hands, almost believing they belonged to someone else. When I tried to get up, I had no balance, no equilibrium, and the room spun around and around. I tried to take a step, but my legs weren't strong enough to carry my weight. I fell back on the bed, my clock radio crashing to the floor.

My mother appeared in my room and for some reason she didn't seem real. "Mom? Mom? Is that you?" I think I was yelling.

She was holding a question in her eyes. "Yes," she said. She seemed so serious.

"I fell," I said.

She said something—but I couldn't translate what she was saying. Everything was so strange and I thought maybe I was dreaming, but her hand on my arm felt like a real touch. "You're burning up," she said.

I felt her hands on my face.

I kept wondering where I was, so I asked her. "Where are we?"

She held me for a moment. "Shhh."

The world was so silent. There was a barrier between me and the world, and I thought for a moment that the world had never wanted me and now it was taking the opportunity to get rid of me.

I looked up and saw my mom standing in front of me, holding out two aspirin, a glass of water.

I sat up and reached for the pills and put them in my mouth. When I held the glass, I could see my hands trembling.

She put a thermometer under my tongue.

She studied the time on her watch, then pulled the thermometer out of my mouth.

"A hundred and four," she said. "We've got to break that fever." She shook her head. "It's all those germs at the pool."

The world seemed closer for an instant. "It's just a cold," I whispered. But it seemed like someone else was talking.

"I think you have the flu."

But it's summer. The words were on my tongue but I couldn't say them. I couldn't stop shivering. She placed another blanket over me.

Everything was spinning but when I closed my eyes, the room was motionless and dark.

And then the dreams came.

Birds were falling from the sky. Sparrows. Millions and millions of sparrows. They were falling like rain and they were hitting me as they fell and I had their blood all over me and I couldn't find a place to protect myself. Their beaks were breaking my skin like arrows. And Buddy Holly's plane was falling from the sky and I could hear Waylon Jennings singing "La Bamba." I could hear Dante crying—and when I turned around to see where he was, I saw that he was holding Richie Valens's limp body in his arms. And then the plane came falling down on us. All I saw was the shadow and the earth on fire.

And then the sky disappeared.

I must have been screaming, because my mom and dad were in the room. I was trembling and everything was soaked in my sweat. And then I realized that I was crying and I couldn't make myself stop.

My dad picked me up and rocked me in the chair. I felt small and weak and I wanted to hold him back but I couldn't because there wasn't any strength in my arms, and I wanted to ask him if he had held me like this when I was a boy because I didn't remember and why didn't I remember. I started to think that maybe I was still dreaming, but my mother was changing the sheets on my bed so I knew that everything was real. Except me.

I think I was mumbling. My father held me tighter and whispered something, but not even his arms or his whispers could keep me from trembling. My mom dried my sweaty body with a towel and she and my dad changed me into a clean T-shirt and clean underwear. And then I said the strangest thing, "Don't throw my T-shirt away. Dad gave it to me." I knew I was crying, but I didn't know why because I wasn't the kind of guy who cried, and I thought that maybe it was someone else who was crying.

I could hear my father whisper, "Shhhh. It's okay." He laid me back down on the bed and my mother sat next to me and made me drink some water and take more aspirin.

I saw the look on my dad's face and I knew he was worried. And I was sad that I had made him worry. I wondered if he had really held me and I wanted to tell him that I didn't hate him, it was just that I didn't understand him, didn't understand who he was and I wanted to, I wanted so much to understand. My mother said something to my father in Spanish and he nodded. I was too tired to care about words in any language.

The world was so quiet.

I fell asleep—and the dreams came again. It was raining outside and there was thunder and lightning all around me. And I could see myself as I ran in the rain. I was looking for Dante and I was yelling because he was lost, "Dante! Come back! Come back!" And then I wasn't looking for Dante anymore, I was looking for my dad and I was yelling for him, "Dad! Dad! Where did you go? Where did you go?"

When I woke again, I was soaked in my own sweat again.

My dad was sitting on my rocking chair, studying me.

My mom walked into the room. She looked at my father—then at me.

"I didn't mean to scare you." I couldn't make myself talk above a whisper.

My mother smiled and I thought she must have been really pretty when she was a girl. She helped me sit up. "*Amor*, you're soaked. Why don't you take a nice shower?"

"I had nightmares."

I leaned my head on her shoulder. I wanted the three of us to stay that way forever.

My dad helped me to the shower. I felt weak and washed out and when the warm water hit my body, I thought of my dreams . . . Dante, my dad. And I wondered what my dad looked like when he was my age. My mother had told me he was beautiful. I wonder if he'd been as beautiful as Dante. And I wondered why I thought that.

When I went back to bed, my mom had changed the sheets again. "Your fever's gone," she said. She gave me another glass of water. I didn't want it but I drank all of it. I didn't know how thirsty I'd been, and I asked her for more water.

My father was still there, sitting on my rocking chair.

We studied each other for a moment as I lay in bed.

"You were looking for me," he said.

I looked at him.

"In your dream. You were looking for me."

"I'm always looking for you," I whispered.

Two

THE NEXT MORNING, WHEN I WOKE, I THOUGHT I HAD
died. I knew it wasn't true—but the thought was there. Maybe a part
of you died when you were sick. I don't know.

My mom's solution to my predicament was to make me drink
gallons of water—one painful glass at a time.

I finally went on strike and refused to drink anymore. "My blad-
der's turned into a water balloon that's about to explode."

"That's good," she said, "You're flushing your system out."

"I'm done flushing," I said.

The water wasn't the only thing I had to deal with. I had to deal
with her chicken soup. Her chicken soup became my enemy.

The first bowl was incredible. I had never been that hungry. Not
ever. She mostly gave me broth.

The soup returned the next day for lunch. That was okay too,
because now I got all the chicken and the vegetables in the soup
with warm corn tortillas and my mother's *sopa de arroz*. But the
soup came back in the form of an afternoon snack. And for dinner.

I was sick of water and chicken soup. I was sick of being sick.
After four days in bed, I finally decided that it was time to move on.

I made an announcement to my mother. "I'm well."

"You're not," my mother said.

"I'm being held hostage." That's the first thing I said to my father when he came home from work.

He grinned at me.

"I'm fine now, Dad. I am."

"You still look a little pale."

"I need some sun."

"Give it one more day," he said. "Then you can go out into the world and cause all the trouble you want."

"Okay," I said. "But no more chicken soup."

"That's between you and your mother."

He started to leave my room. He hesitated for a moment. He had his back to me. "Have you had any more bad dreams?"

"I always have bad dreams," I said.

"Even when you're not sick?"

"Yeah."

He stood at my doorway. He turned around and faced me. "Are you always lost?"

"In most of them, yeah."

"And are you always trying to find me?"

"Mostly I think I'm trying to find me, Dad." It was strange to talk to him about something real. But it scared me too. I wanted to keep talking, but I didn't know exactly how to say what I was holding inside me. I looked down at the floor. Then I looked up at him and shrugged like *no big deal*.

"I'm sorry," he said. "I'm sorry I'm so far away."

"It's okay," I said.

"No," he said. "No, it's not." I think he was going to say something else, but he changed his mind. He turned and walked out of the room.

I kept staring down at the floor. And then I heard my father's voice in the room again. "I have bad dreams too, Ari."

I wanted to ask him if his dreams were about the war or about my brother. I wanted to ask him if he woke up as scared as me.

All I did was smile at him. He'd told me something about himself.

I was happy.

Three

I WAS ALLOWED TO WATCH TELEVISION. BUT I DISCOVERED something about myself. I didn't really like television. I didn't like it at all. I switched the TV off and found myself watching my mother as she sat at the kitchen table, looking over some of her old lesson plans.

"Mom?"

She looked up at me. I tried to imagine my mother standing in front of her class. I wondered what the guys thought of her. I wondered how they saw her. I wondered if they liked her. Hated her? Respected her? I wondered if they knew she was a mother. I wondered if that mattered to them.

"What are you thinking?"

"You like teaching?"

"Yes," she said.

"Even when your students don't care?"

"I'll tell you a secret. I'm not responsible for whether my students care or don't care. That care has to come from them—not me."

"Where does that leave you?"

"No matter what, Ari, my job is to care."

"Even when they don't?"

"Even when they don't."

"No matter what?"

"No matter what."

"Even if you teach kids like me, who think life is boring?"

"That's the way it is when you're fifteen."

"Just a phase," I said.

"Just a phase." She laughed.

"You like fifteen-year-olds?"

"Are you asking me if I like you, or are you asking me if I like my students?"

"Both, I guess."

"I adore you, Ari, you know I do."

"Yeah, but you adore your students, too."

"Are you jealous?"

"Can I go outside?" I could avoid questions as skillfully as she could.

"You can go out tomorrow."

"I think you're being a fascist."

"That's a big word, Ari."

"Thanks to you, I know all about the different forms of government. Mussolini was a fascist. Franco was a fascist. And Dad says Reagan is a fascist."

"Don't take your father's jokes too literally, Ari. All he's saying is that he thinks President Reagan is too heavy-handed."

"I know what he's saying, Mom. Just like *you* know what *I'm* saying."

"Well, it's good to know that you think your mother is more than a form of government."

"You kind of are," I said.

"I get your point, Ari. You're still not going outside."

There were days when I wished I had it in me to rebel against my mother's rules.

"I just want to get out of here. I'm bored out of my skull."

She got up from where she was sitting. She placed her hands on my face. "*Hijo de mi vida*," she said, "I'm sorry that you think I'm too strict on you. But I have my reasons. When you're older—"

"You always say that. I'm fifteen. How old do I have to be? How old, Mom, before you think I'm smart enough to get it? I'm not a little boy."

She took my hand and kissed it. "You are to me," she whispered. There were tears running down her cheeks. There was something I wasn't getting. First Dante. Then me. And now my mom. Tears all over the damned place. Maybe tears were something you caught. Like the flu.

"It's okay, Mom," I whispered. I smiled at her. I think I was hoping for a full explanation for her tears, but I was going to have to work to get it. "Are you okay?" I said.

"Yes," she said, "I'm okay."

"I don't think you are."

"I'm trying hard not to worry about you."

"Why do you worry? I just had the flu."

"That's not what I mean."

"What?"

"What do you do when you leave the house?"

"Stuff."

"You don't have any friends." She started to place her hand over her mouth, then stopped herself.

69

I wanted to hate her for that accusation. "I don't want any."

She looked at me, almost as if I were a stranger.

"And how can I have friends if you don't let me go outside?"

I got one of her looks.

"I *do* have friends, Mom. I have school friends. And Dante. He's my friend."

"Yes," she said. "Dante."

"Yes," I said. "Dante."

"I'm glad for Dante," she said.

I nodded. "I'm okay, Mom. I'm just not the kind of guy—" I didn't know what I was trying to say. "I'm just different." I didn't even know what I meant.

"You know what I think?"

I didn't want to know what she thought. I didn't. But I was going to hear it anyway. "Sure," I said.

She ignored the attitude.

"I don't think you know how loved you are."

"I *do* know."

She started to say something, but she changed her mind. "Ari, I just want you to be happy."

I wanted to tell her that happy was hard for me. But I think she already knew that. "Well," I said, "I'm at that phase where I'm supposed to be miserable."

That made her laugh.

We were okay.

"You think it would be all right if Dante came over?"

70

Four

DANTE ANSWERED THE PHONE ON THE SECOND RING.
"You haven't been going to the pool." He sounded mad.

"I've been in bed. I caught the flu. Mostly I've been sleeping, having really bad dreams, and eating chicken soup."

"Fever?"

"Yeah."

"Achy bones?"

"Yeah."

"Night sweats?"

"Yeah."

"Bad stuff," he said. "What were your dreams about?"

"I can't talk about them."

That seemed okay with him.

Fifteen minutes later, he showed up at my front door. I heard the doorbell. I could hear him talking to my mother. Dante never had any trouble starting up conversations. He was probably telling my mom his life story.

I heard him walking down the hall in his bare feet. And then there he was, standing at the doorway to my room, wearing a T-shirt that was so worn you could almost see through it, and a ratty pair of jeans with holes in them.

"Hi," he said. He was carrying a book of poems, a sketch pad, and some charcoal pencils.

"You forgot your shoes," I said.

"I donated them to the poor."

"Guess the jeans are next."

"Yeah." We both laughed.

He studied me. "You look a little pale."

"I still look more Mexican than you do."

"Everybody looks more Mexican than I do. Pick it up with the people who handed me their genes." There was something in his voice. The whole Mexican thing bothered him.

"Okay, okay." I said. "Okay, okay" always meant it was time to change the subject. "So you brought your sketch pad."

"Yeah."

"Are you going to show me your drawings?"

"Nope. I'm going to sketch you."

"What if I don't want to be sketched?"

"How am I going to be an artist if I can't practice?"

"Don't artists' models get paid?"

"Only the ones that are good-looking."

"So I'm not good-looking?"

Dante smiled. "Don't be an asshole." He seemed embarrassed. But not as embarrassed as I was.

I could feel myself turning red. Even guys with dark skin like me could blush. "So you're really going to be an artist?"

"Absolutely." He looked right at me. "You don't believe me?"

"I need evidence."

He sat in my rocking chair. He studied me. "You still look sick."

"Thanks."

"Maybe it's your dreams."

"Maybe." I didn't want to talk about my dreams.

"When I was a boy, I used to wake up thinking that the world was ending. I'd get up and look in the mirror and my eyes were sad."

"You mean like mine."

"Yeah."

"My eyes are always sad."

"The world isn't ending, Ari."

"Don't be an asshole. Of course it's not ending."

"Then don't be sad."

"Sad, sad, sad," I said.

"Sad, sad, sad," he said.

We were both smiling, trying to hold in our laughter—but we just couldn't do it. I was happy that he'd come over. Being sick made me feel fragile, like I might break. I didn't like feeling like that. Laughing made me feel better.

"I want to draw you."

"Can I stop you?"

"You're the one who said you needed evidence."

He tossed me the book of poems he'd brought along. "Read it. You read. I'll draw." Then he got real quiet. His eyes started searching everything in the room: me, the bed, the blankets, the pillows, the light. I felt nervous and awkward and self-conscious and uncomfortable. And Dante's eyes on me, well, I didn't know if I liked that or didn't like that. I just knew I felt naked. But there was something happening between Dante and his drawing pad that made me feel invisible. And that made me relax.

"Make me look good," I said.

"Read," he said. "Just read."

It didn't take long for me to forget Dante was drawing me. And I just read. I read and I read and I read. Sometimes I would glance over at him, but he was lost in his work. I returned to the book of poems. I read a line and tried to understand it: "from what we cannot hold the stars are made." It was a beautiful thing to say, but I didn't know what it meant. I fell asleep thinking what the line might mean.

When I woke, Dante was gone.

He hadn't left any of the sketches that he'd done of me. But he did leave a sketch of my rocking chair. It was perfect. A rocking chair against the bare walls of my room. He'd captured the afternoon light streaming into the room, the way the shadows fell on the chair and gave it depth and made it appear as if it was something more than an inanimate object. There was something sad and solitary about the sketch and I wondered if that's the way he saw the world or if that's the way he saw *my* world.

I stared at the sketch for a long time. It scared me. Because there was something true about it.

I wondered where he'd learned to draw. I was suddenly jealous of him. He could swim, he could draw, he could talk to people. He read poetry and he liked himself. I wondered how that felt, to really like yourself. And I wondered why some people didn't like themselves and others did. Maybe that's just the way it was.

I looked at his drawing, then looked at my chair. That's when I saw the note he'd left.

Ari,

> *I hope you like the sketch of your chair. I miss you at the pool. The lifeguards are jerks.*

> *Dante*

After dinner, I picked up the phone and called him.

"Why did you leave?"

"You needed to rest."

"I'm sorry I fell asleep."

Then neither one of us said anything.

"I liked the sketch," I said.

"Why?"

"Because it looks just like my chair."

"Is that the only reason?"

"It holds something," I said

"What?"

"Emotion."

"Tell me," Dante said.

"It's sad. It's sad and it's lonely."

"Like you," he said.

I hated that he saw who I was. "I'm not sad all the time," I said.

75

"I know," he said.

"Will you show me the others?"

"No."

"Why?"

"I can't."

"Why not?"

"For the same reason you can't tell me about your dreams."

Five

THE FLU DIDN'T SEEM TO WANT TO LET ME GO.

That night, the dreams came again. My brother. He was on the other side of the river. He was in Juárez and I was in El Paso and we could see each other. And I yelled, "Bernardo, come over!" and he shook his head. And then I thought he didn't understand, so I yelled at him in Spanish. "*Vente pa'aca, Bernardo!*" I thought that if I only knew the right words or spoke them in the right language, then he would cross the river. And come home. If only I knew the right words. If only I spoke the right language. And then my dad was there. He and my brother stared at each other and I couldn't stand the look on their faces, because it seemed like there was the hurt of all the sons and all the fathers of the world. And the hurt was so deep that it was way beyond tears and so their faces were dry. And then the dream changed and my brother and father were gone. I was standing in the same place where my father had been standing, on the Juárez side, and Dante was standing across from me. And he was shirtless and shoeless and I wanted to swim toward him but I couldn't move. And then he said something to me in English and I couldn't understand him. And I said something to him in Spanish, and he couldn't understand me.

And I was so alone.

And then all the light was gone and Dante disappeared into the darkness.

I woke up and I felt lost.

I didn't know where I was.

The fever was back. I thought that maybe nothing would ever be the same. But I knew it was just the fever. I fell asleep again. The sparrows were falling from the sky. And it was me who was killing them.

Six

DANTE CAME OVER TO VISIT. I KNEW I WASN'T A LOT
of fun. He knew it too. It didn't seem to matter.

"Do you want to talk?"

"No," I said.

"Do you want me to go?"

"No," I said.

He read poems to me. I thought about the sparrows falling from
the sky. As I listened to Dante's voice, I wondered what my brother
would sound like. I wondered if he'd ever read a poem. My mind was
full and crowded—falling sparrows, my brother's ghost, Dante's voice.

Dante finished reading a poem, then went looking for another.

"Aren't you afraid of catching what I have?" I said.

"No."

"You're not afraid?"

"No."

"You're not afraid of anything."

"I'm afraid of lots of things, Ari."

I could have asked *What? What are you afraid of?* I don't think
he would have told me.

Seven

THE FEVER WAS GONE.

But the dreams stayed.

My father was in them. And my brother. And Dante. In my dreams. And sometimes my mother, too. I had this image stuck in my mind. I was four and I was walking down the street, holding my brother's hand. I wondered if it was a memory or a dream. Or a hope.

I lay around and thought about things. All the ordinary problems and mysteries of my life that mattered only to me. Not that thinking about things made me feel better. I decided that my junior year at Austin High School was going to suck. Dante went to Cathedral because they had a swim team. My mom and dad had wanted to send me to school there, but I'd refused. I didn't want to go to an all-boy Catholic school. I'd insisted to myself and to my parents that all the boys there were rich. My mom argued that they gave scholarships to smart boys. I argued back that I wasn't smart enough to get a scholarship. My mom argued back that they could afford to send me there. "I hate those boys!" I'd begged my father not to send me there.

I never said anything to Dante about hating Cathedral boys. He didn't have to know.

I thought about my mom's accusation. "You don't have any friends."

I thought of my chair and how really it was a portrait of me.

I was a chair. I felt sadder than I'd ever felt.

I knew I wasn't a boy anymore. But I still felt like a boy. Sort of. But there were other things I was starting to feel. Man things, I guess. Man loneliness was much bigger than boy loneliness. And I didn't want to be treated like a boy anymore. I didn't want to live in my parents' world and I didn't have a world of my own. In a strange way, my friendship with Dante had made me feel even more alone.

Maybe it was because Dante seemed to make himself fit everywhere he went. And me, I always felt that I didn't belong anywhere. I didn't even belong in my own body—*especially* in my own body. I was changing into someone I didn't know. The change hurt but I didn't know why it hurt. And nothing about my own emotions made any sense.

When I was younger, I'd had this idea that I wanted to keep a journal. I sort of wrote things down in this little leather book I bought, filled with blank pages. But I was never disciplined about the whole thing. The journal turned into a random thing with random thoughts and nothing more.

When I was in the sixth grade, my parents gave me a baseball glove and a typewriter for my birthday. I was on a team so the glove made sense. But a typewriter? What was it about me that made them think of getting me a typewriter? I pretended to like it. But I wasn't a good pretender.

Just because I didn't talk about things didn't make me a good actor.

The funny thing was, I learned how to type. At last, a skill. The baseball thing didn't work out. I was good enough to make the team. But I hated it. I did it for my father.

I didn't know why I was thinking about all these things—except that's what I always did. I guess I had my own personal television in my brain. I could control whatever I wanted to watch. I could switch the channels anytime I wanted.

I thought about calling Dante. And then I thought that maybe I wouldn't call him. I didn't really feel like talking to anyone. I just felt like talking to myself.

I got to thinking about my older sisters and how they were so close to each other but so far away from me. I knew it was the age thing. That seemed to matter. To them. And to me. I was born "a little late." That's the expression my sisters used. One day, they were talking to each other at the kitchen table and they were talking about me and that's the expression they used. It wasn't the first time I'd heard someone say that about me. So I decided to confront my sisters because I just didn't like being thought of that way. I don't know, I just sort of lost it. I looked at my sister, Cecilia, and said: "You were born a little too early." I smiled at her and shook my head. "Isn't that sad? Isn't that just too fucking sad?"

My other sister, Sylvia, lectured me. "I hate that word. Don't talk that way. That's so disrespectful."

Like they respected me. Yeah, sure they did.

They told my mom I was using language. My mother hated "language." She looked at me with the look. "The 'f' word shows an extreme lack of respect and an extreme lack of imagination. And don't roll your eyes."

But I got in worse trouble for refusing to apologize.

The good thing was that my sisters never used the expression "born too late" ever again. Not in front of me, anyway.

I think I was mad because I couldn't talk to my brother. And I was mad because I couldn't really talk to my sisters either. It's not that my sisters didn't care about me. It's just that they mostly treated me more like a son than a brother. I didn't need three mothers. So really, I was alone. And being alone made me want to talk to someone my own age. Someone who understood that using the "f" word wasn't a measure of my lack of imagination. Sometimes using that word just made me feel free.

Talking to myself in my journal qualified as talking to someone my own age.

Sometimes I would write down all the bad words I could think of. It made me feel better. My mother had her rules. For my father: no smoking in the house. And for everyone: no cussing. She didn't go for that. Even when my father let out a string of interesting words, she looked at him and said, "Take it outside, Jaime. Maybe you can find a dog who'll appreciate that kind of language."

My mom was soft. But she also very strict. I think that's how she survived. I wasn't going to get into the whole cussing thing with my mom. So I did most of my cussing in my head.

And then there was this whole thing with my name. Angel Aristotle Mendoza. I hated the name Angel and I'd never let anybody call me that. Every guy I knew who was named Angel was a real asshole. I didn't care for Aristotle either. And even though I knew I was named after my grandfather, I also knew I had inherited the name of the world's most famous philosopher. I hated that. Everyone expected something from me. Something I just couldn't give.

So I renamed myself Ari.

If I switched the letter, my name was Air.

I thought it might be a great thing to be the air.

I could be something and nothing at the same time. I could be necessary and also invisible. Everyone would need me and no one would be able to see me.

Eight

MY MOM INTERRUPTED MY THOUGHTS—IF THAT'S what they were. "Dante's on the phone."

I walked past the kitchen and noticed my mom was cleaning out all her cabinets. Whatever summer meant, for Mom it meant work.

I threw myself on the couch in the living room and grabbed the phone.

"Hi," I said.

"Hi," he said. "What are you doing?"

"Nothing. I'm still not feeling great. My mom's taking me to the doctor this afternoon."

"I was hoping we could go swimming."

"Shit," I said, "I can't. I just, you know—"

"Yeah, I know. So you're just hanging out?"

"Yeah."

"Are you reading something, Ari?"

"No. I'm thinking."

"About what?"

"Stuff."

"Stuff?"

"You know, Dante, things."

"Like what, Ari?"

"You know, like how my two sisters and my brother are so much older than me and how that makes me feel."

"How old are they, your sisters and brother?"

"My sisters are twins. They're not identical, but they look alike. They're twenty-seven. My mom had them when she was eighteen."

"Wow," he said. "Twenty-seven."

"Yeah, wow."

"I'm fifteen and I have three nieces and four nephews."

"I think that's really cool, Ari."

"Trust me, Dante, it's not that cool. They don't even call me Uncle Ari."

"So how old is your brother?"

"He's twenty-five."

"I always wanted a brother."

"Yeah, well, I might as well not have one."

"Why?"

"We don't talk about him. It's like he's dead."

"Why?"

"He's in prison, Dante." I'd never told anyone about my brother. I'd never said a word about him to another human being. I felt bad for talking about him.

Dante didn't say anything.

"Can we not talk about him?" I said.

"Why?"

"It makes me feel bad."

86

"Ari, you didn't do anything."

"I don't want to talk about him, okay, Dante?"

"Okay. But you know, Ari, you have this really interesting life."

"Not really," I said.

"Yes, really," he said. "At least you have siblings. Me, I only have a mother and a father."

"What about cousins?"

"They don't like me. They think I'm—well, they think I'm a little different. They're really Mexican, you know. And I'm sort of, well, what did you call me?"

"A *pocho*."

"That's exactly what I am. My Spanish isn't great."

"You can learn it," I said.

"Learning it at school is different than learning it at home or on the street. And it's really hard because most of my cousins are on my mom's side—and they're really poor. My mom's the youngest and she really fought her family so she could go to school. Her father didn't think a girl should go to college. So my mom said, 'Screw it, I'm going anyway.'"

"I can't picture your mom saying, 'screw it.'"

"Well, she probably didn't say that—but she found a way. She was really smart and she worked her way through college and then she got some kind of fellowship to go to graduate school at Berkeley. And that's where she met my dad. I was born somewhere in there. They had their studies. My mom was turning herself into a psychologist. My dad was turning himself into an English professor. I mean, my dad's parents were born in Mexico. They live in a small little house in East LA and they speak no English and own a little restaurant. It's like my mom and dad created a whole new world for themselves. I live in their new world. But they understand the old world, the world they came from—and I don't. I don't belong anywhere. That's the problem."

"You do," I said. "You belong everywhere you go. That's just how you are."

"You've never seen me around my cousins. I feel like a freak."

I knew what it was like to feel like that. "I know," I said. "I feel like a freak too."

"Well, at least you're a real Mexican."

"What do I know about Mexico, Dante?"

The quiet over the phone was strange. "Do you think it will always be this way?"

"What?"

"I mean, when do we start feeling like the world belongs to us?"

I wanted to tell him that the world would never belong to us. "I don't know," I said. "Tomorrow."

Nine

I WENT INTO THE KITCHEN AND WATCHED MY MOM AS she cleaned out her cabinets.

"What were you and Dante talking about?"

"Stuff."

I wanted to ask her about my brother. But I knew I wasn't going to ask. "He was telling me about his mom and dad, about how they met at graduate school at Berkeley. How he was born there. He said he remembered his parents reading books and studying all the time."

My mom smiled. "Just like me and you," she said.

"I don't remember."

"I was finishing my bachelor's degree when your father was at war. It helped me take my mind off things. I worried all the time. My mom and my aunts helped me take care of your sisters and your brother while I went to school and studied. And when your father came back, we had you." She smiled at me and did that combing-my-hair-with-her-fingers thing.

"Your father got on with the post office and I kept going to school. I had you and I had school. And your father was safe."

"Was it hard?"

"I was happy. And you were such a good baby. I thought I'd died and gone to heaven. We bought this house. It needed work, but it was ours. And I was doing what I had always wanted to do."

"You always wanted to be a teacher?"

"Always. When I was growing up, we didn't have anything, but my mom understood how much school meant to me. She cried when I told her I was going to marry your father."

"She didn't like him?"

"No, it wasn't that. She just wanted me to keep going to school. I promised her that I would. It took me a while but I kept my promise."

That was the first time that I really saw my mother as a person. A person who was so much more than just my mother. It was strange to think of her that way. I wanted to ask her about my father, but I didn't know how. "Was he different? When he came back from the war?"

"Yes."

"How was he different?"

"There's a wound somewhere inside of him, Ari."

"But what is it? The hurt? What is it?"

"I don't know."

"How can you not know, Mom?"

"Because it's his. It's just his, Ari."

I understood that she had just accepted my father's private wound. "Will it ever heal?"

"I don't think so."

"Mom? Can I ask you something?"

"You can ask me anything."

"Is it hard to love him?"

"No." She didn't even hesitate.

"Do you understand him?"

"Not always. But Ari, I don't always have to understand the people I love."

"Well, maybe I do."

"It's hard for you, isn't it?"

"I don't know him, Mom."

"I know you're going to get mad at me when I say this, Ari, but I'm going to say it anyway. I think someday you *will* understand."

"Yeah," I said. "Someday."

Someday, I would understand my father. Someday he would tell me who he was. Someday. I hated that word.

Ten

I LIKED WHEN MY MOM TOLD ME ABOUT HOW SHE FELT about things. She seemed to be able to do that. Not that we talked that much, but sometimes we did and it was good and I felt like I knew her. And I didn't feel like I knew a lot of people. When she talked to me, she was different than when she was being my mother. When she was being my mother, she had a lot of ideas about who I should be. And I hated that, fought her on that, didn't want her input.

I didn't think it was my job to accept what everyone said I was and who I should be. *Maybe if you weren't so quiet, Ari . . . Maybe if you could just be more disciplined . . .* Yeah, everyone had suggestions as to what was wrong with me and what I should become. Especially my older sisters.

Because I was the youngest.

Because I was the surprise.

Because I was born too late.

Because my older brother was in prison and maybe my mother and father blamed themselves. If only they'd said something, done something. They weren't going to make that mistake again. So I was stuck with my family's guilt—a guilt that not even my mother would talk about. She sometimes mentioned my brother in passing. But she never said his name.

So now I was the only son. And I felt the weight of a son in a Mexican family. Even though I didn't want it. But that was the way it was.

It made me mad that I'd felt like I'd betrayed my family by mentioning my brother to Dante. It didn't feel good. There were so many ghosts in our house—the ghost of my brother, the ghosts of my father's war, the ghosts of my sister's voices. And I thought that maybe there were ghosts inside of me that I hadn't even met yet. They were there. Lying in wait.

I picked up my old journal and thumbed through the pages. I found an entry that I'd written a week after I turned fifteen:

I don't like being fifteen.

I didn't like being fourteen.

I didn't like being thirteen.

I didn't like being twelve.

I didn't like being eleven.

*Ten was good. I liked being ten. I don't know why but
I had a very good year when I was in the fifth grade.*

*The fifth grade was very good. Mrs. Pedregon was a
great teacher and for some reason, everyone seemed
to like me. A good year. An excellent year. Fifth grade.
But now, at fifteen, well, things are a little awkward.
My voice is doing funny things and I keep running
into things. My mom says my reflexes are trying to
keep up with the fact that I'm growing so much.*

I don't much care for this growing thing.

*My body's doing things I can't control and I just
don't like it.*

*All of a sudden, I have hair all over the place. Hair
under my arms and hair on my legs and hair around
my—well—hair between my legs. Okay, I'm not
liking it. I even got hair growing on my toes. What's
that about?*

*And my feet keep getting bigger and bigger. What's
with the big feet? When I was ten, I was kinda small
and I wasn't worried about hair. The only thing
I was worried about was trying to speak perfect
English. I made up my mind that year—when I
was ten—that I wasn't going to sound like another
Mexican. I was going to be an American. And when
I talked I was going to sound like one.*

So what if I don't look exactly like an American.

What does an American look like, anyway?

*Does an American have big hands and big feet and
hair around his—well, hair between his legs?*

Reading my own words embarrassed the hell out me. I mean,
what a *pendejo*. I had to be the world's biggest loser, writing about
hair, and stuff about my body. No wonder I stopped keeping a journal. It was like keeping a record of my own stupidity. Why would
I want to do that? Why would I want to remind myself what an
asshole I was?

I don't know why I didn't throw the journal across the room.
I kept thumbing through it randomly. And then I found a section
about my brother.

There are no pictures of my brother in our house.

*There are pictures of my two older sisters on their
wedding days. There are pictures of my mother in her
first communion dress. There are pictures of my father
when he was in Vietnam. There are pictures of me as
a baby, me on the first day of school, me holding a first
place trophy with my little league teammates.*

There are pictures of my three nieces and four nephews.

There are pictures of my grandparents, who are all dead.

All over the house, there are pictures.

But there are no pictures of my brother.

Because he's in prison.

No one in my house talks about him.

It's like being dead.

It's worse than being dead. At least the dead get talked about and you get to hear stories about them. People smile when they tell those stories. And they even laugh. Even the dog we used to have gets talked about.

Even Charlie, the dead dog, gets a story.

My brother doesn't get any stories.

He has been erased from our family history. It doesn't seem right. My brother is more than a word written on a chalkboard. I mean I have to write an essay on Alexander Hamilton and I even know what he looks like.

I'd rather write an essay on my brother.

I don't think anyone at school would be interested in reading that essay.

I wondered if I would ever have the courage to ask my parents to tell about my brother. I asked my older sisters once. Cecilia and Sylvia both shot me a look. "Don't ever bring him up."

I remember thinking that if they'd had a gun, she'd have shot me.

I caught myself whispering over and over again, "my brother is in prison, my brother is in prison, my brother is in prison." I wanted to feel those words in my mouth as I spoke them aloud. Words could be like food—they felt like something in your mouth. They tasted like something. "My brother is in prison." Those words tasted bitter.

But the worst part was that those words were living inside me. And they were leaking out of me. Words were not things you could control. Not always.

I didn't know what was happening to me. Everything was chaos and I was scared. I felt like Dante's room before he'd put everything in order. Order. That was what I needed. So I took my journal and started writing:

These are the things that are happening in my life (in no particular order):

- I got the flu and I feel terrible and I also feel terrible inside.

-I have always felt terrible inside. The reasons for this keep changing.

- I told my father I always had bad dreams. And that was true. I'd never told anyone that before. Not even myself. I only knew it was true when I said it.

- I hated my mom for a minute or two because she told me I didn't have any friends.

- I want to know about my brother. If I knew more about him, would I hate him?

- My father held me in his arms when I had a fever and I wanted him to hold me in his arms forever.

- The problem is not that I don't love my mother and father. The problem is that I don't know how to love them.

- Dante is the first friend I've ever had. That scares me.

- I think that if Dante really knew me, he wouldn't like me.

Eleven

WE HAD TO WAIT OVER TWO HOURS AT THE DOCTOR'S office. But my mom and I came prepared. I brought the book of poems Dante had brought over, the book of poems by William Carlos Williams—and Mom, she brought a novel she was reading, *Bless Me, Ultima.*

I was sitting across from her in the waiting room and I knew that sometimes, she was studying me. I felt her eyes on me. "I didn't know you liked poetry."

"It's Dante's book. His father has poetry books all over the house."

"It's a wonderful thing, what his father does."

"You mean being a professor?"

"Yes. How wonderful."

"I guess so," I said.

"When I went to the university, I never had one Mexican-American professor. Not one." There was a look on her face, almost anger.

I knew so little about her. About what she'd been through—about what it felt like to be her. I'd never cared, not really. I was starting to care, starting to wonder. Starting to wonder about everything.

"You like poetry, Ari?"

"Yeah. I guess I do."

"Maybe you'll be a writer," she said. "A poet."

It sounded like such a beautiful thing when she said it. Too beautiful for me.

Twelve

THERE WAS NOTHING WRONG WITH ME. THAT'S WHAT the doctor said. Just recovering normally from a severe flu. An afternoon wasted. Except I'd seen rage appear on my mother's face for an instant. That was something I would have to think about.

Just when she was becoming less of a mystery, she became more of one.

I finally got to leave the house.

I met Dante at the swimming pool, but I got winded easily. Mostly, I watched Dante swim.

It looked like it was going to rain. They always came this time of year, the rains. I heard the distant thunder. As we were walking toward Dante's house, it began to rain. And then it began to pour.

I looked at Dante. "I won't run if you don't."

"I won't run."

So we walked in the rain. I wanted to walk faster, but instead I slowed down. I looked at Dante. "Can you take it?"

He smiled.

Slowly, we made our way to his house. In the rain. Soaked.

Dante's father made us change into dry clothing when we got to his house, and gave us a lecture. "I already know that Dante doesn't have an ounce of common sense. But, Ari, I thought you were a little more responsible."

Dante couldn't help but interrupt. "Fat chance, Dad."

"He just got over a flu, Dante."

"I'm okay now," I said. "I like the rain." I looked down at the floor. "I'm sorry."

He put his hand on my chin and lifted it up. He looked at me. "Summer boys," he said.

I liked the way he looked at me. I thought he was the kindest man in the world. Maybe everybody was kind. Maybe even my father. But Mr. Quintana was brave. He didn't care if the whole world knew he was kind. Dante was just like him.

I asked Dante if his father ever got mad.

"He doesn't get mad very often. Hardly at all. But when he *does* get mad, I try to stay out of his way."

"What does he get mad at?'

"I threw out all his papers once."

"You did that?"

"He wasn't paying any attention to me."

"How old were you?"

"Twelve."

"So you made him mad on purpose."

"Something like that."

Out of nowhere I started coughing. We gave each other a panicked look. "Hot tea," Dante said.

I nodded. Good idea.

We sat, drinking our tea and watching the rain fall on his front porch. The sky was almost black and then it started hailing. It was so beautiful and scary, I wondered about the science of storms and how sometimes it seemed that a storm wanted to break the world and how the world refused to break.

I was staring at the hail when Dante tapped me on the shoulder. "We need to have a conversation."

"A conversation?"

"A talk."

"We talk every day."

"Yeah, but. I mean a talk."

"About what?"

"About, you know, what we're like. Our parents. Stuff like that."

"Did anybody ever tell you that you weren't normal?"

"Is that something I should aspire to?"

"You're not. You're not normal." I shook my head. "Where did you come from?"

"My parents had sex one night."

I could almost imagine his parents having sex—which was a little weird. "How do you know it was night?"

"Good point."

We busted out laughing.

"Okay," he said. "This is serious."

"Is this like a game?"

"Yes."

"I'll play."

"What's your favorite color?"

"Blue."

"Red. Favorite car?"

"Don't like cars."

"Me neither. Favorite song?"

"Don't have one. Yours?"

"'The Long and Winding Road.'"

"'The Long and Winding Road'?"

"The Beatles, Ari."

"Don't know it."

"Great song, Ari."

"Boring game, Dante. Are we interviewing each other?"

"Something like that."

"What position am I applying for?"

"Best friend."

"I thought I already had the job."

"Don't be so sure, you arrogant son of a bitch." He reached over and punched me. Not hard. But not soft either.

That made me laugh. "Nice mouth."

"Sometimes don't you just want to stand up and yell out all the cuss words you've learned?"

"Every day."

"Every day? You're worse than me." He looked at the hail. "It's like pissed off snow," he said.

That made me laugh.

Dante shook his head. "We're too nice, you know that?"

"What do you mean?"

"Our parents turned us into nice boys. I hate that."

"I don't think I'm so nice."

"Are you in a gang?"

"No."

"Do you do drugs?"

"No."

"Do you drink?"

"I'd like to."

"Me too. But that wasn't the question."

"No, I don't drink."

"Do you have sex?"

"Sex?"

"Sex, Ari."

"No, never had sex, Dante. But I'd like to."

"Me too. See what I mean? We're nice."

"Nice," I said. "Shit."

"Shit," he said.

And then we busted out laughing.

All afternoon, Dante shot questions at me. I answered them. When it stopped hailing and raining, the hot day had suddenly turned cool. The whole world seemed to be quiet and calm and I wanted to be the world and feel like that.

Dante got up from the step of the porch and stood on the sidewalk. He held up his arms toward the heavens. "It's all so damned beautiful," he said. He turned around. "Let's go for a walk."

"Our tennis shoes," I said.

"Dad put them in the dryer. Who cares?"

"Yeah, who cares?"

I knew I had done that before, walked barefoot on a wet side-walk, knew I had felt the breeze against my face. But it didn't feel like I'd ever done that. It felt like this was happening for the first time.

Dante was saying something but I wasn't really listening. I was staring at the sky, the dark clouds, listening to the distant thunder.

I looked at Dante, the breeze alive in his long, dark hair.

"We're leaving for a year," he said.

I was suddenly sad. No, not exactly sad. It felt like someone had punched me. "Leaving?"

"Yeah."

"Why? I mean, when?"

"My dad's going to be a visiting professor for a year at the University of Chicago. I think they're interested in hiring him."

"That's great," I said.

"Yeah," he said.

I'd been happy, and then, just like that, I was sad. I couldn't stand it, how sad I was. I didn't look at him. I just looked up at the sky. "That's really great. So when are you leaving?"

"At the end of August."

Six weeks. I smiled. "That's great."

"You keep saying '*that's great.*'"

"Well, it is."

"Yeah, it is."

"Aren't you sad, that I'm leaving?"

"Why would I be sad?"

He smiled and then, I don't know, there was this look on his face and it was so hard to tell what he was thinking or feeling, which was strange because Dante's face was a book that the whole world could read.

"Look," he said. He pointed at a bird in the middle of the street that was trying to fly. I could tell that one of his wings was broken.

"He's going to die," I whispered.

"We can save it."

Dante walked into the middle of the street and tried to pick up the bird. I watched him as he picked up the frightened bird. That's the last thing I remember before the car swerved around the corner. *Dante! Dante!* I knew the screams were coming from inside me. *Dante!*

I remember thinking that it was all a dream. All of it. It was just another bad dream. I kept thinking that the world was ending. I thought about the sparrows falling from the sky.

Dante!

The End of Summer

Do you remember
the summer of the rain . . .
You must let everything fall that wants to fall.
—Karen Fiser

One

I REMEMBER THE CAR SWERVING AROUND THE CORNER and Dante standing in the middle of the street holding a bird with a broken wing. I remember the slippery streets after the hail storm. I remember screaming his name. *Dante!*

I woke up in a hospital room.

Both of my legs were in a cast.

So was my left arm. Everything seemed really far away and my whole body hurt and I kept thinking *what happened?* I had a dull headache. *What happened? What happened?* Even my fingers hurt. I swear they did. I felt like a soccer ball after a game. Shit. I must have groaned or something, because all of a sudden my mom and dad were standing right beside my bed. My mom was crying.

"Don't cry," I said. My throat was really dry and I didn't sound like me. I sounded like someone else.

She bit her lip and reached over and combed my hair with her fingers.

I just looked at her. "Just don't cry, okay?"

"I was afraid you'd never wake up." She just sobbed into my father's shoulder.

Part of me was beginning to register everything. Another part of me just wanted to be somewhere else. Maybe none of this was really happening. But it was happening. It was. It didn't seem real. Except that I was in some serious pain. And that *was* real. It was the most real thing I had ever known.

"It hurts," I said.

That's when my mom just shut off her tears and became herself again. I was glad. I hated to see her weak and crying and falling apart. I wondered if that's the way she felt when my brother was taken away to prison. She pushed a button on my IV—then put it in my hand. "If you're in a lot of pain, you can push this every fifteen minutes."

"What is it?"

"Morphine."

"At long last I get to do drugs."

She ignored my joke. "I'll get the nurse." My mom, she was always moving into action. I liked that about her.

I looked around the room and wondered why I'd woken up. I kept thinking that if I could only get back to sleep, then it wouldn't hurt anymore. I preferred my bad dreams to the pain.

I looked at my dad. "It's okay," I said. "Everything's okay." I didn't really believe what I was saying.

My father was wearing a serious smile. "Ari, Ari," he said. "You're the bravest boy in the world."

"I'm not."

"You are."

"I'm the guy who's afraid of his own dreams, Dad. Remember?"

I loved his smile. Why couldn't he just smile all the time?

I wanted to ask him what happened. But I was afraid. I don't know. . . . My throat was dry and I just couldn't talk, and then it all came back to me and the image of Dante holding a wounded bird flashed in my head. I couldn't catch my breath and I was afraid, and I thought that maybe Dante was dead, and then there was all this panic living inside of me. I could feel this awful thing going on in my heart. "Dante?" I heard his name in my mouth.

The nurse was standing next to me. She had a nice voice. "I'm going to check your blood pressure," she said. I just lay there and let her do what she wanted. I didn't care. She smiled. "How's your pain?"

"My pain is fine," I whispered.

She laughed. "You gave us a good scare, young man."

"I like scaring people," I whispered.

My mother shook her head.

"I like the morphine," I said. I closed my eyes. "Dante?"

"He's fine," my mother said.

I opened my eyes.

I heard my father's voice. "He's scared. He's really scared."

"But he's okay?"

"Yes. He's okay. He's been waiting for you to wake up." My mother and father looked at each other. I heard my mother's voice. "He's here."

He was alive. Dante. I felt myself breathe. "What happened to the bird he was holding?"

My father reached over and squeezed my hand. "Crazy boys," he whispered. "Crazy, crazy boys." I watched him as he left the room.

My mother just kept staring at me.

"Where did Dad go?"

"He went to get Dante. He hasn't left. He's been here for the last thirty-six hours—waiting for you to—"

"Thirty-six hours?"

"You had surgery."

"Surgery?"

"They had to repair your bones."

"Okay."

"You'll have scars."

"Okay."

"You were awake for a little while after the surgery."

"I don't remember."

"You were in pain. They gave you something. Then you were out again."

"I don't remember."

"The doctor said you probably wouldn't."

"Did I say anything?"

"You just moaned. You asked for Dante. He wouldn't leave. He's a very stubborn young man."

That made me smile. "Yeah, well, he wins all our arguments. Just like the ones I have with you."

"I love you," she whispered. "Do you know how much I love you?"

It was nice the way she said that. She hadn't said that to me in a long time.

"Love you more." When I was a boy, I used to say that to her.

I thought she was going to cry again. But she didn't. Well, there were tears, but no real crying. She handed me a glass of water and I drank a little bit from a straw. "Your legs," she said. "The car ran over your legs."

"It wasn't the driver's fault," I said.

She nodded. "You had a very, very fine surgeon. All the breaks are below the knees. God—" She stopped. "They thought you might lose your legs—" She stopped and wiped the tears from her face. "I'm never going to let you out of the house, ever again."

"Fascist," I whispered.

She kissed me. "You sweet, beautiful kid."

"I'm not that sweet, Mom."

"Don't argue with me."

"Okay," I said. "I'm sweet."

She started crying again.

"It's okay," I said. "Everything's okay."

Dante and my dad walked into the room.

We looked at each other and smiled. He had some stitches above his left eye and the left side of his face was all scraped up. He had two black eyes and he was wearing a cast on his right arm. "Hi," he said.

"Hi," I said.

"We sort of match," he said.

"I got you beat," I whispered.

"Finally, you get to win an argument."

"Yeah, finally," I said. "You look like shit."

He was standing right next to me. "So do you."

We just looked at each other. "You sound tired," he said.

"Yeah."

"I'm glad you woke up."

"Yeah, I woke up. But it hurts less when I sleep."

"You saved my life, Ari."

"Dante's hero. Just what I always wanted to be."

"Don't do that, Ari. Don't make fun. You almost got yourself killed."

"I didn't do it on purpose."

He started crying. Dante and his tears. Dante and his tears. "You pushed me. You pushed me and you saved my life."

"Looks like I pushed you and beat the crap out of your face."

"I've got character now," he said.

"It was that damned bird," I said. "We can blame it all on the bird. The whole thing."

"I'm done with birds."

"No you're not."

He started crying again.

"Knock it off," I said. "My mom's been crying, and now you're crying—and even Dad looks like he wants to cry. Rules. I have rules. No crying."

"Okay," he said, "No more crying. Boys don't cry."

"Boys don't cry," I said. "Tears make me really tired."

Dante laughed. And then he got really serious. "You took a dive like you were in a swimming pool."

"We don't have to talk about this."

He just kept talking. "You dove at me, like, I don't know, like some kind of football player diving at the guy with the ball, and you pushed me out of the way. It all happened so fast and yet, you just, I don't know, you just knew what to do. Only you could have gotten yourself killed." I watched the tears falling from his face. "And all because I'm an idiot, standing in the middle of the road trying to save a stupid bird."

"You're breaking the no-crying rule again," I said. "And birds aren't stupid."

"I almost got you killed."

"You didn't do anything. You were just being you."

"No more birds for me."

"I like birds," I said.

"I've given them up. You saved my life."

"I told you. I didn't do it on purpose."

That made everybody laugh. God, I was tired. And it hurt so much and I remember Dante squeezing my hand and saying over and over, "I'm sorry I'm sorry Ari Ari Ari forgive me forgive me."

I guess the aftereffects of the surgery and the morphine made me feel a little high.

I remember humming. "La Bamba." I know that Dante and my mom and dad were still in the room, but I couldn't stay awake.

I remember Dante squeezing my hand. And I remember thinking, *Forgive you? For what, Dante? What is there to forgive?*

I don't know why, but there was rain in my dreams.

Dante and I were barefoot. The rain wouldn't stop.

And I was afraid.

Two

I DON'T KNOW HOW LONG I WAS IN THE HOSPITAL. A few days. Four days. Maybe five. Six. Hell, I don't know. It felt like forever.

They ran tests. That's what they do in hospitals. They were checking to make sure I had no other internal injuries. Especially brain injuries. I had a neurologist come in and see me. I didn't like him. He had dark hair and really deep green eyes that didn't like looking at people. He didn't seem to care. Either that or he cared too much. But the thing was, he wasn't very good with people. He didn't talk to me very much. He took a lot of notes.

I learned that nurses liked to make small talk and were in love with taking your vitals. That's what they did. They gave you a pill to help you sleep, then they woke you up all night. Shit. I wanted to sleep. I wanted to sleep and wake to see that my casts were gone. That's what I told one of the nurses. "Can't you just put me to sleep and wake me up when they take my casts off?"

"Silly boy," the nurse said.

Yeah. Silly boy.

I remember this one thing: My room was full of flowers. Flowers from all my mom's church-lady friends. Flowers from Dante's mother and father. Flowers from my sisters. Flowers from the neighbors. Flowers from my mother's garden. Flowers. Shit. I never had an opinion about flowers until then. I decided I didn't like them.

I sort of liked my surgeon. He was all about sports injuries. He was kind of young and I could tell he was a jock, you know this big gringo with big hands and long fingers and I wondered about that. He had the hands of a pianist. I remember thinking that. But I didn't know shit about pianists' hands or surgeons' hands and I remember dreaming them. His hands. In my dream, he healed Dante's bird and set it free into the summer sky. It was a nice dream. I didn't have those very often.

Dr. Charles. That was his name. He knew what he was doing. A good guy. Yeah, that's what I thought. He answered all my questions. And I had lots of them.

"Do I have pins in my legs?"

"Yes."

"Permanently?"

"Yes."

"And you won't have to go in again?"

"Hope not."

"Big talker, huh, Doc?"

He laughed. "You're a tough guy, huh?"

"I don't think I'm so tough."

"Well, I think you *are* tough. I think you're tough as hell."

"Yeah?"

"I've been around."

"Really?"

"Yes. Really, Aristotle. Can I tell you something?"

"Call me Ari."

"Ari." He smiled. "I'm surprised at how well you held up during the operation. And I'm surprised how well you're doing right now. It's amazing really."

"It's luck and genes," I said. "The genes I got from my mom and dad. And my luck, well, I don't where that came from. God, maybe."

"You a religious guy?"

"Not really. That would be my mom."

"Yeah, well, moms and God generally get along pretty well."

"Guess so," I said. "When am I going to stop feeling like crap?"

"In no time."

"No time? Am I going to be hurting and itching for eight weeks?"

"It'll get better."

"Sure. And how come, if my legs were broken *below* the knee, my casts are *above* the knee?"

"I just want to keep you still for two or three weeks. I don't want you to be bending. Might hurt yourself again. Tough guys, they push themselves. After a few weeks, I'll change your casts. Then you'll be able to bend your legs."

"Shit."

"Shit?"

"A few weeks?"

"We'll give it three weeks."

"Three weeks without bending my legs?"

"It's not such a long time."

"It's summer."

"And then I'll get you to a physical therapist."

I took a breath. "Shit. And this?" I said, aiming my arm cast at him. I was getting really depressed.

"That fracture wasn't so bad. It'll be off in a month."

"A month? Shit."

"You like that word, don't you?"

"I'd prefer to use other words."

He smiled. "Shit will do just fine."

I wanted to cry. I did. Mostly I was mad and frustrated and I knew he was going to tell me that I needed to be patient. And that's exactly what he said.

"You just need to be patient. You'll be good as new. You're young. You're strong. You have great, healthy bones. I have every reason to believe that you're going to heal very nicely."

Very nicely. Patient. Shit.

He checked the feeling in my toes, had me breathe, had me follow his fingers with my left eye, then my right eye. "You know," he said, "that's a helluva thing you did for your friend, Dante."

"Look, I wish people would stop talking about that."

He looked at me. He had this look on his face. "You could have wound up a paraplegic. Or worse."

"Worse?"

"Young man, you could have been killed."

Killed. Okay. "People keep saying that. Look, Doc, I'm alive."

"You don't much like being a hero, do you?"

"I told Dante I didn't do it on purpose. Everyone thought that was funny. It wasn't a joke. I don't even remember diving toward him. It wasn't as if I said to myself, *I'm going to save my friend, Dante.*

It wasn't like that. It was just a reflex, you know, like when someone hits your funny bone below the knee. Your leg just jerks. That's how it was. It just happened."

"Just a reflex? It just happened?"

"Exactly."

"And you're responsible for none of it?"

"It was just one of those things."

"Just one of those things?"

"Yeah."

"I have a different theory."

"Of course you do—you're an adult."

He laughed. "What do you have against adults?"

"They too have many ideas about who we are. Or who we should be."

"That's our job."

"Nice," I said.

"Nice," he said. "Listen, son, I know you don't think of yourself as being brave or courageous or any of those things. Of course you don't."

"I'm just a regular guy."

"Yeah, that's how you see yourself. But, you pushed your friend out of the way of an oncoming car. You did that, Ari, and you didn't think about yourself or what would happen to you. You did that because that's who you are. I'd think about that if I were you."

"What for?"

"Just think about it."

"I'm not sure I want to do all that thinking."

122

"Okay. Just so you know, Ari, I think you're a very rare young man. That's what I think."

"I told you, Doc, it was just a reflex."

He grinned at me and put his hand on my shoulder. "I know your kind, Ari. I'm on to you." I don't know exactly what he meant by that. But he was smiling.

Right after that conversation with Dr. Charles, Dante's mom and dad came to visit. Mr. Quintana came right up to me and kissed me on the cheek. Just like it was this normal thing to do. I guess for him it *was* normal. And really, I thought that the gesture was kind of nice, you know, sweet, but it made me a little bit uncomfortable. It was something I wasn't used to. And he kept thanking me over and over and over. I wanted to tell him to knock it off. But, I just let him go on and on because I knew how much he loved his Dante and he was so happy and I was happy that he was happy. So it was okay.

I wanted to change the subject. I mean, I didn't have a lot to talk about. I felt like crap. But they were there to see me and I could talk and, you know, I could process things even though my mind was still a little foggy. So I said, "So you'll be in Chicago for a year?"

"Yes," he said. "Dante hasn't forgiven me yet."

I sort of just looked at him.

"He's still mad. He says he wasn't consulted."

That made me smile.

"He doesn't want to miss swimming for a year. He told me he could live with you for a year."

That surprised me. Dante kept more secrets than I thought. I closed my eyes.

"Are you okay, Ari?"

"The itching makes me crazy sometimes. So I just close my eyes."

He had this really kind look on his face.

I didn't tell him that my new thing was trying to imagine what my brother looked like every time I couldn't stand the sensation in my legs. "Anyway, it's good to talk," I said. "It keeps my mind off things." I opened my eyes. "So Dante's mad at you."

"Well, I told him there was no way I was going to leave him behind for a year."

I pictured Dante giving his father a look. "Dante's stubborn."

I heard Mrs. Quintana's voice. "He takes after me."

That made me smile. I knew it was true.

"You know what I think?" she said. "I think Dante's going to miss you. I think that's the real reason he doesn't want to leave."

"I'll miss him too," I said. I was sorry I'd said that. It was true, okay, but I didn't have to say it.

His father looked at me. "Dante doesn't have a lot of friends."

"I always thought everybody liked him."

"That's true. Everybody likes Dante. But he's always been something of a loner. He doesn't seem to go along with the crowd. He's always been like that." He smiled at me. "Like you."

"Maybe so," I said.

"You're the best friend he's ever had. I think you should know that."

I didn't want to know that. I didn't know *why* I didn't want to know that. I smiled at him. He was a good man. And he was talking to me. To me. To Ari. And even though I didn't particularly want to have this conversation, I knew I just had to go with it. There weren't that many good people in the world.

"You know, I'm kind of a boring guy when you think about it. Don't know what Dante sees." I couldn't believe I'd said that to them.

Mrs. Quintana had been standing further away. But she came up and stood right next to her husband. "Why do you think that, Ari?"

"What?"

"Why do you think you're boring?"

God, I thought, *the therapist has shown up*. I just shrugged. I closed my eyes. Okay, I knew when I opened my eyes, they would still be there. Dante and I were cursed with parents who cared. Why couldn't they just leave us alone? What ever happened to parents who were too busy or too selfish or just didn't give a shit about what their sons did?

I decided to open my eyes again.

I knew Mr. Quintana was going to say something else. I could just feel it. But maybe he sensed something about me. I don't know. He didn't say anything else.

We started talking about Chicago. I was glad we weren't talking about me or Dante or what happened. Mr. Quintana said the university had found them a small place. Mrs. Quintana was taking an eight-month leave from her practice. So really they wouldn't be gone a whole year. Just a school year. Not such a long time.

I don't remember everything that the Quintanas talked about. They were trying so hard, and a part of me was happy they were there but another part of me just didn't give a damn. And, of course, the conversation changed back to me and Dante. Mrs. Quintana said she was going to take Dante to a counselor. "He feels so bad," she said. She said maybe it would be a good idea if I went to see a counselor too. Yeah, the therapist thing to say. "I'm worried about the both of you," she said.

"You should have coffee with my mother," I said. "You can worry together."

Mr. Quintana thought that was funny, but really I didn't say it to be funny.

Mrs. Quintana grinned at me. "Aristotle Mendoza, you're not the least bit boring."

After a while, I was just really tired and stopped concentrating.

I don't know why I couldn't stand the gratitude in Mr. Quintana's eyes when he said good-bye. But it was Mrs. Quintana who really got to me. Unlike her husband, she wasn't the kind of woman who let people see what she really felt. Not that she wasn't nice and decent and all of that. Of course she was. It was just that when Dante said that his mother was inscrutable, I knew exactly what he was saying.

Before she left, Mrs. Quintana took my face between her two hands, looked right into my eyes, and whispered, "Aristotle Mendoza, I will love you forever." Her voice was soft and sure and fierce and there weren't any tears in her eyes. Her words were serene and sober and she looked right at me because she wanted me to know that she meant every word of what she'd said to me.

This is what I understood: a woman like Mrs. Quintana didn't use the word "love" very often. When she said that word, she meant it. And one more thing I understood: Dante's mother loved him more than he would ever know. I didn't know what to do with that piece of information. So I just kept it inside. That's what I did with everything. Kept it inside.

Three

I GOT A PHONE CALL FROM DANTE. "SORRY, I HAVEN'T gone to see you," he said.

"It's okay," I said. "I'm not really in the mood to talk to people."

"Me neither," he said. "Did my mom and dad tire you out?"

"No. They're nice."

"My mom says I have to go to a counselor."

"Yeah, she said something like that."

"Are you gonna go?"

"I'm not going anywhere."

"Your mom and my mom, they talked."

"Bet they did. So are you gonna go?"

"When Mom thinks something is a good idea, there's no escape. It's best to go along quietly."

That made me laugh. I wanted to ask him what he'd tell the counselor. But I don't think I really wanted to know. "How's your face?" I said.

"I like staring at it."

"You're really weird. Maybe it is a good idea for you to see a counselor."

I liked hearing him laugh. It made things seem normal. A part of me thought things would never be normal again.

"Does it still hurt a lot, Ari?"

"I don't know. It's as if my legs own me. I can't think about anything else. I just want to yank the casts off and, shit, I don't know."

"It's all my fault." I hated that thing in his voice.

"Listen," I said. "Can we have some rules here?"

"Rules? More rules. You mean like the no-crying rule?"

"Exactly."

"Did they take you off the morphine?"

"Yes."

"You're just in a bad mood."

"This isn't about my mood. It's about rules. I don't know what the big deal is—you love rules."

"I hate rules. I like to break them mostly."

"No, Dante, you like to make your own rules. So long as the rules are yours, you like them."

"Oh, so now you're analyzing me?"

"See, you don't have to go to a counselor. You have me."

"I'll tell my mom."

"Let me know what she says." I think we were both smiling. "Look, Dante, I just want to say that we have to have some rules here."

"Post-op rules?"

"You can call them that if you want."

"Okay, so what are the rules?

"Rule number one: We won't talk about the accident. Not ever.

Rule number two: Stop saying thank you. Rule number three: This whole thing is not your fault. Rule number four: Let's just move on."

"I'm not sure I like the rules, Ari."

"Take it up with your counselor. But those are the rules."

"You sound like you're mad."

"I'm not mad."

I could tell Dante was thinking. He knew I was serious. "Okay," he said. "We won't ever talk about the accident. It's a stupid rule, but okay. And can I just say 'I'm sorry' one more time? And can I say 'thank you' one more time?"

"You just did. No more, okay?"

"Are you rolling your eyes?"

"Yes."

"Okay, no more."

That afternoon, he took the bus and came to visit me. He looked, well, not so good. He tried to pretend it didn't hurt him to look at me but he could never hide anything that he felt. "Don't feel sorry for me," I said. "The doctor said I was going to heal very nicely."

"Very nicely?"

"That's exactly what he said. So give me eight to ten or twelve weeks, and I'm going to be myself again. Not that being myself is such a great thing."

Dante laughed. Then he looked at me. "Are you going to initiate a no-laughing rule?"

"Laughing is always good. Laughing works."

"Good," he said. He sat down and took out some books from his backpack. "I brought you reading material. *The Grapes of Wrath* and *War and Peace*."

"Great," I said.

He gave me a look. "I could have brought you more flowers."

"I hate flowers."

"Somehow I guessed that." He grinned at me.

I stared at the books. "They're fucking long," I said.

"That's the point."

"Guess I have time."

"Exactly."

"You've read them?"

"'Course I have."

"'Course you have."

He slid the books onto the stand next to my bed.

I shook my head. Yeah. Time. Shit.

He took out his sketch pad.

"You going to sketch me in my casts?"

"Nope. I just thought that maybe you'd want to look at some of my sketches."

"Okay," I said.

"Don't get too excited."

"It's not that. The pain comes and goes."

"Does it hurt right now?"

"Yes."

"Are you taking anything?"

"I'm trying not to. I hate the way whatever the hell they give me makes me feel." I pushed the button on the bed, so I could sit up. I wanted to say "I hate this" but I didn't. I wanted to scream.

Dante handed me the sketch pad.

I started to open it.

"You can look at it after I leave."

I guess I was holding a question on my face.

"You have rules. I have rules too."

It was good to laugh. I wanted to laugh and laugh and laugh until I laughed myself into becoming someone else. The really great thing about laughing was that it made me forget about the strange and awful feeling in my legs. Even if it was only for a minute.

"Tell me about the people on the bus," I said.

He smiled. "There was a man on the bus who told me about the aliens in Roswell. He said that . . ." I don't know that I really listened to the story. I guess it was enough just to hear the sound of Dante's voice. It was like listening to a song. I kept thinking about the bird with the broken wing. Nobody told me what happened to the bird. And I couldn't even ask because I would be breaking my own rule about not talking about the accident. Dante kept telling the story about the man on the bus and the aliens in Roswell and how some had escaped to El Paso and were planning on taking over the transportation system.

As I watched him, the thought came into my head that I hated him.

He read me some poems. They were nice I guess. I wasn't in the mood.

When he finally left, I stared at his sketch pad. He'd never let anybody look at his sketches. And now he was showing them to me. To me. Ari.

I knew he was only letting me see his work because he was grateful.

I hated all that gratitude.

Dante felt he owed me something. I didn't want that. Not that.

I took his sketch pad in my hands and flung it across the room.

Four

IT WAS JUST MY LUCK THAT MY MOTHER WAS WALKING into the room as Dante's sketch pad hit the wall.

"You want to tell me what that was about?"

I shook my head.

My mother picked up the sketch pad. She sat down. She was going to open it.

"Don't do that," I said

"What?"

"Don't look at it."

"Why?"

"Dante doesn't like people to look at his sketches."

"Only you?"

"I guess so."

"Then why'd you throw it across the room?"

"I don't know."

"I know you don't want to talk about this, Ari, but I think—"

"I don't want to know what you think, Mom. I just don't want to talk."

"It's not good for you to keep everything inside. I know this is hard. And the next two or three months or so are going to be very difficult. Keeping everything bottled up inside you isn't going to help you heal."

"Well, maybe you'll have to take me to see some counselor and have me talk about my difficulties."

"I know sarcasm when I hear it. And I don't think a counselor would be such a bad idea."

"You and Mrs. Quintana making backroom deals?"

"You're a wise guy."

I closed my eyes and opened them. "I'll make a deal with you, Mom." I could almost taste the anger on my tongue. I swear. "You talk about my brother and I'll talk about what I feel."

I saw the look on her face. She looked surprised and hurt. And angry.

"Your brother has nothing to do with any of this."

"You think you and Dad are the only ones who can keep things on the inside? Dad keeps a whole war inside of him. I can keep things on the inside too."

"One thing has nothing to do with the other."

"That's not how I see it. You go to a counselor. Dad goes to a counselor. And maybe after that, I'll go to a counselor."

"I'm going to have a cup of coffee," she said.

"Take your time." I closed my eyes. I guess that was going to be my new thing. I couldn't exactly storm away in anger. I'd just have to close my eyes and shut out the universe.

Five

MY DAD VISITED ME EVERY EVENING.

I wanted him to go away.

He tried to talk to me but it wasn't working. He pretty much just sat there. That made me crazy. I got this idea into my head. "Dante left two books," I said. "Which one do you want to read? I'll read the other."

He chose *War and Peace*.

The Grapes of Wrath was fine with me.

It wasn't so bad, me and my father sitting in a hospital room. Reading.

My legs itched like crazy.

Sometimes, I would just breathe.

Reading helped.

Sometimes I knew my father was studying me.

He asked me if I was still having dreams.

"Yes," I said. "Now I'm looking for my legs."

"You'll find them," he said.

My mom never brought up the conversation we'd had about my brother. She just pretended it hadn't happened. I'm not sure how I felt about that. The good thing was, she wasn't pushing me to talk. But, you know, she just hung out, trying to make sure I was comfortable. *I wasn't comfortable.* Who in the hell could be comfortable with two leg casts? I needed help doing everything. And I was tired of bedpans. And I was tired of taking rides in a wheelchair. My best friend, the wheelchair. And my best friend, my mom. She was making me crazy. "Mom, you're hovering. You're going to make me say the 'f' word. You really are."

"Don't you dare say that word in front of me."

"I swear I'm going to, Mom, if you don't stop."

"What is this wise guy role you've been playing?"

"It's not a role, Mom. I'm not in a play." I was desperate. "Mom, my legs hurt and when they don't hurt, they itch. They've taken the morphine away—"

"Which is a good thing," my mother interrupted.

"Yeah, okay, Mom. We can't have a little addict running around, now can we?" As if I could run around. "Shit. Mom, I just want to be alone. Is that okay with you? That I just want to be alone?"

"Okay," she said.

She gave me more space after that.

Dante never came back to visit. He'd call twice a day just to say hi. He'd gotten sick. The flu. I felt bad for him. He sounded terrible. He said he had dreams. I told him I had dreams too. One day he called and said, "I want to say something to you, Ari."

"Okay," I said.

And then he didn't say anything.

"What?" I said.

"Never mind," he said. "It doesn't matter."

I thought it probably mattered a lot. "Okay," I said.

"I wish we could swim again."

"Me too," I said.

I was glad he called. But I was also glad he couldn't come to see me. I don't know why. For some reason I thought: *My life will be different now.* And I kept repeating that to myself. I wondered what it would have been like to lose my legs. And in a sense, I had lost them. Not forever. But for a while.

I tried using crutches. It just wasn't going to happen. Not that the nurses and my mom didn't warn me. I guess I just had to see for myself. It was just impossible with both my legs completely straight and my left arm in a cast.

It was hard to do everything. The worst thing for me was that I had to use a bedpan. I guess you could say that I found it humiliating. That was the word. I couldn't even really take a shower—and I didn't really have the use of both hands. But the good thing was that I could use all my fingers. That was something I guess.

I got to practice using a wheelchair with my legs out. I named the wheelchair Fidel.

Dr. Charles came to visit me one last time.

"Have you thought about what I told you?"

"Yup," I said.

"And?"

"And I think you made a really good decision by becoming a surgeon. You would have made a lousy therapist."

"So you've always been a wiseass, huh?"

"Always."

"Well, you can go home and be a wiseass there. How does that sound?"

I wanted to hug him. I was happy. I was happy for about ten seconds. And then I started to feel really anxious.

I gave my mom a lecture. "When we get home, you're not allowed to hover."

"What is this about making all these rules, Ari?"

"No hovering. That's all."

"You'll need help," she said.

"But I'll need to be left alone too."

She smiled at me. "Big Brother is watching you."

I smiled back at her.

Even when I wanted to hate my mother, I loved her. I wondered if it was normal for fifteen-year-old boys to love their mothers. Maybe it was. Maybe it wasn't.

I remember getting into the car. I had to stretch out in the backseat. It was a pain in the ass to get me in. It was a good thing my father was strong. Everything was so damned hard and my parents were so afraid of hurting me.

No one said anything in the car.

As I stared out, I looked for birds.

I wanted to close my eyes and let the silence swallow me whole.

Six

THE MORNING AFTER I CAME HOME, MY MOM WASHED
my hair. "You have such beautiful hair," she said.

"I think I'll grow it long," I said. Like I had a choice. A trip to a
barber shop would have been a nightmare.

She gave me a sponge bath.

I closed my eyes and sat still for her.

She shaved me.

When she left the room, I broke down and sobbed. I had never
been this sad. *I have never been this sad. I have never been this sad.*

My heart hurt even more than my legs.

I know my mom heard me. She had the decency to let me cry
alone.

I stared out the window most of the day. I practiced pushing
myself on the wheelchair through the house. My mom kept rear-
ranging things to make it easier.

We smiled at each other a lot.

"You can watch television," she said.

"Brain rot," I said. "I have a book."

"Do you like it?"

"Yeah. It's kind of hard. Not the words. But, you know, what it's about. I guess Mexicans aren't the only poor people in the world."

We looked at each other. We didn't really smile. But we were smiling at each other on the inside.

My sisters came over for dinner. My nephews and nieces signed my cast. I think I smiled a lot and everyone was talking and laughing and it all seemed so normal. And I was glad for my mom and dad because I think it was me who was making the house sad.

When my sisters left, I asked my dad if we could sit on the front porch.

I sat on Fidel. My mother and father sat on their outdoor rocking chairs.

We drank coffee.

My mother and father held hands. I wondered what that was like, to hold someone's hand. I bet you could sometimes find all of the mysteries of the universe in someone's hand.

Seven

IT WAS A RAINY SUMMER. EVERY AFTERNOON, THE clouds would gather like a flock of crows, and it would rain. I fell in love with the thunder. I finished reading the *Grapes of Wrath*. Then I finished reading *War and Peace*. I decided I wanted to read all the books by Ernest Hemingway. My father decided he would read everything that I read. Maybe that was our way of talking.

Dante came over every day.

Mostly Dante would talk and I would listen. He decided that he should read *The Sun Also Rises* to me aloud. I wasn't going to argue with him. I was never going to out-stubborn Dante Quintana. So every day he would read a chapter of the book. And then we would talk about it.

"It's a sad book," I said.

"Yeah. That's why you like it."

"Yeah," I said. "That's exactly right."

He never asked me anything about what I thought of his sketches. I was glad about that. I had placed his sketchbook under my bed and refused to look at it. I think I was punishing Dante. He had given me a piece of himself that he had never given to another human being.

And I hadn't even bothered to look at it. Why was I doing that?

One day he blurted out that he'd finally gone to see a counselor.

I was hoping he wouldn't tell me anything about his counseling session. He didn't. I was glad about that. And then I was sort of mad he didn't. Okay, so I was moody. And inconsistent. Yeah, that's what I was.

Dante kept looking at me.

"What?"

"Are you going to go?"

"Where?"

"To see a counselor, you idiot."

"No."

"No?"

I looked at my legs.

I could see he wanted to say "I'm sorry" again. But he didn't.

"It helped," he said. "Going to the counselor. It wasn't so bad. It really did help."

"Are you going back?"

"Maybe."

I nodded. "Talking doesn't help everybody."

Dante smiled. "Not that you'd know."

I smiled back. "Yeah. Not that I'd know."

Eight

I DON'T KNOW HOW IT HAPPENED, BUT ONE MORNING Dante came over and decided he'd be the one to give me a sponge bath. "Is it okay?" he said.

"Well, it's kind of my mom's job," I said.

"She said it was okay," he said.

"You asked her?"

"Yeah."

"Oh," I said. "Still, it's really her job."

"Your dad? He's never bathed you?"

"No."

"Shaved you?"

"No. I don't want him to."

"Why not?"

"I just don't."

He was quiet. "I won't hurt you."

You've already hurt me. That's what I wanted to say. Those were the words that entered my head. Those were the words I wanted to slap him with. The words were mean. I was mean.

"Let me," he said.

Instead of telling him to go screw himself, I said okay.

I'd learned to make myself perfectly passive when my mother bathed and shaved me. I would shut my eyes and think about the characters in the book I was reading. Somehow that got me through.

I closed my eyes.

I felt Dante's hands on my shoulders, the warm water, the soap, the washcloth.

Dante's hands were bigger than my mother's. And softer. He was slow, methodical, careful. He made me feel as fragile as porcelain.

I never once opened my eyes.

We didn't say a word.

I felt his hands on my bare chest. On my back.

I let him shave me.

When he was done, I opened my eyes. Tears were falling down his face. I should have expected that. I wanted to yell at him. I wanted to tell him that it was me who should be crying.

Dante had this look on his face. He looked like an angel. And all I wanted to do was put my fist through his jaw. I couldn't stand my own cruelty.

Nine

THREE WEEKS AND TWO DAYS AFTER THE ACCIDENT, I went to the doctor's office to get new casts and x-rays. My father took the day off. On the way to the doctor's office, my dad was very talkative—which was very weird. "August thirtieth," my dad said.

Okay, so that was my birthday.

"I thought maybe you'd like a car."

A car. Shit. "Yeah," I said. "I don't drive."

"You can learn."

"You said you didn't want me driving."

"I never said that. It was your mom who said that."

I couldn't see my mom's face from the backseat. And I couldn't exactly lean over. "And what does my mom think?"

"You mean your mom, the fascist?"

"Yeah, her," I said.

We all busted out laughing.

"So, what do you say, Ari?"

My dad sounded like a boy. "I think I'd like, you know, one of those low-rider cars."

My mother didn't skip a beat. "Over my dead body."

I lost it. I think I probably laughed for five minutes straight. My father joined in the fun. "Okay," I said finally. "Seriously?"

"Seriously."

"I'd like an old pickup truck."

My mother and father exchanged glances.

"We can make that happen," my mother said.

"I only have two questions. The first question is this: Are you getting me a car because you feel bad that I'm an invalid?"

My mother was ready for that one. "No. You'll be in invalid for another three or four weeks. Then you'll do some therapy. Then you'll be fine. And you won't be invalid. You'll just return to being a pain in the ass."

My mother never cussed. This was serious business.

"What was your second question?"

"Which of the two of you are going to give me driving lessons?"

They both answered at the same time. "I am."

I figured I'd let them fight it out.

Ten

I HATED LIVING IN THE SMALL AND CLAUSTROPHOBIC atmosphere of my house. It didn't feel like home anymore. I felt like an unwanted guest. I hated being waited on all the time. I hated that my parents were so patient with me. I did. That's the truth. They didn't do anything wrong. They were just trying to help me. But I hated them. And I hated Dante too.

And I hated myself for hating them. So there it was, my own vicious cycle. My own private universe of hate.

I thought it would never be over.

I thought my life would never get better. But it *did* get better with my new casts. I could bend my knees. I used Fidel for another week. Then my arm cast came off and I could use my crutches. I asked my dad to put Fidel in the basement so I wouldn't have to look at that stupid wheelchair ever again.

With the full use of my hands, I could bathe myself. I took out my journal and this is what I wrote: *I TOOK A SHOWER!*

I was actually almost happy. Me, Ari, almost happy.

"Your smile is back." That's what Dante said.

"Smiles are like that. They come and go."

My arm was sore. The physical therapist gave me some

exercises. Look at me, I can move my arm. Look at me.

I woke up one day, made my way to the bathroom and stared at myself in the mirror. *Who are you?* I made my way to the kitchen. My mom was there, drinking a cup of coffee and looking over her lesson plans for the new school year.

"Planning for the future, Mom?"

"I like to be prepared."

I sat myself down across from her. "You're a good girl scout."

"You hate that about me, don't you?"

"Why do you say that?"

"You hated that whole thing, that whole scout thing."

"Dad made me go."

"You ready to go back to school?"

I held up my crutches. "Yeah, I get to wear shorts every day."

She poured me a cup of coffee and combed my hair with her fingers. "You want a haircut?"

"No. I like it."

She smiled. "I like it too."

We drank coffee together, me and my mom. We didn't talk a lot. Mostly I watched her look through her folders. The morning light always came through the kitchen. And just then, she looked young. I thought she was really beautiful. She *was* beautiful. I envied her. She had always known exactly who she was.

I wanted to ask her, *Mom, when will I know who I am?* But I didn't.

Me and my crutches walked back into my room and took out my journal. I'd been avoiding writing in it. I think I was afraid all my anger would spill out on the pages. And I just didn't want to look at all that rage. It was a different kind of pain. A pain I couldn't stand. I tried not to think. I just started writing:

- School starts in five days. Junior year. Guess I'll have to go to school on crutches. Everyone will notice me. Shit.

- I see myself driving down a desert road in a pickup, no one else around. I'm listening to Los Lobos. I see myself lying on the bed of the pickup truck, staring up at all the stars. No light pollution.

- Physical therapy will be coming up soon. Doctor says swimming will be very good. Swimming will make me think of Dante. Shit.

- When I'm well enough, I'm going to start lifting weights. Dad has his old weights in the basement.

- Dante's leaving in a week. I'm glad. I need a break from him. I'm sick of him coming over every day just because he feels bad. I don't know if we will ever be friends again.

- I want a dog. I want to walk him every day.

- Walking every day! I am in love with that thought.

- I don't know who I am.

*- What I really want for my birthday: for someone
to talk about my brother. I want to see his picture on
one of the walls of our house.*

*- Somehow I'd hoped that this would be the summer
that I would discover that I was alive. The world my
mom and dad said was out there waiting for me.
That world doesn't actually exist.*

Dante came over that evening. We sat on the steps of the front porch.

He stretched out his arm, the one that had been broken in the accident.

I stretched out *my* arm, the one that had been broken in the accident.

"All better," he said.

We both smiled.

"When something gets broken, it can be fixed." He stretched out his arm again. "Good as new."

"Maybe not good as new," I said. "But good anyway."

His face had healed. In the evening light, he was perfect again.

"I went swimming today," he said.

"How was it?"

"I love swimming."

"I know," I said.

"I love swimming," he said again. He was quiet for a little while. And then he said, "I love swimming—*and you*."

I didn't say anything.

"Swimming and you, Ari. Those are the things I love the most."

"You shouldn't say that," I said.

"It's true."

"I didn't say it wasn't true. I just said you shouldn't say it."

"Why not?"

"Dante, I don't—"

"You don't have to say anything. I know that we're different. We're not the same."

"No, we're not the same."

I knew what he was saying and I wished to God he was someone else, someone who didn't have to say things out loud. I just kept nodding.

"Do you hate me?"

I don't know what happened just then. Since the accident, I'd been mad at everyone, hated everyone, hated Dante, hated Mom and Dad, hated myself. Everyone. But right then, I knew I didn't really hate everyone. Not really. I didn't hate Dante at all. I didn't know how to be his friend. I didn't know how to be anybody's friend. But that didn't mean I hated him. "No," I said. "I don't hate you, Dante."

We just sat there, not saying anything.

"Will we be friends? When I come back from Chicago?"

"Yes," I said.

"Really?"

"Yes."

"Do you promise?"

I looked into his perfect face. "I promise."

He smiled. He wasn't crying.

Eleven

DANTE AND HIS PARENTS CAME OVER TO OUR HOUSE the day before they left for Chicago. Our moms cooked together. It didn't surprise me they got along so well. They were alike in some ways. It *did* surprise me how well Mr. Quintana and my dad got along. They sat in the living room and drank beer and talked about politics. I mean, I guess they more or less agreed about things.

Dante and I hung out on the front porch.

For some reason, we were both into front porches.

We weren't really talking very much. I think we didn't really know what to say to each other. And then I got this idea into my head. I was playing with my crutches. "Your sketch pad is under my bed. Will you go get it for me?"

Dante hesitated. But then he nodded.

He disappeared into the house and I waited.

When he came back, he handed me the sketchbook.

"I have a confession to make," I said.

"What?"

"I haven't looked at it."

He didn't say anything.

"Can we look at it together?" I said.

He didn't say anything, so I just opened up the sketchbook. The first sketch was a self-portrait. He was reading a book. The second sketch was of his father who was also reading a book. And then there was another self-portrait. Just his own face.

"You look sad in this one."

"Maybe I was sad that day."

"Are you sad now?"

He didn't answer the question.

I flipped the page and stared at a sketch of me. I didn't say anything. There were five or six sketches he'd done of me the day he'd come over. I studied them carefully. There was nothing careless about his sketches. Nothing careless at all. They were exact and deliberate and full of all the things he felt. And yet they seemed to be so spontaneous.

Dante didn't say a word as I looked over his sketches.

"They're honest," I said.

"Honest?"

"Honest and true. You're going to be a great artist someday."

"Someday," he said. "Listen, you don't have to keep the sketchbook."

"You gave it to me. It's mine."

That's all we said. Then we just sat there.

We didn't really say good-bye that night. Not really. Mr. Quintana kissed me on the cheek. That was his thing. Mrs. Quintana placed her hand on my chin and lifted my head up. She looked into my eyes as if she wanted to remind me of what she'd said to me in the hospital.

Dante hugged me.

I hugged him back.

"See you in a few months," he said.

"Yeah," I said.

"I'll write," he said.

I knew he would.

I wasn't so sure I'd write back.

Me and my mom and dad sat out on the front porch after they'd left. It started to rain and we just sat. Sat and watched the rain in silence. I kept seeing Dante standing in the rain holding a bird with a broken wing. I couldn't tell if he was smiling or not. What if he'd lost his smile?

I bit my lip so I wouldn't cry.

"I love the rain," my mother whispered.

I love it too. I love it too.

I felt like I was the saddest boy in the universe. Summer had come and gone. Summer had come and gone. And the world was ending.

Letters on a Page

There are some words I'll never learn to spell.

One

FIRST DAY OF SCHOOL, AUSTIN HIGH SCHOOL, 1987.
"What happened to you, Ari?" I had a one-word answer to that question. "Accident." Gina Navarro accosted me during lunch and said, "Accident?"

"Yup," I said.

"That's no answer."

Gina Navarro. Somehow she felt entitled to hound me because she'd known me since first grade. If there's one thing I knew about Gina it was that she didn't like simple answers. *Life is complicated.* That was her motto. *What to say? What to say?* So I didn't say anything. I just looked at her.

"You're never going to change, are you, Ari?"

"Change is overrated."

"Not that you'd know."

"Yeah, not that I'd know."

"I'm not sure if I like you, Ari."

"I'm not sure if I like you either, Gina."

"Well, not all relationships are based on *like.*"

"Guess not."

"Listen, I'm the closest thing you've ever had to a long-term relationship."

"You're depressing the hell out of me, Gina."

"Don't blame me for your melancholy."

"Melancholy?"

"Look it up. Your sad sack moods are nobody's fault but yours. Just look at yourself why don't you? You're a mess."

"I'm a mess? Take a hike, Gina. Leave me alone."

"That's your problem. Too much alone. Too much Ari Time. Talk."

"Don't want to." I knew she wasn't going to let this go.

"Look, so just tell me what happened."

"I already told you. It was an accident."

"What kind of accident?"

"It's complicated."

"You're mocking me."

"You noticed."

"You're a shit."

"Sure I am."

"Sure you are."

"You're bugging the crap out of me."

"You should thank me. At least I'm talking to you. You're the most unpopular guy in the whole school."

I pointed at Charlie Escobedo who was walking out of the cafeteria. "No, that's the most unpopular guy in the whole school. I'm not even a close second."

Just then Susie Byrd was walking by. She sat right next to Gina.

She stared at my crutches. "What happened?"

"Accident."

"Accident?"

"That's what he claims."

"What kind of accident?"

"He won't say."

"I guess the two of you don't really need me for this conversation, do you?"

Gina was getting mad. The last time I'd seen that look on her face, she'd thrown a rock at me. "Tell us," she said.

"Okay," I said. "It was after a rainstorm. Remember the afternoon it hailed?"

They both nodded.

"That was the day. Well, there was a guy standing in the middle of the road and a car was coming. And I took a dive and shoved him out of the way. I saved his life. The car ran over my legs. And that's the whole story."

"You're so full of shit," Gina said.

"It's true," I said.

"You expect me to believe that you're some kind of hero?"

"Are you going to throw a rock at me again?"

"You really are full of shit." Susie said. "Who was he, the guy you supposedly saved?"

"I don't know. Some guy."

"What was his name?"

I waited for a little while before I answered. "I think his name was Dante."

"Dante? That was his name? Like we believe you?" Gina and Susie gave each other the look: *This guy is fucking unbelievable.* That look. They both got up from the table and walked away.

I was smiling the rest of the day. Sometimes, all you have to do is tell people the truth. They won't believe you. After that, they'll leave you alone.

Two

MY LAST CLASS OF THE DAY WAS ENGLISH WITH MR. Blocker. Brand-new teacher, fresh out of education school, all smiles and enthusiasm. He still thought high school students were nice. He didn't know any better. Dante would have loved him.

He wanted to get to know us. Of course, he did. New teachers, I always felt sorry for them. They tried too hard. It embarrassed me.

The first thing Mr. Blocker did was to ask us to talk about *one* interesting thing that happened to us during the summer. I always hated this icebreaker bullshit. I made up my mind to ask my mother about teachers and icebreaking exercises.

Gina Navarro, Susie Byrd, and Charlie Escobedo were in the same class. I didn't like that. Those three, they were always asking me lots of questions. Questions I didn't want to answer. They wanted to get to know me. Yeah, well, I wasn't interested in being known. I wanted to buy a T-shirt that read: I AM UNKNOWABLE. But that would have only made Gina Navarro ask more questions.

So there I was, stuck in a class with Gina, Susie, and Charlie—and a new teacher who liked to ask questions. I sort of halfway listened in on everybody's ideas of what constituted interesting. Johnny

Alvarez said he'd learned to drive. Felipe Calderón said he'd gone to LA to see his cousin. Susie Byrd said she'd gone to Girls State in Austin. Carlos Gallinar claimed to have lost his virginity. Everyone laughed. *Who was she? Who was she?* Mr. Blocker had to put down a few rules after that. I decided to just check out. I was an excellent daydreamer. I got to thinking about the truck I hoped I'd be getting on my birthday. I was picturing myself driving down a dirt road, clouds in the blue sky, U2 playing in the background. That's when I heard Mr. Blocker's voice aimed in my direction.

"Mr. Mendoza?" At least he said my name right. I looked up at Mr. Blocker. "Are you with us?"

"Yes, sir," I said.

Then I hear Gina's voice yelling out: "Nothing interesting ever happens to him." Everyone laughed.

"That's true," I said.

I thought maybe Mr. Blocker would move on to someone else, but he didn't. He just waited for me to say something.

"One interesting thing, huh? Gina's right," I said. "Nothing really interesting happened to me this summer."

"Nothing?"

"Getting my legs broken in an accident. I guess that counts as interesting." I nodded, but I felt really uncomfortable, so I decided to be a wiseass like everyone else. "Oh," I said, "I'd never tried morphine before. That was interesting." Everybody laughed. Especially Charlie Escobedo, who had committed his life to experimenting with mood-altering substances.

Mr. Blocker smiled. "You must have been in some serious pain."

"Yeah," I said.

"Are you going to be okay, Ari?"

"Yes." I hated this conversation.

"Does it still hurt?"

"No," I said. It was a small lie. The real answer was longer and more complicated. Gina Navarro was right. Life *was* complicated.

Three

I PICKED UP MY JOURNAL AND THUMBED THROUGH it. I studied my handwriting. I had lousy handwriting. Nobody could read it but me. That was the good news. Not that anybody would want to read it. I decided to write something. This is what I wrote:

> *I learned how to swim this summer. No, that's not true. Someone taught me. Dante.*

I tore out the page.

Four

"YOU DO ICEBREAKERS WITH YOUR STUDENTS ON the first day of school?"

"Sure."

"Why?"

"I like to get to know my students."

"What for?"

"Because I'm a teacher."

"You get paid to teach government. The first, second, and third amendments to the Constitution. Stuff like that. Why don't you just dive right in?"

"I teach students. Students are people, Ari."

"We're not that interesting."

"You're more interesting than you think."

"We're difficult."

"That's part of your charm." She had an interesting look on her face. I recognized that look. My mom, she sometimes resided in the space between irony and sincerity. That was part of *her* charm.

Five

THE SECOND DAY OF SCHOOL. NORMAL. EXCEPT THAT after school as I waited for my mom, this girl, Ileana, came up to me. She took out a marker and wrote her name on one of my casts.

She looked into my eyes. I wanted to look away. But I didn't.

Her eyes were like the night sky in the desert.

It felt like there was a whole world living inside her. I didn't know anything about that world.

Six

A 1957 CHEVY PICKUP. CHERRY RED WITH CHROME fenders, chrome hubcaps, and whitewall tires. It was the most beautiful truck in the world. And it was mine.

I remember looking into my dad's dark eyes and whispering, "Thank you."

I felt stupid and inadequate and I hugged him. Lame. But I meant it, the thank you and the hug. I meant it.

A real truck. A real truck for Ari.

What I didn't get: a picture of my brother on one of the walls of our house.

You can't have everything.

I sat in the truck and had to force myself to rejoin the party. I hated parties—even the ones thrown in my honor. Right then, I would have liked to take the truck out onto the open road, my brother sitting next to me. And Dante too. My brother and Dante. That would have been enough of a party for me.

I guess I *did* miss Dante—even though I tried hard to not think about him. The problem with trying hard not to think about something was that you thought about it even more.

Dante.

For some reason I thought of Ileana.

Seven

EVERY DAY, I GOT UP REALLY EARLY AND HOBBLED over to my truck that was sitting in the garage. I backed it up into the driveway. There was a whole universe waiting to be discovered in a pickup truck. Sitting in the driver's seat made everything seem possible. It was strange to feel those moments of optimism. Strange and beautiful.

Turning on the radio and just sitting there was my version of praying.

My mom came out one morning and took a picture of me. "Where are you going to go?" she asked.

"To school," I said.

"No," she said. "That's not what I meant. The first time you get to drive that thing, where are you going to take it?"

"The desert," I said. I didn't tell her I wanted to go out and look at all the stars.

"By yourself?"

"Yup." I said.

I knew she wanted to ask me if I was making any new friends at school. But she didn't. And then her eyes fell on my cast. "Who's Ileana?"

"Some girl."

"Is she pretty?"

"Too pretty for me, Mom."

"Silly boy."

"Yeah, silly boy."

That night I had a bad dream. I was driving down a street in my pickup. Ileana was sitting right next to me. I looked over and smiled at her. I didn't see him, Dante, standing in the middle of the road. I couldn't stop. I couldn't stop. When I woke up, I was drenched in sweat.

In the morning, as I sat in my truck and drank a cup of coffee, my mom came out of the house. She sat on the steps of the porch. She patted the step next to her. She watched me as I awkwardly got down from my truck. She'd stopped hovering.

I made my way toward her and sat next to her on the front steps.

"Casts come off next week," she said.

I smiled. "Yeah."

"Then therapy," she said.

"Then driving lessons," I said.

"Your father's looking forward to teaching you."

"You lost the coin toss?"

She laughed. "Be patient with him, okay?"

"Not a problem, Mom." I knew that she wanted to talk to me about something. I could always tell.

"You miss Dante?"

I looked at her. "I don't know."

"How can you not know?"

"Well, look, Mom, it's, well, Dante, he's like you. I mean, he hovers sometimes."

She didn't say anything.

"I like being alone, Mom. I know you don't get that about me, but I do."

She nodded and it seemed like she was really listening. "You were screaming his name last night," she said.

"Oh," I said. "It was just a dream."

"Bad?"

"Yeah."

"You want to talk about it?"

"Not really."

She gave me that nudge, the *c'mon humor your mom* nudge.

"Mom? Do you ever have bad dreams?"

"Not often."

"Not like me and Dad."

"You and your father, you're fighting your own private wars."

"Maybe so. I hate my dreams." I could feel my mom listening to me. She was always there. I hated her for that. And loved her. "I was driving my truck and it was raining. I didn't see him standing in the middle of the road. I couldn't stop. I couldn't."

"Dante?"

"Yeah."

She squeezed my arm.

"Mom, sometimes I wished I smoked."

"I'll take the truck away."

"Well, at least I know what's going to happen to me when I break the rules."

"Do you think I'm mean?"

"I think you're strict. Too strict sometimes."

"I'm sorry."

"No you're not." I clutched at my crutches. "Someday, I'm going to have to break some of your rules, Mom."

"I know," she said. "Try to do it behind my back, will you?'

"You can bet on that, Mom."

We both sat there and laughed. Like Dante and I used to do.

"I'm sorry about your bad dreams, Ari."

"Did Dad hear?"

"Yes."

"I'm sorry."

"You can't help what you dream."

"I know. I didn't mean to run over him."

"You didn't. It was just a dream."

I didn't tell her that I hadn't been paying attention. I'd been looking at a girl when I should have been driving. And that's why I ran over Dante. I didn't tell her that.

Eight

TWO LETTERS FROM DANTE IN ONE DAY. THEY WERE on my bed when I got home from school. I hated that my mom knew about the letters. Stupid. Why was that? Privacy. That was it. A guy had no privacy.

Dear Ari,

Okay, I really am sort of in love with Chicago. I ride the El sometimes and make up stories in my head about the people. There are more black people here than in El Paso. And I like that. There are lots of Irish types and Eastern Europeans, and, of course, there are Mexicans. Mexicans are everywhere. We're like sparrows. You know, I still don't really know if I'm a Mexican. I don't think I am. What am I, Ari?

I AM NOT ALLOWED TO RIDE THE EL AT NIGHT. I REPEAT: I AM NOT ALLOWED.

My mom and dad always think that something bad is going to happen to me. I don't know if they were like this before the accident. So I tell my dad, "Dad, a car can't run over my ass on an El train." My dad, who is pretty cool about most things just gave me this look. "No riding the El at night."

My dad likes his gig here. He only has to teach one class and prepare for a lecture on some topic. I think he's writing about the long poem after modernism or something like that. I'm sure my mom and I will attend the lecture. I love my dad but I'm not into all this academic stuff. Too much analysis. What ever happened to reading a book because you liked it?

My mom is taking the opportunity to write a book about addictions and young people. Most of her clients are teenage addicts. Not that she really talks about her work all that much. She spends a lot of time in the library these days and I think she's really enjoying herself. My parents, they're both eggheads. I like that about them.

I have some friends. They're okay. Different, I guess. You know, the group of people I got interested in are all goth types. I went to a party and had my first beer. Well, three beers really. I got a little bit high. Not too high, but a little bit. I can't decide if I like beer or not. I'm thinking that when I get older, I'm going to be a wine drinker. I don't mean the cheap stuff either. I don't think I'm a snob. But my mom says I suffer from only-child syndrome. She made that up, I think. And who's fault is that, anyway? Who's stopping them from having another kid?

At the party, I got offered a joint. I took a hit or two. Okay, I don't really want to talk about that.

My mom would kill me if she knew I was experimenting with mood-altering substances. Beer and pot. Not so bad. But my mom would have a different opinion about that. She's talked to me about what she calls "gateway drugs." My eyes glaze over when she gives me the drug talk and she gives me one of her looks.

The pot thing and the beer thing, it was just one of those things that happens at a party. Not such a big deal when you think about it. Not that I'm going to have this discussion with my mom. My dad, either.

Have you drunk a beer? Done pot? Let me know.

I heard my mom and dad talking. They've already decided that if my dad gets a job offer here, he's going to turn it down. "It's not a good place for Dante." They've already decided that. Of course, they don't ask me. Of course not. What about a little input from Dante himself? Dante likes to speak for himself. Yes, he does.

I don't want my parents organizing their world around me. I'm going to disappoint them someday. And then what?

The truth is, Ari, I miss El Paso. When we first moved there, I hated it. But now I think about El Paso all the time.

And I think of you.

Always,
Dante

P.S. I go swimming almost every day after school. I cut my hair. It's really short. But short hair is good for swimming. Long hair sucks when you swim every day. Don't know why I ever had it long.

Dear Ari,

Everyone has parties around here. My dad thinks it's great that I get invited. My mom, well, it's hard to guess what she thinks. I can tell she has her eyes open. She told me my clothes smelled like cigarettes after the last party. "Some people smoke," I said. "Can't help that." I got the look.

So Friday night, I went to this party. And, of course, there was alcohol. I had a beer and have now decided that beer is not for me. I did like the vodka and orange juice. Ari, there were so many people there. Amazing. We were like roaches! You couldn't move without bumping into someone. So, I just walked around talking to people and I was having a good time.

Somehow, I found myself talking to this girl. Her name is Emma and she's smart and nice and beautiful. We were in the kitchen talking and she said she loved my name. And all of a sudden, she leans into me and kisses me. I guess you could say I kissed her back. She tasted like mint and cigarettes and it was, well, Ari, it was nice.

We kissed a long time.

I smoked a cigarette with her and we kissed some more.

She liked touching my face. She told me I was beautiful. No one has ever told me I was beautiful. Moms and dads do not count.

And then we went outside.

She smoked another cigarette. She asked me if I wanted one. I told her one was enough because I was a swimmer.

I'm still thinking about that kiss.

She gave me her number.

I'm not sure about all this.

Your friend,
Dante

Nine

I TRIED TO PICTURE DANTE WITH SHORT HAIR. I TRIED to imagine him kissing a girl. Dante was complicated. Gina would have liked Dante. Not that I was ever going to introduce them.

I lay in bed and thought about writing back to him. Instead, I sat down to write in my journal.

> *What would it be like to kiss a girl? Specifically, Ileana. She wouldn't taste like cigarettes. What does a girl taste like when you kiss her?*

I stopped writing and tried to think of something else. I thought about the stupid essay on the Great Depression that I didn't want to write. I thought about Charlie Escobedo who wanted me to do drugs with him. I started to think about Dante kissing a girl again and then I thought about Ileana. Maybe she *would* taste like cigarettes. Maybe she smoked. I didn't know a damn thing about her.

I sat up on my bed. No, no, no. No thinking about kissing. And then I don't know why, but I felt sad. And then I started thinking about my brother. Every time I felt sad, I thought about him.

Maybe deep down a part of me was always thinking about him. Sometimes, I caught myself spelling out his name. *B-E-R-N-A-R-D-O*. What was my brain doing, spelling out his name without my permission?

I sometimes think that I don't let myself know what I'm really thinking about. That doesn't make much sense but it makes sense to me. I have this idea that the reason we have dreams is that we're thinking about things that we don't know we're thinking about—and those things, well, they sneak out of us in our dreams. Maybe we're like tires with too much air in them. The air has to leak out. That's what dreams are.

And now that I think about it, I'd had a dream about my brother. I was four and he was fifteen and we were taking a walk. He was holding my hand and I was looking up at him. I was happy. It was a beautiful dream. The sky was blue and clear and pure.

Maybe the dream came from a memory. Dreams don't come from nowhere. That's a fact. I think maybe I want to study dreams when I'm old enough to actually choose what I want to study. I sure as hell don't want to study Alexander Hamilton. Yeah, maybe I'll study dreams and where they come from. Freud. Maybe that's what I'll do—I'll write a paper on Sigmund Freud. That way, I'll get a head start.

And maybe I'll help people out who have bad dreams. So they won't have them anymore. I think I'd like to do that.

Ten

I'VE DECIDED THAT I'M GOING TO FIND A WAY TO KISS Ileana Tellez. But when? Where? She's not in any of my classes. I hardly see her.

Find her locker. That's the plan.

Eleven

ON THE WAY BACK FROM THE DOCTOR'S OFFICE, MY mom asked me if I'd written back to Dante.

"Not yet."

"I think you should write to him."

"Mom, I'm your son, not a suggestion box."

She shot me a look.

"Keep your eyes on the road," I said.

When I got back home, I took out my journal and this is what I wrote:

> *If dreams don't come from nowhere, then what does it mean that I ran over Dante in my dream? What does it mean that I had that dream again? Both times I was staring at Ileana when I ran over Dante. Okay, this is not good.*
>
> *The air is leaking out.*
>
> *I don't want to think about this.*

*I can either think about the dreams I have about my
brother or I can think about the dreams I have about
Dante.*

Those are my choices?

I think I should get a life.

Twelve

WHEN I THINK ABOUT THE DREAM ABOUT MY BROTHER, I think about the fact that the last time I saw him was when I was four. So there is a direct connection between the dream and my life. I suppose that's when it all happened. I was four and he was fifteen. That's when he did whatever he did. So now he's in jail. Not jail. Prison. There's a difference. My uncle, he gets drunk sometimes and winds up in jail. That really upsets my mom. But he gets out quick because he doesn't drive when he drinks—he just winds up in stupid places and he gets a little belligerent with people. If the word *belligerent* hadn't been invented, it would have been invented for my uncle when he drinks. But someone always bails him out. In prison, there's no such thing as bailing someone out. You don't get out quick. Prison is a place you get put away for a long time.

So that's where my brother is. Prison.

I don't know if he's in a federal prison or a state prison. I don't know why a guy gets sent to one or the other. It's not something they teach us at school.

I am going to find out why my brother is in prison. It's a research project. I've thought about it. I've thought and thought about it.

Newspapers. Don't they save old newspapers somewhere?

If Dante were here, he could help me. He's smart. He'd know exactly what to do.

I don't need Dante.

I can do this on my own.

Thirteen

DEAR ARI,

I hope you got my letters. Okay, that's a disingenuous start. Of course you got my letters. I'm not going to analyze why you haven't written back. Okay, that's not totally true. I have analyzed why there's no letter waiting for me when I get back from swimming. I won't waste good paper on theories that I come up with when I can't sleep at night. This is the deal, Ari, I'm not going to get on your case about writing back. I promise. If I want to write you, then I'll write to you. And if you don't want to write to me, you don't have to. You have to be who you are. And I have to be who I am. That's the way it is. And anyway, I usually did most of the talking.

I have another favorite thing to do besides riding the El: going to the Art Institute of Chicago. Wow, Ari. You should see the art in that place. It's amazing. I wish you were here and we could see all this art together. You'd go nuts. I swear you would. All kinds of art, contemporary and not-so-contemporary and, well, I could go and on, but I won't. Do you like Andy Warhol?

There is a famous painting, Nighthawks, *by Edward Hopper.
I am in love with that painting. Sometimes, I think everyone
is like the people in that painting, everyone lost in their own
private universes of pain or sorrow or guilt, everyone remote
and unknowable. The painting reminds me of you. It breaks my
heart.*

But Nighthawks *isn't my favorite painting. Not by a long shot.
Did I ever tell you what my favorite painting is? It's* The Raft
of the Medusa *by Géricault. There's a whole story behind that
painting. It's based on a true story about a shipwreck and it
made Géricault famous. See the thing about artists is that they
tell stories. I mean, some paintings are like novels.*

*Someday, I'm going to travel to Paris and go to the Louvre and
stare at that painting all day long.*

*I've done the math and I know that by now your casts are off.
I know you said that the rule was that we couldn't talk about
the accident. I'm going to say this, Ari. That's an incredibly
inane rule. No reasonable person could be expected to keep that
rule—not that I qualify as a reasonable person. So, I hope that
your therapy is going well and that you're normal again. Not
that you're normal. You are definitely not normal.*

*I miss you. Can I say that? Or is there a rule? You know, it's
interesting that you have so many rules for things. Why is that,
Ari? I suppose everyone has rules for things. Maybe we get that*

from our parents. Parents are rule givers. Maybe they gave us too many rules, Ari. Did you ever think about that?

I think we need to do something about rules.

I'm not going to tell you that I miss you anymore.

Your friend,
Dante

Fourteen

I FOUND ILEANA'S LOCKER WITH THE HELP OF SUSIE Byrd. "Don't tell Gina about this."

"I won't," she said. "I promise." She promptly broke her promise.

"She's trouble," Gina said.

"Yeah, and she's eighteen," Susie said.

"So?"

"You're just a boy. She's a woman."

"Trouble," Gina repeated.

I left Ileana a note. "Hi," it said. I signed my name. I'm such a jerk. Hi. What's that?

Fifteen

I SPENT THE EVENING AT THE PUBLIC LIBRARY LOOKING at microfilms of the *El Paso Times*. I was looking for an article on my brother. But I didn't even know if I had the right year and I gave up after about an hour and a half. There had to be a better way of doing this kind of research.

I thought of writing Dante a letter. Instead, I found an art book on the work of Edward Hopper. Dante was right about *Nighthawks*. It was a great painting. And it was true, what Hopper was saying. I felt as if I were looking in a mirror. But it didn't break my heart.

Sixteen

DO YOU KNOW WHAT DEAD SKIN LOOKS LIKE WHEN they take off a cast?

That was my life, all that dead skin.

It was strange to feel like the Ari I used to be. Except that wasn't totally true. The Ari I used to be didn't exist anymore.

And the Ari I was becoming? He didn't exist yet.

I came home and took a walk.

I found myself staring at the spot where I'd seen Dante holding the bird. I don't know why I was there.

I found myself walking in front of Dante's house.

There was a dog across the street at the park staring at me.

I stared back.

He plopped himself on the grass.

I walked across the street and the dog didn't move. He just wagged his tail. That made me smile. I sat down on the grass next to him and took off my shoes. The dog scooted himself up to me and put his head on my lap.

I just sat there and petted him. I noticed he didn't have a collar. After studying him some more, I discovered that he was a she.

"What's your name?"

People talk to dogs. Not that they understand. But maybe they understand enough. I thought of Dante's last letter. I'd had to look up the word *inane*. I got up and walked to the library, which was at the edge of the park.

I found an art book that had a picture of the "Raft of the Medusa."

I went home: Ari, the boy who could walk again without the help of crutches. I wanted to tell Dante that his math had been a little off. *I got them off today, Dante. Today.*

On my walk home, I thought about the accident and Dante and my brother and I wondered if he knew how to swim. I thought about my dad and how he never talked about Vietnam. Even though he had a picture with some of his war buddies hanging on the living room wall, he never talked about that picture or the names of his friends. I asked him once and it was as if he hadn't heard the question. I never asked again. Maybe the problem between me and my father was that we were both the same.

When I got home, I noticed the dog had followed me. I sat on the steps of the front porch and she laid down on the sidewalk looking up at me.

My dad came out. "Getting your legs back?"

"Yeah," I said.

He looked at the dog.

"She followed me home from the park."

"Are you interested in him?"

"It's a she."

We were both smiling.

"And yeah," I said. "I'm very interested."

"Remember Charlie?"

"Yeah. I loved that dog."

"Me too."

"I cried when she died."

"Me too, Ari." We looked at each other. "Seems like a nice dog. No collar?"

"No collar, Dad. Beautiful."

"Beautiful, Ari." He laughed. "Your mother doesn't like dogs in the house."

Seventeen

DEAR DANTE,

Sorry I haven't written. I really am.

I can walk like normal now. Just so you won't feel guilty anymore, okay? The x-rays look good. I've healed, Dante. The doctor says a lot of things could have gone wrong, beginning with the surgery. But, as it happens, nothing went wrong. Imagine, Dante, nothing going wrong. Okay, I've broken my own rule so that's enough about that particular topic.

I have a new dog! Her name is Legs because I found her the day I got my legs back. She followed me home from the park. My dad and I bathed her in the backyard. She's really a great dog. She just stood there and let us bathe her. Really tame and mellow dog. I don't know exactly what kind she is. The vet's best guess was that she's part pit bull, part Labrador and part God-knows-what-else. She's white,

medium-sized, and has brown circles around her eyes.
Really good-looking dog. My mom's only response was: "The
dog stays in the yard."

That rule didn't last. At night, I let the dog into my bedroom.
The dog sleeps at my feet. On the bed. Mom hates that. She
gave in pretty easily though. "Well, at least you have a friend,"
she said.

My mom doesn't think I have any friends. That's sort of true.
But I'm not good at making friends. I'm okay with that.

Not much to report other than the dog. No, wait, guess what?
I got a 1957 Chevy pickup for my birthday! Lots of chrome.
I love the truck. A real Mexican truck, Dante! All I need are
hydraulics to bounce around in. Like that's going to happen.
Hydraulics. My mom just looked at me. "Who's going to pay
for it?"

"I'll get a job," I said.

Dad gave me my first driving lesson. We went out on some
deserted farm road in the upper valley. I did pretty well. I have
to get the gear thing down. I'm not very smooth about shifting
and I killed the truck a couple of times trying to shift into
second. It's all timing. Push in the clutch, shift, gas, clutch, shift,
gas, drive. Someday soon I'm going to learn to do all of those

*things in one smooth motion. It will be like walking. I won't
even have to think about it.*

*After the first lesson, we parked the truck and my dad smoked
a cigarette. He smokes sometimes. But never in the house.
Sometimes, he smokes in the backyard, but not very often.
I asked him if he was ever going to quit. "It helps with the
dreams." I know his dreams are about the war. I sometimes
try to picture him in the jungles of Vietnam. I never ask him
anything about the war. I guess it's something he has to keep to
himself. Maybe it's a terrible thing, to keep a war to yourself.
But maybe that's the way it has to be. So, instead of asking him
about the war, I asked him if he ever dreamed about Bernardo.
My brother. "Sometimes." That's all he said. He drove my truck
back home and didn't say another word.*

*I think I upset him by bringing up my brother. I don't want to
upset him, but I do. I always upset him. And other people too.
I guess that's what I do. And I upset you too. I know that. And
I'm sorry. I'm doing the best I can, okay? So if I don't write as
many letters as you do, don't be upset. I'm not doing it to upset
you, okay? This is my problem. I want other people to tell me
how they feel. But I'm not so sure I want to return the favor.*

I think I'll go sit in my truck and think about that.

Ari

Eighteen

THIS IS THE LIST OF WHAT MY LIFE IS NOW:

-studying to get my driver's license and studying hard
to get into college. (This makes my mom happy.)

-lifting weights in the basement.

-running with Legs, who is not only a great dog, but
also a great runner.

-reading Dante's letters (sometimes I get two a week).

-arguing with Gina Navarro and Susie Byrd (about
anything).

-trying to find ways of running into Ileana at school.

-looking through microfilms of the El Paso Times at the
library trying to find out something about my brother.

-writing in my journal.

-washing my truck once a week.

-having bad dreams. (I keep running Dante down on that rainy street.)

-working twenty hours at the Charcoaler. Flipping burgers isn't so bad. Four hours on Thursday after school, six hours on Friday nights and eight hours on Saturday. (Dad won't let me cover extra shifts.)

That list just about covered all my life. Maybe my life isn't all that interesting but at least I'm busy. Busy doesn't mean happy. I know that. But at least I'm not bored. Being bored is the worst.

I like having money and I like the fact that I'm not dedicating too much time to feeling sorry for myself.

I get invited to parties and don't go.

Well, I did go to one party—just to see if Ileana was there. I left the party just as Gina and Susie were arriving. Gina accused me of being a misanthrope. She said I was the only boy in the whole damn school who had never kissed a girl. "And you'll never kiss one if you leave parties just as they're starting to get good."

"Really?" I said. "I've never kissed a girl? And how exactly did you come by this bit of information?"

"Just a hunch," she said.

"You're trying to get me to tell you things about my life," I said. "It's not going to work."

"Who have you kissed?"

"Put a lid on it, Gina."

"Ileana? I don't think so. She's just toying with you."

I just kept walking and flipped her a bird.

Gina, what was with that girl? Seven sisters and no brothers—that was her problem. I guess she thought she could just borrow me. I could be the brother she could bug. She and Susie Byrd used to go by the Charcoaler on Friday nights around closing time. Just to keep bugging me. Just to piss me off. They'd order their burgers and fries and cherry Cokes and park and honk and wait for me to close up and just bug, bug, bug me and piss me off. Gina was learning to smoke and she'd flash her cigarettes around like she was Madonna.

One time, they had beer. They offered me some. Okay, I had some beers with them. It was fine. It was okay.

Except Gina kept asking me who I'd kissed.

But then I got an idea that would make her just stop hounding me. "You know what I think," I said. "I think you want me to lean into you and give you the kiss of your life."

"That's disgusting," she said.

"Why the interest, then?" I said. "You'd love to know what I taste like."

"You're an idiot," she said. "I'd rather have a bird crap in my mouth."

"Sure you would," I said.

Susie Byrd said I was being mean. That Susie Byrd, you always had to be nice around her. If you said the wrong thing, she cried. I didn't like that crying stuff. She was a nice girl. But she didn't help herself out with all that crying.

Gina never brought up the subject of kissing ever again. That was the good thing.

Ileana would find me sometimes. She would smile at me and I was falling a little bit in love with her smile. Not that I knew a damn thing about love.

School was okay. Mr. Blocker was still all about the sharing thing. But he was a good teacher. He made us write a lot. I liked that. For some reason, I was really getting into writing. The only class that I was having a hard time with was my art elective. I couldn't draw worth a damn. I was pretty good at trees. I sucked at drawing faces. But in art class, all you had to do was try. I was getting an A for work. But not for talent. The story of my life.

I knew I didn't have it so bad. I had a dog, a driver's license, and two hobbies: looking for my brother's name on microfilm and looking for a way to kiss Ileana.

Nineteen

MY DAD AND I GOT INTO A ROUTINE. WE'D GET UP really early on Saturdays and Sundays for my driving lessons. I thought—I don't know what I thought. I guess I thought that maybe my dad and I would talk about stuff. But we didn't. We talked about driving. It was all business. It was all about the learning-to-drive thing.

Dad was patient with me. He could explain things about driving a truck and his philosophy of paying attention and watching out for the other guy. He was actually a really good teacher, never got upset (except the time I brought up my brother). He said something once that really made me smile. "You can't expect to go both ways when you're driving on a one-way street." I thought that was a funny and interesting thing to say. I laughed when he said it. He hardly ever made me laugh.

But he never asked me any questions about my life. Unlike my mom, he left me to my private world. My dad and I, we were like that Edward Hopper painting. Well almost—but not exactly. I noticed that somehow my dad seemed more relaxed with himself when he and I were out on those mornings. He seemed so at ease with himself, like he was at home. Even though he didn't talk much, he didn't seem as remote. That was nice. He sometimes whistled, like he was happy to be with me. Maybe my dad just didn't need words to get by in the world. I wasn't like that. Well, I *was* like that on the outside, pretending not to need words. But I *wasn't* like that on the inside.

I'd figured something out about myself: on the inside, I wasn't like my dad at all. On the inside I was more like Dante. That really scared me.

Twenty

I HAD TO TAKE MY MOM OUT FOR A DRIVE BEFORE she'd let me go out on my own. "You drive a little fast," she said.

"I'm sixteen," I said. "And I'm a boy."

She didn't say anything. But then she said, "If I even suspect that you've taken one sip of alcohol and driven this truck, I'm going to sell it."

For some reason that made me smile. "That's not fair. Why should I have to pay for the fact that you have a suspicious mind? Like that's my fault."

She just looked at me. "Fascists are like that."

We both smiled at each other. "No drinking and driving."

"What about drinking and walking?"

"None of that either."

"I guess I knew that."

"Just making sure."

"I'm not afraid of you, Mom. Just so you know."

That made her laugh.

So my life was more or less uncomplicated. I got letters from Dante and I didn't always write back. When I did write back, my letters were short. *His* letters were *never* short. He was still experimenting with kissing girls even though he said he'd rather be kissing boys. That's exactly what he said. I didn't know exactly what to think about that, but Dante was going to be Dante and if I was going to be his friend, I would just have to learn to be okay with it. And, because he was in Chicago and I was in El Paso, it was easy to be okay with it. Dante's life was way more complicated than mine—at least when it came to kissing boys or girls. On the other hand, he didn't have to wonder about a brother who was in prison, a brother his parents pretended didn't exist.

I think I was trying to make my life uncomplicated because everything inside me felt so confusing. And I had the bad dreams to prove it. One night I dreamed I didn't have any legs. They were just gone. And I couldn't get out of bed. I woke up screaming.

My dad came into the room and whispered, "It's just a dream, Ari. Just a bad dream."

"Yeah," I whispered. "Just a bad dream."

But you know, I was used to them in a way, the bad dreams. But why was it that some people never remembered their dreams? And why wasn't I one of those people?

Twenty-One

DEAR DANTE,

*I got my license! I took my mom and dad for a drive. I drove
them to Mesilla, New Mexico. We ate lunch. I drove them back
home and I think they more or less approved of my driving.
But the best part was this. I went out at night and drove into
the desert and parked. I listened to the radio and lay down in
the back of my pickup and looked out at all the stars. No light
pollution, Dante. It was really beautiful.*

Ari

Twenty-Two

ONE NIGHT, MY PARENTS WENT OUT TO SOME WEDDING dance. Mexicans. They loved wedding dances. They wanted to drag me out with them but I said no thanks. Watching my parents dance to Tex-Mex music was my idea of hell. I told them I was tired from flipping burgers all day and that I was just going to stay home and relax.

"Well, if you feel like going out," my dad said, "just leave a note."

I had no plans.

I made myself comfortable and was about to make myself a quesadilla when Charlie Escobedo came knocking on my door and asked me, "'Sup?"

And I said: "Not much. I'm making a quesadilla."

And he said: "Cool."

I was not about to ask him if he wanted me to make him one even if the guy looked hungry as hell. But that was his look. He had this hungry way about him. He was the skinny type. Always looked like a coyote in the middle of a drought. I knew about coyotes. I was way into coyotes. So we sort of looked at each other and I said: "You hungry?" I couldn't believe I said that.

And then he said: "Nah." And then he said: "You ever shoot up?"

And I said: "Nope."

And he said: "You wanna?"

And I said: "Nope."

And he said: "You should try. It's fantastic. You know we could score some and go out into the desert in your truck and, you know, get high. It's sweet. So sweet, dude."

And I said: "I'm really into chocolate."

And he said: "What the fuck are you talking about?"

And I said: "Sweet. You said sweet. I think I'll get my sweet from chocolate."

And then he got mad and called me a *pinchi joto* and all sorts of other names and he said he was gonna kick my ass all the way to the border. And who the fuck did I think I was, thinking that I was too good to shoot up or even smoke cigarettes and didn't I know that nobody liked me because I thought of myself as Mr. *Gabacho*.

Mr. *Gabacho*.

I hated that. I was as Mexican as he was. And I was bigger than he was too. I wasn't exactly afraid of the little son of a bitch. And I said, "Why don't you get someone else to do drugs with you, *vato*?" I figured the guy was lonely. But he didn't have to be an asshole about it.

And he said, "You're gay, *vato*, you know that?"

What the hell was the guy talking about? I was gay because I didn't want to shoot up heroin?

And then I said: "Yeah, I'm gay and I want to kiss you."

And then he got this really disgusted look on his face and said: "I ought to kick your ass."

And I said: "Go ahead."

Then he just flipped me off and, and well, he just took off—which was okay with me. I mean, I sort of liked the guy before he got into all this mood-altering substance abuse thing and to tell myself the truth, I was really curious about the heroin thing, but, you know, I just wasn't ready.

A guy has to be ready for important things. That's how I saw it.

I got to thinking about Dante and how he'd had a few beers and I thought about the couple of beers I'd had with Gina and Susie and I wondered what it would be like to get drunk. I mean really drunk. I wondered if it felt good. I mean, Dante had even tried pot. I got to thinking about my brother again. Maybe he got into drugs. Maybe that's why he was in the slammer.

I think I really loved him when I was a little boy. *I think I really did*. Maybe that's why I felt sad and empty—because I'd missed him all my life.

I don't know why I did what I did. But I did it. I went out and found an old drunk loitering around the Circle K in Sunset Heights, begging for money. He looked like hell and smelled even worse. But it's not like I was interested in being his friend. I asked him to buy me a six-pack. I told him I'd buy him a six-pack too. He was game. I parked my truck around the corner. When he came out and handed me my six-pack, he smiled at me and said, "How old are you?"

"Sixteen," I said. "You?"

"Me. I'm forty-five." He looked a lot older. I mean the guy looked as old as dirt. And then I felt bad—for using the guy. But he was using me too. So that was the math on that one.

206

At first I started to drive out into the desert to drink my six-pack. But then I thought that maybe that wasn't such a good idea. I kept hearing my mom's voice in my head and it really pissed me off that her voice was there. So I just decided to go home. I knew my parents wouldn't be home for a long time. I had all night to drink my beer.

I parked my truck in the driveway and just sat there. Drinking my beer. I let Legs in the truck with me and she tried to lick my beer can so I had to tell her that beer wasn't good for dogs. Probably, beer wasn't good for boys either. But, you know, I was experimenting. You know, discovering the secrets of the universe. Not that I thought I'd find the secrets of the universe in a Budweiser.

I got this idea into my head that if I chugged the first two or three beers then maybe I'd get a good buzz. And that's exactly what I did. And it worked. It felt kind of nice, you know.

I got to thinking about things.

My brother.

Dante.

My dad's bad dreams.

Ileana.

After chugging three beers I wasn't feeling any pain. Sort of like morphine. But different. And then, I opened up another beer. Legs put her head on my lap and we just sat there. "I love you, Legs." It was true. I loved that dog. And life didn't seem so bad, me sitting there in my truck with my dog and a beer.

There were a lot of guys in the world that would have killed to have what I had. So why wasn't I more grateful? Because I was an ingrate, that's why. That's what Gina Navarro said about me.

She was a smart girl. She wasn't wrong about me.

I had my window rolled down and I felt the cold. The weather had changed and winter was coming. Summer hadn't brought me what I wanted. I didn't think winter would do me any better. Why did the seasons exist anyway? The cycle of life. Winter, spring, summer, fall. And then it began again.

What do you want, Ari? That's what I kept asking myself. Maybe it was the beer. *What do you want, Ari?*

And then I answered myself: "A life."

"What's a life, Ari?"

"Like I know the answer to that?"

"Deep inside you know, Ari."

"No, I don't."

"Shut up, Ari." So I *did* shut up. And then the thought entered my head that I'd like to kiss someone. It didn't matter who. Anyone. Ileana.

When I finished all my beers, I stumbled into bed.

I didn't dream anything that night. Nothing at all.

Twenty-Three

OVER CHRISTMAS BREAK, I WAS WRAPPING SOME Christmas gifts for my nephews. I went looking for a pair of scissors. I knew my mom kept a junk drawer in the dresser in the spare bedroom. So that's where I went looking for them. And there they were, the scissors, right on top of an extra large brown envelope with my brother's name written over the top. BERNARDO.

I knew that the envelope contained everything about my brother's life.

A whole life in one envelope.

And I knew there were photographs of him in there too.

I wanted to rip it open but that's not what I did. I left the scissors there and pretended I hadn't seen the envelope. "Mom," I asked, "Where are the scissors?" She got them for me.

That night I wrote an entry in my journal. I wrote his name again and again:

> *Bernardo*
>
> *Bernardo*
>
> *Bernardo*
>
> *Bernardo*
>
> *Bernardo*
>
> *Bernardo*

Twenty-Four

DEAR ARI,

I have this picture in my head of you lying on the bed of your pick-up looking up at all the stars. I have the sketch in my head. I'm sending you a picture of me standing next to our Christmas tree. And I'm sending you a gift. I hope you like it.

Merry Christmas, Ari.
Dante

When I opened the gift, I smiled.

And then I laughed.

A pair of miniature tennis shoes. I knew exactly what I was supposed to do with them. Hang them from my rearview mirror. And that's exactly what I did.

Twenty-Five

THE DAY AFTER CHRISTMAS, I WORKED AN EIGHT-HOUR shift at the Charcoaler. My dad let me pick up extra shifts since it was the Christmas break. I didn't mind the job. Okay, there was this guy that I worked with who was a real jerk. But I just let him talk and most of the time he didn't even notice that I wasn't listening. He wanted to hang out after our shift and I said, "I got plans."

"Date?" he said.

"Yup," I said.

"Got a girlfriend?"

"Yup," I said.

"What's her name?"

"Cher."

"Screw you, Ari," he said

Some guys can't take a joke.

When I got home, my mom was in the kitchen warming up some tamales for dinner. I loved homemade tamales. I liked to warm them up in the oven which was really strange because that wasn't the standard way of warming up tamales. I liked the way the oven sort of dried out the tamales so they got a little crispy and you could smell the corn leaves sort of burning and it smelled really great so my mom put some in the oven for me. "Dante called," she said.

"Really?"

"Yeah."

"He's going to call you back in a while. I told him you were working."

I nodded.

"He didn't know you worked. He said you never mentioned anything about that in your letters."

"Why does it matter?"

She shook her head. "Guess it doesn't." I knew she was doing some math in her head about this, but she was keeping the math to herself. That was okay with me. That was when the phone rang again. "It's probably Dante," she said.

It *was* Dante.

"Hi."

"Hi."

"Merry Christmas."

"Did it snow in Chicago?"

"No. Just cold. And gray. I mean really cold."

"Sounds nice."

"I kind of like it. But I'm tired of the gray days. They say it will be worse in January. February too, probably."

"That sucks."

"Yeah, it does suck."

There was a little silence on the phone.

"So you're working?"

"Yeah, flipping burgers at the Charcoaler. Trying to save up some money."

"You didn't tell me."

"Yeah, it's not important. Just a shitty job."

"Well, you're not going to save too much money buying nice art books for your friends." I could tell he was smiling.

"So you got the book?"

"I'm holding it in my lap. *Gericault's Raft of the Medusa* by Lorenz E. A. Eitner. It's a beautiful book, Ari."

I thought he was going to cry. And I whispered in my own brain, *don't cry don't cry*. And it was like he heard me—and he didn't cry. And then he said, "How many burgers did you flip to buy the book?"

"That's a very Dante question," I said.

"That's a very Ari answer," he said.

And then we started laughing and couldn't stop. And I missed him so much.

When I hung up the phone, I felt a little sad. And a little happy. For a few minutes I wished that Dante and I lived in the universe of boys instead of the universe of almost-men.

I went out for a slow run. Legs and me. It's true what they say that every guy should have a dog. Gina says every boy *is* a dog. That Gina. She was like my mother. I had her voice in my head.

Halfway through the run, it started to rain. The movie of the accident played through my brain. For a few seconds, there was a pain in my legs.

Twenty-Six

ON NEW YEAR'S EVE, I GOT CALLED IN TO WORK AT THE Charcoaler. I was good with that. I didn't have any plans and I didn't feel like being in my head.

"You're going in to work?" My mom wasn't happy.

"Social interaction," I said.

She shot me a look. "Everybody's coming over."

Yeah, the family thing. Uncles. Cousins. My mom's menudo and more tamales. I was burnt out on tamales. Beer. Wine for my mom and my sisters. I wasn't big on family gatherings. Too many intimate strangers. I smiled a lot, but really I never knew what to say.

I smiled at my mom. "1987. Glad that's over."

She shot me another look. "It was a good year, Ari."

"Well, there was that small incident in the rain."

She smiled. "Why is it so hard for you to give yourself some credit?"

"Because I'm like my father." I raised my cup of coffee toward her in a toast. "Here's to '88. And to Dad."

My mother reached over and combed my hair with her fingers. She hadn't done that in a while. "You're looking more and more like a man," she said.

I raised my cup of coffee again. "Well, here's to manhood."

Work wasn't so busy. The rain kept people away, so the four of us who were working took turns trying to sing our favorite songs of 1987. The Los Lobos version of "La Bamba" was my favorite, hands down. I couldn't sing worth a damn so I sang it on purpose because I knew everyone would tell me, *don't sing don't sing*, which is exactly what they said. So I was off the hook. Alma kept singing "Faith." Didn't care for George Michael. Lucy kept pretending she was Madonna and even though she had a good voice, I was not into Madonna. Somewhere toward the end of the shift we all started singing U2 songs. "I Still Haven't Found What I'm Looking For." Yeah, that was a good song. My theme song. But really I thought it was everybody's theme song.

At five minutes to ten, I heard a voice at the drive-in ordering a burger and fries. Gina Navarro. I'd know that voice anywhere. I couldn't decide if I really liked her or I was just used to her. When her order was done, I took it out to her beat-up Volkswagen Beetle, where she and Susie Byrd were parked.

"You guys going out with each other?"

"Hardee-har, you asshole."

"Happy New Year to you too."

"You almost done?"

"We gotta clean up before I get off."

Susie Byrd smiled. I gotta say she had a sweet smile. "We came to invite you to a party."

"Party. I don't think so," I said.

"There's beer," Gina said.

"And girls you might want to kiss," Susie said.

My own personal dating service. Just what I wanted for the new year. "Maybe," I said.

"No maybes," Gina said. "Loosen up."

I don't know why I said yes, but that's just what I said. "Just give me the address and I'll meet you there. I have to go home and tell my parents."

I was hoping my mom and dad would say "no way." But that's not what happened. "You're actually going to a party?" my mother said.

"Surprised that I'm invited, Mom?"

"No. Just surprised that you want to go."

"It's New Year's."

"Will there be drinking?"

"I don't know, Mom."

"You're not driving your truck there. Period."

"Guess I can't go."

"Where's the party?"

"Corner of Silver and Elm."

"That's just down the street. You can walk."

"It's raining."

"It stopped."

My mom was practically throwing me out of the house. "Go. Have a good time."

Shit. A good time.

And guess what? I *did* have a good time.

I kissed a girl. No, she kissed me. Ileana. She was there. Ileana. She just walked up to me and said, "It's New Year's. So Happy New

Year." And then she just leaned into me and kissed me.

We kissed. For a long time. And then she whispered, "You're the best kisser in the world."

"No," I said, "I'm not."

"Don't argue with me. I know about these things."

"Okay," I said, "I won't argue with you." And then we kissed again.

And then she said, "I gotta go." And then she just left.

I didn't even have time to take the whole thing in before Gina was standing in front of me. "I saw that," she said.

"So fucking what?"

"How was it?"

I just looked at her. "Happy New Year." And then I hugged her. "I have a New Year's resolution for you."

That made her laugh. "I have a whole list for you, Ari."

We stood there laughing our asses off.

It was strange to have a good time.

Twenty-Seven

ONE DAY, WHEN I WAS ALONE IN THE HOUSE, I OPENED the drawer. The drawer with the large manila envelope marked BERNARDO. I wanted to open it. I wanted to know all the secrets that were contained there.

Maybe I would be free. But why wasn't I free? I wasn't in prison, was I?

I put the envelope back.

I didn't want to do it this way. I wanted my mother to hand it to me. To say, "This is the story of your brother."

Maybe I wanted too much.

Twenty-Eight

DANTE WROTE ME A SHORT LETTER.

Ari,

Do you masturbate? I'm thinking you think that's a funny question. But it's a very serious question. I mean, you're pretty normal. At least, you're more normal than me.

So maybe you masturbate or maybe you don't. Maybe I'm a little obsessed with this topic lately. Maybe it's just a phase. But, Ari, if you do masturbate, what do you think about?

I know I should ask my dad about this, but I don't feel like it. I love my dad—but do I have to tell him everything?

Sixteen-year-olds masturbate, right? How many times a week is normal?

> *Your friend,*
> *Dante*

It really made me mad that he sent that letter. Not that he wrote it, but that he sent it. I was really embarrassed by the whole thing. *I am not interested in having a conversation about masturbation with Dante.*

I am not interested in having a conversation about masturbation with anyone.

What the hell was wrong with that guy?

Twenty-Nine

JANUARY, FEBRUARY, MARCH, APRIL. THE MONTHS SORT of ran together. School was okay. I studied. I worked out. I ran with Legs. I worked at the Charcoaler. I played hide-and-seek with Ileana. Or rather she played hide-and-seek with me. I just didn't get her.

Some Friday nights, I'd drive my truck out into the desert after work. I'd lie in the bed of my pickup and look out at the stars.

One day I just flat out asked Ileana to go out on a date. I was tired of the flirting thing. It wasn't working anymore. "Let's just go to a movie," I said. "You know, maybe hold hands."

"I can't," she said.

"You can't?"

"Not ever."

"So why'd you kiss me then?"

"Because you're good-looking."

"That's the only reason?"

"And you're nice."

"So what's the problem?" I was beginning to figure out that Ileana was playing a game that I just didn't like.

Sometimes she would come by the Charcoaler on Friday nights when I was closing up and we would sit in my pickup and talk. But we really didn't talk about anything important. She was even more private than I was.

There was this prom thing coming up and I thought maybe I'd ask her to go. It didn't matter that she'd turned me down already. And wasn't she the one coming to see me at the Charcoaler? A couple of weeks before the prom, she showed up at the Charcoaler as I was closing up. We sat in my truck. "So you want to go the prom with me?" I said. I was trying to sound confident but I don't think it came out exactly right.

"I can't," she said.

"Okay," I said.

"Okay?"

"Yeah, it's okay."

"Don't you want to know why, Ari?"

"If you wanted to tell me why, you'd tell me."

"Okay, I'll tell you why I can't go."

"You don't have to."

"I have a boyfriend, Ari."

"Oh," I said. I said it like nothing. "So I'm just, this, well, what am I, Ileana?"

"You're a guy I like."

"Okay," I said. I heard Gina's voice in my head. *She's just toying with you.*

"He's in a gang, Ari."

"Your boyfriend?"

"Yeah. And if he knew I was here, something bad would happen to you."

"I'm not afraid."

"You should be."

"Why don't you just break up with him?"

"It's not that easy."

"Why?"

"You're a good boy, you know that, Ari?"

"Yeah, well, that sucks, Ileana. I don't want to be a good boy."

"Well, you *are*. I love that about you."

"Well, here's the thing," I said, "I get to be the good boy. And the gang guy gets the girl. I don't like this movie."

"You're mad. Don't be mad."

"Don't tell me not to be mad."

"Ari, please don't be mad."

"Why did you kiss me? Why did you kiss me, Ileana?"

"I shouldn't have. I'm sorry." She just looked at me. Before I could say anything else, she got out of my truck.

On Monday, I looked for her at school. But I could never find her. I got Gina and Susie on the case. They were good detectives. Gina came back with a report, "Ileana dropped out of school."

"Why?"

"She just did, Ari."

"Can she do that? Isn't it against the law or something?"

"She's a senior, Ari. She's eighteen. She's an adult. She can do whatever she wants."

"She doesn't know what she wants."

I found her address. Her dad's number was listed in the book. I went to her house and knocked on her door. Her brother came out. "Yeah?" He just looked at me.

"I'm looking for Ileana."

"What do you want her for?"

"She's a friend. From school."

"Friend?" He just kept nodding his head. "Look, *vato*, she got married."

"What?"

"She got knocked up. She married the guy."

I didn't know what to say. So I didn't say anything at all.

I sat in my truck that night with Legs. I kept thinking that I took this kissing way too seriously. I promised myself that I was going to become the world's most casual kisser.

Kissing didn't mean a damn thing.

Thirty

DEAR ARI,

Seven to one. That's the ratio of Dante Letters to Ari Letters. Just so you know. When I get back this summer, I'm going to take you swimming and drown you. Almost drown you. Then I'll give you mouth-to-mouth and revive you. How does that sound? Sounds good to me. Am I freaking you out yet?

So on the business of kissing. This girl who've I've been experimenting with. I mean with the kisses. She's a good kisser. She's taught me a lot in that department. But she finally said to me, "Dante, I think that when you kiss me, you're kissing someone else."

"Yeah," I said. "Guess so."

"Are you kissing another girl? Or are you kissing a boy?"

I thought that was a very interesting and forward question.

"A boy," I said.

"Anyone I know?" she asked.

"No," I said. "I think I'm just making up a boy in my head."

"Any boy?"

"Yeah," I said. "A good-looking boy."

"Well, yeah," she said. "As good-looking as you?"

I shrugged. It's nice that she thought I was good-looking. We're friends now. And it's nice because now I don't feel like I'm leading her on. And anyway, she confessed to me that the only reason she liked kissing me at all those parties was because she was trying to make this guy she really likes jealous. That made me laugh. She said it wasn't working. "Maybe he'd rather be kissing you than me," she said. Ha, ha, I said. I didn't know which guy she was talking about but to tell you the honest truth, Ari, even though it's been a real trip hanging out with privileged Chicago kids who can afford lots of beer and liquor and pot, they're really not all that interesting. Not to me anyway.

I want to go back home.

That's what I told my mom and dad. "Can we go now? Are we done here?" Of course, my dad, who can be a real wise ass, *looks me straight in the eyes and says: "I thought you hated El Paso? Isn't that what you said when I told you we were moving to El Paso? You said: "Just shoot me, Dad."*

I know what he was after. He wanted me to say I was wrong. Well, I looked right back at him and said: "I was wrong, Dad. Are you happy?"

He gets this grin on his face. "Happy about what, Dante?"

"Happy that I was wrong?"

He kissed me on the cheek and said, "Yeah, I'm happy, Dante."

The thing is I love my dad. My mom too. And I keep wondering what they're going to say when I tell them that someday I want to marry a boy. I wonder how that's going to go over? I'm the only son. What's going to happen with the grandchildren thing? I hate that I'm going to disappoint them, Ari. I know I've disappointed you too.

I'm a little worried that we won't be friends when I get back. I guess I have to deal with these things. I hate lying to people, Ari. I especially hate lying to my parents. You know how I feel about them.

I guess I'm just going to tell my dad. I have this little speech. It starts something like this. "Dad, I have something to say to you. I like boys. Don't hate me. Please don't hate me. I mean,

Dad, you're a boy too." The speech doesn't really fit together very well. It needs some work. It sounds too needy. I hate that. I don't want to be needy. Just because I'm playing for the other team doesn't mean that I'm this pathetic human being who's begging to be loved. I have more self-respect than that.

Yeah, I know, I'm droning on and on. Three more weeks and I'll be home. Home. Another summer, Ari. You think we're too old to play in the streets? Probably. Maybe not. Look, I just want you to know that I don't want you to feel like you have to be my friend when I get back. I'm not exactly best-friend material, am I?

> Your friend,
> Dante

P.S. It would be very weird not be friends with the guy who saved your life, don't you think? Am I breaking the rules?

Thirty-One

ON THE LAST DAY OF SCHOOL, GINA ACTUALLY GAVE me a compliment. "You know all that working out has turned you into a hunk."

I smiled at her. "That's the nicest thing you've ever said to me."

"So how are you going to celebrate the beginning of summer?"

"I'm working tonight."

She smiled. "So serious."

"You and Susie going to a party?"

"Yeah."

"Don't you get tired of parties?"

"Don't be stupid. I'm seventeen, you idiot. Of course I don't get tired of parties. You know what, you're an old man trapped in the body of a seventeen-year-old guy."

"I won't be seventeen until August."

"It gets worse."

We both laughed.

"You want to do me a favor?" I said.

"What?"

"If I go out to the desert and get plastered tonight, will you and

Susie drive me back home?" I didn't even know I was going to say that.

She smiled. She had a great smile. A really great smile.

"Sure," she said.

"What about your party?"

"Watching you loosen up, Ari. That's a party. We'll even score the beer for you," she said. "To celebrate the end of school."

Gina and Susie were waiting for me on my front steps when I got home from work. They were talking to my mom and dad. Of course they were. I cursed myself for telling them to meet me at my house. What the hell was I thinking? And I didn't even have an explanation. *Yeah, Mom, we're going out to the desert and I'm going to get shit faced.*

Gina and Susie were cool, though. No hint of the beer they said they were going to score. They played good girls to my parents. Not that they weren't good girls. That's exactly what they were: good girls who wanted to pretend they were bad girls but who never would be bad girls because they were too decent.

When I drove up, my mom was ecstatic. Not that she behaved ecstatically. But I knew that look. *Friends at last! You're going to a party!* Yeah, okay, I really did love my mom. My mom. My mom who knew Gina's parents, who knew Susie's parents, who knew everybody. Of course she did.

I remember changing clothes in my room and washing up. I remember staring at myself in the mirror. I remember whispering, *"You are a beautiful boy."* I didn't believe it—but I wanted to.

So the first people to enter into my truck other than Legs and my mother and father, were Gina Navarro and Susie Byrd. "You guys are breaking in my virgin truck," I said. They rolled their eyes—then just laughed their asses off.

We stopped at Gina's cousin's house and picked up an ice chest full of beer and Cokes. I let Gina drive to make sure she knew how to drive a stick shift. She was a pro. She drove better than I did. Not that I told her. It was a perfect night and there was still some coolness in the desert breeze, the heat of the summer was still a step away.

Me and Susie and Gina sat in the bed of my truck. I drank beer and looked up at all the stars. And I found myself whispering, "Do you think we'll ever discover all the secrets of the universe?"

I was surprised to hear Susie's voice answering my question. "That would be a beautiful thing, wouldn't it, Ari?"

"Yeah." I whispered, "Really beautiful."

"Do you think, Ari, that love has anything to do with the secrets of the universe?"

"I don't know. Maybe."

Susie smiled. "Did you love Ileana?"

"No. Maybe a little bit."

"Did she break your heart?"

"No. I didn't even know her."

"Have you ever been in love?"

"Does my dog count?"

"Well, counts for something." We all laughed.

Susie was nursing a Coke as I drank beer after beer. "Are you drunk yet?"

"Sort of."

"So why do you want to get drunk?"

"To feel something."

"You're an idiot," she said. "You're a good guy, Ari, but you're definitely an idiot."

We all lay down on the back of the pickup, me and Gina and Susie, and just kept looking out at the night sky. I didn't really get all that drunk. I just let myself mellow out. I listened to Gina and Susie talk and I thought it was nice that they knew how to talk and how to laugh and how to be in the world. But it maybe it was easier for girls.

"It's good you brought a blanket," I said. "Good thinking."

Gina laughed. "That's what girls do, good thinking."

I wondered what it would be like, to love a girl, to know how a girl thinks, to see the world through a girl's eyes. Maybe they knew more than boys. Maybe they understood things that boys could never understand.

"Too bad we can't lie out here forever."

"Too bad," Susie said.

"Too bad," Gina said.

Too bad.

Remember the Rain

turning the pages patiently
in search of meanings
—W. S. Merwin

One

SUMMER WAS HERE AGAIN. SUMMER, SUMMER, SUMMER. I loved and hated summers. Summers had a logic all their own and they always brought something out in me. Summer was supposed to be about freedom and youth and no school and possibilities and adventure and exploration. Summer was a book of hope. That's why I loved and hated summers. Because they made me want to believe.

I had that Alice Cooper song in my head.

I made up my mind that this was going to be *my* summer. If summer was a book then I was going to write something beautiful in it. In my own handwriting. But I had no idea what to write. And already the book was being written for me. Already it wasn't all that promising. Already it was about more work and commitments.

I'd gone on full time at the Charcoaler. I'd never worked forty hours a week. I liked the hours though: eleven in the morning to seven thirty at night, Monday through Thursday. That meant I could always sleep in, and if I wanted, I could go out. Not that I knew where I wanted to go out. On Fridays I went in late and closed at ten. Not a bad schedule—and I had weekends off. So, it was okay.

But this was summer! And Saturday afternoons, my mom signed me up for the food bank. I didn't argue with her.

My life was still someone else's idea.

I got up early on the first Saturday after school let out. I was in my jogging shorts in the kitchen, having a glass of orange juice. I looked over at my mom who was reading the newspaper. "I have to work tonight."

"I thought you didn't work on Saturdays?"

"I'm just filling in for a couple of hours for Mike."

"He your friend?"

"Not really."

"It's decent of you to fill in for him."

"I'm not doing it for free, I'm getting paid. And, anyway, you raised me to be decent."

"You don't sound too thrilled."

"What's so thrilling about being decent? I want to be bad boy, if you want to know the truth."

"A bad boy?"

"You know. Che Guevara. James Dean."

"Who's stopping you?"

"I'm looking at her."

"Yeah, blame it all on your mother." She laughed.

Me, I was trying to decide if I was joking or not.

"You know, Ari, if you really wanted to be a bad boy, you'd just do it. The last thing bad boys need is their mother's approval."

"You think I need your approval?"

"I don't know how to answer that."

We looked at each other. I always wound up getting into these conversations with my mother that I didn't want to have. "What if I quit my job?"

She just looked at me. "Fine."

I knew that tone. "Fine" meant I was full of crap. I knew the code. We looked at each other for about five seconds—which seemed like forever.

"You're too old for an allowance," she said.

"Maybe I'll just mow lawns."

"That's imaginative."

"Too Mexican for you, Mom?"

"No. Just too unreliable."

"Flipping burgers. That's reliable. Not very imaginative, but reliable. Come to think of it, it's the perfect job for me. I'm reliable and unimaginative."

She shook her head. "Are you going to spend your life beating up on yourself?"

"You're right. Maybe I'll take the summer off."

"You're in high school, Ari. You're not looking for a profession. You're just looking for a way to earn some money. You're in transition."

"In transition? What kind of a Mexican mother are you?"

"I'm an educated woman. That doesn't un-Mexicanize me, Ari."

She sounded a little angry. I loved her anger and wished I had more of it. Her anger was different than mine or my father's. Her anger didn't paralyze her. "Okay, I get your point, Mom."

"Do you?"

"Somehow, Mom, I always feel like a case study around you."

"Sorry," she said. Though she wasn't. She looked at me. "Ari, do you know what an ecotone is?"

"It's the terrain where two different ecosystems meet. In an ecotone, the landscape will contain elements of the two different ecosystems. It's like a natural borderlands."

"Smart boy. In transition. I don't have to say any more, do I?"

"No mom, you don't. I live in an ecotone. Employment must coexist with goofing off. Responsibility must coexist with irresponsibility."

"Something like that."

"Do I get an A in Sonhood 101?"

"Don't be mad at me, Ari."

"I'm not."

"Sure you are."

"You're such a school teacher."

"Look, Ari, it's not my fault you're almost seventeen."

"And when I'm twenty-five, you'll still be a schoolteacher."

"Well, that was mean."

"Sorry."

She studied me.

"I am, Mom. I'm sorry."

"We always begin every summer with an argument, don't we?"

"It's a tradition," I said. "I'm going running."

As I turned away, she grabbed my arm. "Look, Ari, I'm sorry too."

"It's okay, Mom."

"I know you, Ari," she said.

I wanted to tell her the same thing I wanted to tell Gina Navarro. *Nobody knows me.*

Then she did what I knew she was going to do—she combed my hair with her fingers. "You don't have to work if you don't want to. Your father and I will be happy to give you money."

I knew she meant it.

But that wasn't what I wanted. I didn't know what I wanted. "It's not about the money, Mom."

She didn't say anything.

"Just make it a nice summer, Ari."

The way she said that. The way she looked at me. Sometimes there was so much love in her voice that I just couldn't stand it.

"Okay, Mom," I said. "Maybe I'll fall in love."

"Why not?" she said.

Sometimes parents loved their sons so much that they made a romance out of their lives. They thought our youth could help us overcome everything. Maybe moms and dads forgot about this one small fact: being on the verge of seventeen could be harsh and painful and confusing. Being on the verge of seventeen could really suck.

Two

IT WASN'T EXACTLY AN ACCIDENT THAT LEGS AND I ran by Dante's house. I knew he was coming back—though I didn't know exactly when. He'd sent a postcard on the day he left Chicago: *We're driving back today via Washington, D.C. My dad wants to look something up at the Library of Congress. See you soon. Love, Dante.*

When I got to the park, I let Legs off the leash, even though I wasn't supposed to. I loved watching her run around. I was in love with the innocence of dogs, the purity of their affection. They didn't know enough to hide their feelings. They existed. A dog was a dog. There was such a simple elegance about being a dog that I envied. I called her back and put her on the leash and started my run again.

"Ari!"

I stopped, then turned around. And there he was, Dante Quintana standing on his porch, waving at me with that honest and sincere smile of his, that same smile he wore when he asked me if I wanted to learn how to swim.

I waved back and walked toward his house. We stood there, looking at each other for a minute. It was strange, that we didn't have any words. And then he just leapt off his porch and hugged me. "Ari!

Look at you! Long hair! You look like Che Guevara without the mustache."

"Nice," I said.

Legs barked at him. "You have to pet her," I said. "She hates to be ignored."

Dante got down on his knees and petted her. Then kissed her. Legs licked his face. It was hard to say which of the two of them was more affectionate. "Legs, Legs, so nice to meet you." He looked so happy and I wondered about that, his capacity for happiness. Where did that come from? Did I have that kind of happiness inside me? Was I just afraid of it?

"Where'd you get all those muscles, Ari?"

I looked at him, standing in front of me, him and all his uncensored questions.

"My dad's old weights in the basement." I said. And then I realized that he was now taller than me. "How'd you grow so much?" I said.

"Must have been the cold," he said. "Five eleven. I'm exactly as tall as my dad." He studied me. "You're shorter—but your hair makes you look taller."

That made me laugh though I didn't know why. He hugged me again and whispered, "I missed you so much, Ari Mendoza."

Typically, I didn't know what to say so I didn't say anything.

"Are we going to be friends?"

"Don't be crazy, Dante. We *are* friends."

"Will we always be friends?"

"Always."

"I'll never lie to you about anything," he said.

"I might lie to you," I said. And then we laughed. And I thought, *Maybe this will be the summer when there is nothing but laughter. Maybe this will be the summer.*

"Come and say hi to Mom and Dad," he said. "They'll want to see you."

"Can they come out? I have Legs."

"Legs can come in."

"I don't think your mom would like that."

"If it's your dog, the dog can come in. Trust me on that one." He lowered his voice to a whisper. "My mom isn't about to forget that incident in the rain."

"That's ancient history."

"My mom is an elephant when it comes to remembering."

But we didn't have to test Dante's mom about dogs in the house because just then, Mr. Quintana was at the front door and he was shouting at his wife, "Soledad, guess who's here?"

They were all over me, hugging me and saying nice things, and I wanted to cry. Because their affection was so real and somehow, I felt I didn't deserve it or felt maybe that they were hugging the guy who had saved their son's life. I wanted them to hug me just because I was Ari and I would never be just Ari to them. But I had learned how to hide what I felt. No, that's not true. There was no learning involved. I had been born knowing how to hide what I felt.

They were so happy to see me. And the truth was that I was happy to see them, too.

I remember telling Mr. Quintana that I was working at the

Charcoaler. He smirked at Dante. "Work, Dante, there's a thought."

"I'm going to get a job, Dad. I really am."

Mrs. Quintana looked different. I don't know, it was like she was holding the sun inside her. I had never seen a woman look more beautiful. She looked younger than the last time I'd seen her. Younger, not older. Not that she was old. She'd had Dante when she was twenty, I knew that. So she was thirty-eight or so. But she looked younger than that in the morning light. Maybe that's what it was, the morning light.

I heard Dante's voice as I listened to his parents talk about their year in Chicago. "When do I get a ride in the truck?"

"How about after work?" I said. "I get off at seven thirty."

"You have to teach me how to drive, Ari."

I saw the look on his mother's face.

"Aren't dads supposed to do that?" I said.

"My dad is the worst driver in the universe," he said.

"That's not true," Mr. Quintana said. "Just the worst driver in El Paso." He was the only man I'd ever met who actually admitted he was a bad driver. Before I left, his mother managed to pull me aside. "I know you're going to let Dante drive your truck sooner or later."

"I won't," I said.

"Dante's very persuasive. Just promise me you'll be careful."

"I promise." I smiled at her. Something about her made me feel perfectly confident and at ease. I just didn't feel that way around most people. "I can see that I'm going to have to deal with two mothers this summer."

"You're a part of this family," she said. "There's no use fighting it."

"I'm sure I'll disappoint you someday, Mrs. Quintana."

"No," she said. And even though her voice could be so firm, right then her voice was almost as kind as my own mother's. "You're so hard on yourself, Ari."

I shrugged. "Maybe that's just the way it is with me."

She smiled at me. "Dante's not the only one who missed you."

It was the most beautiful thing an adult who wasn't my mom or dad had ever said to me. And I knew that there was something about me that Mrs. Quintana saw and loved. And even though I felt it was a beautiful thing, I also felt it was a weight. Not that she meant it to be a weight. But love was always something heavy for me. Something I had to carry.

Three

LEGS AND I PICKED DANTE UP AT AROUND EIGHT
o'clock. The sun was still out, but it was sinking fast and it was hot.
I honked the horn and Dante was standing at the door. "That's your
truck! It's amazing! It's beautiful, Ari!"

Yeah, I knew I must have had a stupid grin on my face. A guy who
loves his truck needs other people to admire his driving machine.
Yeah, *needs*. That's the truth. I don't know why, but that's the way
truck guys are.

He shouted back toward his house. "Mom! Dad! Come look
at Ari's truck!" He bounded down the stairs like a kid. Always so
uncensored. Legs and I hopped out of the truck and watched Dante
walk around the truck admiring it. "Not a scratch," he said.

"That's because I don't drive it to school."

Dante smiled. "Real chrome rims," he said. "You're a real Mexican,
Ari."

That made me laugh. "So are you, you jerk."

"Nah, I'll never be a real Mexican."

Why did it matter so much to him? But it mattered to me too.
He was about to say something, but he noticed his parents walking
down the front steps of his house.

"Great truck, Ari! Now, that's a classic." Mr. Quintana reacted just like Dante with that uncensored enthusiasm.

Mrs. Quintana just smiled. The two of them walked around the truck, inspecting it, smiling at it as if they had run into an old friend. "It's a beautiful truck, Ari." I hadn't expected that from Mrs. Quintana. Dante had already redirected his attention to Legs who was licking his face. I don't know what came over me, but I tossed Mr. Quintana my keys. "You can take your girlfriend out for a spin if you want," I said.

There was no hesitation in his smile. I could tell Mrs. Quintana was trying to suppress the girl that was still living inside her. But even without her husband's smile, what she was holding inside of her seemed far more profound to me. It was as if I was coming to understand Dante's mother. I knew that it mattered. I wondered why.

I liked watching them, all three of them around my truck. I wanted time to stop because everything seemed so simple, Dante and Legs falling in love with each other, Dante's mom and dad remembering something about their youth as they examined my truck, and me, the proud owner. I had something of value—even if it was just a truck that brought out a sweet nostalgia in people. It was as if my eyes were a camera and I was photographing the moment, knowing that I would keep that photograph forever.

Dante and I sat on his steps and watched his dad start up my truck, his mother leaning into him like a girl on a first date.

"Buy her a milk shake!" Dante yelled. "Girls like it when you buy them something!"

We could see them laughing as they drove off.

"Your parents," I said. "Sometimes they're like kids."

"They're happy," he said. "Your parents? Are they happy?"

"Mom and Dad, they're not at all like your mom and dad. But, my mom adores my dad. I know that. And I think my dad adores my mom too. He's just not demonstrative."

"Demonstrative. That's not an Ari word."

"You're making fun. I've expanded my vocabulary." I nudged him. "I'm preparing for college."

"How many new words a day?"

"You know, a few. I like the old words better. They're like old friends."

Dante nudged me back. "Demonstrative. Is that word ever going to be an old friend?"

"Maybe not."

"You're like your father, aren't you?"

"Yeah, I guess I am."

"My mom struggles with that too, you know? She doesn't naturally display her feelings. That's why she married my dad. That's what I think. He drags it out of her, all those feelings she has."

"Then it's a good match."

"Yeah, it is. The funny thing is, I sometimes think my mother loves my father more than he loves her. Does that make sense?"

"Yeah, I guess so. Maybe. Is love a contest?"

"What does that mean?"

"Maybe everyone loves differently. Maybe that's all that matters."

"You do realize you're talking, don't you? I mean you're really talking."

"I talk, Dante. Don't be a shit."

"Sometimes you talk. Other times you just, I don't know, you just avoid."

"I'm doing the best I can."

"I know. Are there going to be rules for us, Ari?"

"Rules?"

"You know what I'm talking about."

"Yeah, I guess I do."

"So what are the rules?"

"I don't kiss boys."

"Okay, so the first rule is: No trying to kiss Ari."

"Yeah, that's the first rule."

"And I have a rule for you."

"Okay, that's fair."

"No running away from Dante."

"What does that mean?"

"I think you know what it means. Someday, someone will walk up to you and say: 'Why are you hanging out with that queer?' If you can't stick by me as a friend, Ari, if you can't do that, then maybe it's better that you just, you know—it would kill me. You know it would kill me if you—"

"Then it's a question of loyalty."

"Yes."

I laughed. "I have a harder rule to follow."

He laughed too.

He touched my shoulder—then smiled. "Bullshit, Ari. You have the harder rule to follow? Buffalo shit. Coyote shit. All you have to

248

do is be loyal to the most brilliant guy you've ever met—which is like walking barefoot through the park. I, on the other hand, have to refrain from kissing the greatest guy in the universe—which is like walking barefoot on hot coals."

"I see you still have the barefoot thing going on."

"I'll always hate shoes."

"We'll play that game," I said. "That game you made up to beat the hell out of your tennis shoes."

"It was fun, wasn't it?"

The way he said that. Like he knew we would never play that game again. We were too old now. We'd lost something and we both knew it.

We didn't say anything for a long time.

We just sat there on his front steps. Waiting. I looked over and saw Legs resting her head on Dante's lap.

Four

DANTE AND I AND LEGS DROVE OUT TO THE DESERT
that night. To my favorite spot. It was just past twilight and the stars
were coming out from wherever it was they hid during the day.

"Next time we'll bring my telescope."

"Good idea," I said.

We lay down on the bed of my truck and stared out at the new
night. Legs was exploring the desert and I had to call her back. She
hopped on the truck and made a space for herself between me and
Dante.

"I love Legs," Dante said.

"She loves you back."

He pointed up at the sky. "See Ursa Major?"

"No."

"Over there."

I studied the sky. "Yes. Yes. I see it."

"It's so amazing."

"Yes, it *is* amazing."

We were quiet. We just lay there.

"Ari?"

"Yeah?"

"Guess what?"

"What?"

"My mother's pregnant."

"What?"

"My mom's going to have a baby. Can you believe that?"

"No shit."

"Chicago was cold and my parents figured out a way to keep warm." That really made me laugh.

"You think parents ever outgrow sex?"

"I don't know. I don't think it's something you outgrow, is it? What do I know, I'm just waiting to grow into it."

"Me too."

We were quiet again.

"Wow, Dante," I whispered. "You're going to be a big brother."

"Yeah, a really big brother." He looked over at me. "Does that make you think of—what was your brother's name?"

"Bernardo."

"Does that make you think of him?"

"Everything makes me think of him. Sometimes, when I'm driving along in my pickup, I think of him and I wonder if he liked trucks and I wonder what he's like and I wish I knew him and—I don't know—I just can't let it go. I mean, it's not as if I ever really knew him. So why does it matter so much?"

"If it matters, then it matters."

I didn't say anything.

"Are you rolling your eyes?"

251

"Yeah, I guess."

"I think you should confront your parents. You should just sit them down and make them tell you. Make them be adults."

"You can't make anyone be an adult. Especially an adult." That really made Dante laugh and we got to laughing so hard that Legs started barking at us.

"You know," Dante said, "I need to take my own advice." He paused. "I hope to God that my mother has a boy. And he better like girls. Because if he doesn't, I'll kill him."

That got us to laughing again. And that got Legs to barking again.

When we finally got quiet again, I heard Dante's voice and it seemed so small in the desert night. "I have to tell them, Ari."

"Why?"

"Because I have to."

"But what if you fall in love with a girl?"

"That's not going to happen, Ari."

"They'll always love you, Dante."

He didn't say anything. And then I heard him crying. So I just let him cry. There was nothing I could do. Except listen to his pain. I could do that. I could hardly stand it. But I could do that. Just listen to his pain.

"Dante," I whispered. "Can't you see how much they love you?"

"I'm going to disappoint them. Just like I've disappointed you."

"You haven't disappointed me, Dante."

"You're just saying that because I'm crying."

"No, Dante." I got up from where I was lying and sat on the edge of the open tailgate of the truck. He sat up and we stared at each other. "Don't cry, Dante. I'm not disappointed."

On the way back to town we stopped off at a drive-in burger joint and had a root beer. "So what are you going to do this summer?" I said.

"Well, I'm going to practice with the Cathedral swim team and I'm going to work on some paintings and I'm going to get a job."

"Really. You're going to get a job?"

"God, you sound like my dad."

"Well, why do you want to work?"

"To learn about life."

"Life," I said. "Work. Shit. Ecotone."

"Ecotone?"

Five

ONE NIGHT, DANTE AND I WERE HANGING OUT IN HIS room. He'd graduated to working on canvas. He was working on a large painting on an easel. It was covered over.

"Can I see?"

"No."

"When you finish?"

"Yes. When I finish."

"Okay," I said.

He was lying on his bed and I was sitting on his chair.

"Read any good books of poems lately?" I said.

"No, not really." He seemed a little distracted.

"Where are you, Dante?"

"Here," he said. He sat up on his bed. "I was thinking about the kissing thing," he said.

"Oh," I said.

"I mean, how do you know that you don't like kissing boys if you've never kissed one?"

"I think you just know, Dante."

"Well, have you ever?"

"You know I haven't. Have you?"

"No."

"Well, maybe you don't really like kissing guys. Maybe you just think you do."

"I think we should try an experiment."

"I know what you're going to say and the answer is no."

"You're my best friend, right?"

"Yes. But right now I'm really regretting it."

"Let's just try it."

"No."

"I won't tell anyone. C'mon."

"No."

"Look, it's just a kiss. You know. And then we'll both know."

"We already do know."

"We won't really know until we actually do it."

"No."

"Ari, please."

"Dante."

"Stand up."

I don't know why I did it, but I did it. I stood up.

And then he stood right in front of me.

"Close your eyes," he said.

So I closed my eyes.

And he kissed me. And I kissed him back.

And then he started really kissing me. And I pulled away.

"Well?" he said.

"Didn't work for me," I said.

"Nothing?"

"Nope."

"Okay. It sure worked for me."

"Yeah. I think I get that, Dante."

"So, well, that's over with then, huh?"

"Yeah."

"Are you mad at me?"

"A little."

He sat back down on his bed. He looked sad. I didn't like seeing him that way. "I'm more mad at myself," I said. "I always let you talk me into things. It's not your fault."

"Yeah," he whispered.

"Don't cry, okay?"

"Okay," he said.

"You're crying."

"I'm not."

"Okay."

"Okay."

Six

I DIDN'T CALL DANTE FOR A FEW DAYS.

He didn't call me either.

But somehow I knew he was sulking. He felt bad. And I felt bad too. So after a couple of days passed, I called him. "You want to go running in the morning?" I said.

"What time?" he said.

"Six thirty."

"Okay," he said.

For someone who wasn't a runner, he ran really well. I ran a lot slower with Dante along, but that was okay. We talked a little. And laughed. And afterward, we played Frisbee with Legs in the park and we were all right. And I needed us to be all right. And he needed us to be all right too. And so we were.

"Thanks for calling," he said. "I thought maybe you wouldn't call anymore."

Life seemed strangely normal for a while. Not that I wanted my summer to be normal. But, normal was okay. I could settle for normal. I went for a run in the mornings and worked out. I went to work.

Sometimes Dante called me and we talked. Not about anything in particular. He was working on a painting and he'd gotten a job at the drugstore in Kern Place. He said he liked working there because when he got off he could go to the university and spend some time in the library. Being a professor's son had its privileges. Also he said, "You won't believe who buys condoms."

I don't know if he said that to make me laugh. But it worked.

"And Mom's teaching me how to drive," he said. "Mostly we fight."

"I'll let you drive my pickup," I said.

"My mother's worst nightmare," he said.

We were laughing again. And that was good. It wouldn't be summer without Dante's laughter. We talked a lot on the phone, but we didn't see each other very much those first few weeks of summer.

He was busy. I was busy.

Mostly I think we were busy avoiding each other. Even though we hadn't wanted that kiss to be a big thing, it had been a big thing. It took a while for the ghost of that kiss to disappear.

One morning, when I came back from my run, my mom was gone. She left a note telling me she was going to spend the day reorganizing the food bank. "When are you going to start your Saturday afternoon shift? You promised."

I don't know why, but I decided to call Dante. "I've been volunteered to work at the food bank on Saturday afternoons. Want to volunteer with me?"

"Sure. What are we supposed to do?"

"I'm sure my mom will train us," I said.

I was glad I asked. I missed him. I missed him more now that he was back than when he had been gone.

I didn't know why.

I took a shower and looked at the clock. I had some time to kill. I found myself opening the drawer in the spare bedroom. I found myself holding the envelope labeled BERNARDO. I wanted to rip it open. Maybe if I ripped it open, I would also be ripping open my life.

But I just couldn't. I threw it back in the drawer.

All day, I thought of my brother. But I didn't even remember what he looked like. I kept screwing up the orders at work. The manager told me to pay attention. "I'm not paying you to be pretty."

There was a cuss word in my head. But I didn't let it pass my lips.

I drove by Dante's house after work. "Want to get drunk?" I said.

He studied my face. "Sure." He had the decency not to ask me what was wrong.

I went back home and showered, washing the smell of french fries and onion rings off my skin. My dad was reading. The house seemed quiet to me. "Where's Mom?"

"She and your sisters are in Tucson visiting your Aunt Ophelia."

"Oh, yeah. I forgot."

"It's just you and me."

I nodded. "Sounds like fun." I hadn't meant to sound so sarcastic.

I could tell he was studying me. "Is there something wrong, Ari?"

"No. I'm going out. Dante and I, we're going to go riding around."

He nodded. He kept looking at me. "You seem different, Ari."

"Different how?"

"Angry."

If I had been braver this is what I would have said: *Angry? What have I got to be angry about? You know something, Dad? I don't really care that you can't tell me about Vietnam. Even though I know that war owns you, I don't care if you don't want to talk about it. But I do care that you won't talk about my brother. Damn it to hell, Dad, I can't stand to live with all your silence.*

I imagined his answer: *All that silence has saved me, Ari. Don't you know that? And what is this obsession you have with your brother?*

I imagined my argument: *Obsession, Dad? You know what I've learned from you and Mom? I've learned not to talk. I've learned how to keep everything I feel buried deep inside of me. And I hate you for it.*

"Ari?"

I knew I was about to cry. I knew he could see that. I hated letting my dad see all that sadness inside of me.

He reached for me. "Ari—"

"Don't touch me, Dad. Just don't touch me."

I don't remember driving to Dante's. I just remember sitting there in my truck, parked outside his house.

His parents were sitting on the front steps. They waved at me. I waved back. And then they were standing right there. At the door of my truck. And I heard Mr. Quintana's voice. "Ari, you're crying."

"Yeah, that happens sometimes," I said.

"You should come inside," Mrs. Quintana said.

"No."

And then Dante was there. He smiled at me. And then he smiled at his mom and dad. "Let's go," he said.

His parents didn't ask any questions.

I just drove. I could have driven forever. I don't know how I managed to find my spot in the desert, but I found it. It was as if I had a compass hidden somewhere inside me. One of the secrets of the universe was that our instincts were sometimes stronger than our minds. When I stopped the truck, I got out, slamming the door. "Shit! I forgot about the beer."

"We don't need the beer," Dante whispered.

"We need the beer! We need the fucking beer, Dante!" I don't know why I was yelling. The yelling turned into sobs. I fell into Dante's arms and cried.

He held me and didn't say a word.

Another secret of the universe: Sometimes pain was like a storm that came out of nowhere. The clearest summer morning could end in a downpour. Could end in lightning and thunder.

Seven

IT WAS STRANGE NOT HAVING MY MOM AROUND.

I wasn't used to making the coffee.

My dad left a note. *Are you okay?*

Yeah, Dad.

I was glad that Legs broke the silence of the house when she began barking. Her way of telling me it was time to go for a run.

Legs and I ran faster that morning. I tried not to think of anything as I ran, but it didn't work. I thought of my dad and my brother and Dante. I was always thinking of Dante, always trying to figure him out, always wondering why it was that we were friends and why it seemed to matter so much. To both of us. I hated thinking about things and people—especially when they were mysteries I couldn't solve. I changed the topic in my head to Aunt Ophelia in Tucson. I wondered why I never went to visit her. It's not as if I didn't love her. She lived alone and I could have made an effort. But I never did. I did call her sometimes. It was strange, but I could talk to her. She always made me feel so loved. I wondered how she did that.

When I was drying myself off after my shower, I stared at my naked body in the mirror. I studied it. How strange to have a body.

Sometimes it felt that way. Strange. I remembered what my aunt had told me once. "The body is a beautiful thing." No adult had ever said that to me. And I wondered if I would ever feel like my own body was beautiful. My Aunt Ophelia had solved a few of the many mysteries of the universe. I felt as though I hadn't solved any at all.

I hadn't even solved the mystery of my own body.

RIGHT BEFORE I WENT IN TO WORK, I STOPPED OFF AT the drugstore where Dante was working. I think I just wanted to see that he really had a job. When I walked into the drugstore, he was behind the counter, placing cigarettes on the shelf.

"Are you wearing shoes?" I said.

He smiled. I stared at his name tag. *Dante Q.*

"I was just thinking of you," he said.

"Yeah?"

"Some girls came in a little while ago."

"Girls?"

"They knew you. We got to talking."

I knew which girls they were before he told me. "Gina and Susie," I said.

"Yeah. They're nice. Pretty, too. They go to school with you."

"Yeah, they're nice and pretty. And pushy, too."

"They looked at my name tag. And then they looked at each other. And then one of them asked me if I knew you. I thought that it was a funny question to ask."

"What did you tell them?"

"I told them yeah. I said you were my best friend."

"You told them that?"

"You are *my* best friend."

"Did they ask you anything else?"

"Yeah, they asked if I knew anything about an accident and you breaking your legs."

"I can't believe it. I can't believe it!"

"What?"

"Did you tell them?"

"Of course I told them."

"You told them?"

"Why are you getting mad?"

"You told them about what happened?"

"Of course I did."

"There's a rule, Dante."

"You're mad? You're mad at me?"

"The rule was we weren't supposed to talk about the accident."

"Wrong. The rule was we weren't supposed to talk about the accident with each other. The rule doesn't apply to anyone else."

There was a line forming behind me.

"I have to get back to work," Dante said.

Later that afternoon, Dante called me at work. "Why are you mad?"

"I just don't like other people to know."

"I don't get you, Ari." He hung up the phone.

What I knew was going to happen, happened. Gina and Susie showed up at the Charcoaler just as I was getting off work.

"You were telling us the truth," Gina said.

"So what?" I said.

265

"So what? You saved Dante's life."

"Gina, let's not talk about it."

"You sound upset, Ari."

"I don't like to talk about it."

"Why not, Ari? You're a hero." Susie Byrd had this thing in her voice.

"And how come," Gina said, "we don't know anything about your best friend?"

"Yeah, how come?"

I looked at both of them.

"He's so cute. I'd have thrown myself in front of a moving car for him too."

"Shut up, Gina," I said.

"How come he's such a secret?"

"He's not a secret. He just goes to Cathedral."

Susie had this gaga look on her face. "Cathedral boys are so cute."

"Cathedral boys suck," I said.

"So when are we going to get to know him?"

"Never."

"Oh, so you want him all to yourself."

"Knock it off, Gina, you're really pissing me off."

"You're really touchy about things, you know that, Ari?"

"Go to hell, Gina."

"You really don't want us to know him, do you?"

"I don't really care. You know where he works. Go badger him. Maybe that way, you'll leave me alone."

266

"I DON'T UNDERSTAND WHY YOU'RE SO UPSET."

"Why did you tell Gina and Susie about the whole thing?"

"What's with you, Ari?"

"We agreed not to talk about it."

"I don't get you."

"I don't get me either."

I got up from the steps of his front porch where we were sitting. "I gotta go." I looked out across the street. I remembered Dante running after two boys who were shooting at a bird.

I opened the door to my truck and climbed in. I slammed the door. Dante was standing in front of me. "Do you wish you hadn't saved my life? Is that it? Do you wish I was dead?"

"Of course not," I whispered.

He just stood there, looking at me.

I didn't look back. I started my truck.

"You are the most inscrutable guy in the universe."

"Yeah," I said. "I guess I am."

Dad and I ate dinner together. We were both quiet. We took turns feeding Legs scraps of food. "Mom wouldn't approve."

"No, she wouldn't."

We smiled awkwardly at each other.

"I'm going bowling. You want to go?"

"Bowling?"

"Yeah. Sam and I, we're going bowling."

"You're going bowling with Dante's dad?"

"Yeah. He invited me. I thought it would be good to get out. You and Dante want to come along?"

"I don't know," I said.

"You guys have an argument?"

"No."

I called Dante on the phone. "Our dads are going bowling tonight."

"I know."

"My dad wanted to know if we wanted to go."

"Tell him no," Dante said.

"Okay."

"I have a better idea."

Mr. Quintana picked my dad up to go bowling. I thought that was really strange. I didn't even know my dad bowled. "Boys' night out," Mr. Quintana said.

"Don't drink and drive," I said.

"Dante's wearing off on you," he said. "What's happened to that respectful young man?"

"He's still here," I said. "I'm not calling you Sam, am I?"

My dad shot me a look.

"Bye," I said.

I watched them drive off. I looked at Legs, "Let's go." She hopped in the truck and we drove to Dante's house. He was sitting on the front porch, talking to his mother. I waved. Legs and I leapt out of the truck. I walked up the stairs and leaned down and gave Mrs. Quintana a kiss. The last time I'd seen her, I'd said hi and shaken her hand. I'd felt stupid. "A kiss on the cheek will do, Ari," she'd said. So that was our new greeting.

The sun was setting. Even though it had been a really hot day, the breeze was picking up, the clouds were gathering, and it looked like it might storm. Looking at Mrs. Quintana's hair in the breeze made me think of my mother. "Dante's making a list of names for his baby brother."

I looked at Dante. "What if it's a girl?"

"He'll be a boy." There was no doubt in his voice. "I like Diego. I like Joaquin. I like Javier. Rafael. I like Maximiliano."

"Those names sound pretty Mexican," I said.

"Yeah, well, I'm shying away from ancient classical names. And besides, if he has a Mexican name, then maybe he'll *feel* more Mexican."

The look on his mother's face told me they'd had this discussion more than a few times.

"What about Sam?" I said.

"Sam's okay," he said.

Mrs. Quintana laughed. "Does the mother get a say?"

"No," Dante said. "The mother just gets to do all the work."

She leaned over and kissed him. She looked up at me. "So you two are going stargazing?"

"Yeah, stargazing with the naked eye. No telescopes," I said. "And it's us three. You forgot Legs."

"Nope," she said, "Legs is staying with me. I feel like some company."

"Okay," I said. "If you want."

"She's a wonderful dog."

"Yeah, she is. So you like dogs now?"

"I like Legs. She's sweet."

"Yeah," I said. "Sweet."

It's almost as if Legs knew what the score was. When Dante and I hopped into the truck, she stayed right beside Mrs. Quintana. How strange, I thought, that dogs sometimes understood the needs and behaviors of human beings.

Mrs. Quintana called out to me before I started the truck. "Promise me you'll be careful."

"I promise."

"Remember the rain," she said.

Ten

AS I WAS DRIVING TOWARD MY SPOT IN THE DESERT,
Dante took out the goods. He waved the two joints in the air.

We both smiled, then laughed.

"You're a bad boy," I said.

"You're a bad boy too."

"Just what we've always wanted to be."

"If our parents knew," I said.

"If our parents knew," he said.

We laughed.

"I've never done this."

"It's not hard to learn."

"Where'd you score this?"

"Daniel. This guy I work with. I think he likes me."

"Does he want to kiss you?"

"I think so."

"Do you want to kiss him back?"

"Not sure."

"But you talked him into giving you some pot, didn't you?"

Even though I kept my eye on the road, I knew he was smiling.

"You like talking people into things, don't you?"

"I'm not going to answer that."

There was lightning in the sky and thunder and the smell of rain. Dante and I got out of the truck. We didn't say a word. He lit the joint, inhaled, then held the smoke in his lungs. Then finally, he let it out. Then he did it again, and handed the joint to me. I did exactly as he did. I have to say I liked the smell, but the pot was harsh in my lungs. I fought not to cough. If Dante didn't cough, then I wasn't going to cough. We sat there passing the joint until it was gone.

I felt light and breezy and happy. It was strange and wonderful and everything seemed far away and yet kind of close. Dante and I kept looking at each other as we sat on the tailgate of my truck. We started laughing and couldn't stop.

Then the breeze became a wind. And the thunder and lightning was close and closer and it started to rain. We ran inside the truck. We couldn't stop laughing, didn't want to stop laughing. "It's crazy," I said. "It feels so crazy."

"Crazy," he said. "Crazy, crazy, crazy."

"God, crazy."

I wanted us to laugh forever. We listened to the downpour. God, it was really raining. Like that night.

"Let's go out there," Dante said. "Let's go out in the rain." I watched him as he took off all his clothes: his shirt, his shorts, his boxers. Everything except his tennis shoes. Which was really funny. "Well," he said. He had his hand on the handle of the door. "Ready?"

"Wait," I said. I stripped off my T-shirt and all my clothes. Except my tennis shoes.

We looked at each other and laughed. "Ready?" I said.

"Ready," he said.

We ran out into the rain. God, the drops of rain were so cold. "Shit!" I yelled.

"Shit!" Dante yelled.

"We're fucking crazy."

"Yeah, yeah!" Dante laughed. We ran around the truck, naked and laughing, the rain beating against our bodies. Around and around the truck, we ran. Until we were both tired and breathless.

We sat inside the truck, laughing, trying to catch our breaths. And then the rain stopped. That was the way it was in the desert. The rain poured down, then stopped. Just like that. I opened the door to the truck and stepped out into the damp and windy night air.

I stretched my arms out toward the sky. And closed my eyes.

Dante was standing next to me. I could feel his breath.

I don't know what I would have done if he had touched me.

But he didn't.

"I'm starving," he said.

"Me too."

We got dressed and drove back into town.

"What should we eat?" I said.

"Menudo," he said.

"You like menudo."

"Yeah."

"I think that makes you a real Mexican."

"Do real Mexicans like to kiss boys?"

"I don't think liking boys is an American invention."

"You could be right."

"Yeah, I could be." I shot him a look. He hated when I was right. "How about Chico's Tacos?"

"They don't have menudo."

"Okay, how about the Good Luck Café on Alameda?"

"My dad loves that place."

"Mine too."

"They're bowling," I said.

"They're bowling." We were laughing so hard I had to pull over.

When we finally got to the Good Luck Café, we were so hungry that we both had a plate of enchiladas and two bowls of menudo.

"Are my eyes red?"

"No," I said.

"Good. I guess we can go home."

"Yeah," I said.

"I can't believe we did that."

"Me neither."

"But it was fun," he said.

"God," I said. "It was fantastic."

Eleven

DAD WOKE ME EARLY. "WE'RE GOING TO TUCSON," he said.

I sat up in bed. I stared at him.

"There's coffee."

Legs followed him out the door.

I wondered if he was mad at me, wondered why we had to go to Tucson. I felt a little groggy, like I'd been woken in a middle of a dream. I slipped on a pair of jeans and headed for the kitchen. Dad handed me a cup of coffee. "You're the only kid I know who drinks coffee."

I tried to go with the small talk, tried to pretend I hadn't had that imaginary conversation with him. Not that he knew what I'd said. *But I knew.* And I knew I'd meant to say those things, even if I hadn't. "Someday, Dad, kids all over the world will be drinking coffee."

"I need a cigarette," he said.

Legs and I followed him into the backyard.

I watched him light his cigarette. "How was bowling?"

He smiled crookedly. "It was kind of fun. I'm a crappy bowler. Luckily, so is Sam."

"You should get out more," I said.

"You too," he said. He took a drag off his cigarette. "Your mom called late last night. Your aunt had a very serious stroke. She's not going to make it."

I remembered living with her one summer. I was a small boy and she was a kind woman. She'd never married. Not that it mattered. She knew about boys and knew how to laugh and knew how to make a boy feel as though he was the center of the universe. She'd lived a life separate from the rest of family for reasons no one had ever bothered to explain to me. I never cared about that.

"Ari? Are you listening?"

I nodded.

"You go away sometimes."

"No, not really. I was just thinking. I spent a summer with her when I was little."

"Yes, you did. You didn't want to come back home."

"I didn't? I don't remember."

"You fell in love with her." He smiled.

"Maybe I did. I can't remember not loving her. And that's weird."

"Why is that weird?"

"I don't feel that way about my other uncles and aunts."

He nodded. "The world would be lucky to have more like her. She and your mother wrote to each other every week. A letter a week for years and years and years. Did you know that?"

"No. That's a lot of letters."

"She saved them all."

I took a sip of my coffee.

"Can you make arrangements at work, Ari?"

I could imagine him in the military. Taking charge. His voice calm and undisturbed.

"Yeah. It's only a job flipping burgers. What can they do, fire me?" Legs barked at me. She was used to her morning run. I looked at my dad. "What are we going to do about Legs?"

"Dante," he said.

His mother answered the phone. "Hi," I said. "It's Ari."

"I know," she said. "You're up early."

"Yeah." I said. "Is Dante up?"

"Are you kidding, Ari? He gets up a half hour before he has to be in to work. He won't get up a minute earlier."

We both laughed.

"Well," I said, "I sort of need a favor."

"Okay," she said.

"Well, my aunt had a stroke. My mom was visiting her. My dad and I are leaving as soon as we can. But, then, there's Legs, and I thought maybe—" She didn't let me finish my sentence.

"Of course we'll take her. She's great company. She fell asleep on my lap last night."

"But you work and Dante works."

"It will be fine, Ari. Sam's home all day. He's finishing his book."

"Thanks," I said.

"Don't thank me, Ari." She sounded so much happier and lighter than the woman I'd first met. Maybe it was because she was going to have a baby. Maybe that was it. Not that she still didn't get after Dante.

I hung the phone up, packed a few things. The phone rang. It was Dante. "Sorry about your aunt. But, hey, I get Legs!" He could be such a boy. Maybe he would always be a boy. Like his dad. "Yeah, you get Legs. She likes to run in the morning. Early."

"How early?"

"We get up at five forty-five."

"Five forty-five! Are you crazy? What about sleep?"

That guy could always make me laugh. "Thanks for doing this," I said.

"Are you okay?" he said.

"Yeah."

"Did your dad give you hell for coming in so late?"

"No. He was asleep."

"My mom wanted to know what we were up to."

"What did you tell her?"

"I told her we didn't get to watch any stars because of the storm. I said it was raining like hell and we just got stuck in the storm. And we just sat in the truck and talked. And when the rain stopped, we got hungry so we went out for menudo.

"She looked at me funny. She said: 'Why don't I believe you?' And I said: 'Because you have a very suspicious nature.' And then she dropped the whole thing."

"Your mom has hyper instincts," I said.

"Yeah, well, she can't prove a thing."

"I bet she knows."

"How would she know?"

"I don't know. But I bet she knows."

"You're making me paranoid."

"Good."

We both cracked up laughing.

We dropped off Legs at Dante's house later that morning. My dad gave Mr. Quintana a key to our house. Dante got stuck with watering my mom's plants. "And don't steal my truck," I said.

"I'm Mexican," he said. "I know all about hotwiring." That really made me laugh. "Look," I said. "Eating menudo and hotwiring a truck are two totally different forms of art."

We smirked at each other.

Mrs. Quintana shot us a look.

We drank a cup of coffee with Dante's mom and dad. Dante gave Legs a tour around the house. "I'm betting Dante's going to encourage Legs to chew up all his shoes." We all laughed except my dad. He didn't know about Dante's war against shoes. We laughed even harder when Legs and Dante walked back into the kitchen. Legs was carrying one of Dante's shoes in her mouth. "Look what she found, Mom."

Twelve

MY FATHER AND I DIDN'T TALK ALL THAT MUCH ON THE
drive to Tucson. "Your mother's sad," he said. I knew he was thinking
back.

"You want me to drive?"

"No," he said. But then he changed his mind. "Yes." He got off at
the next exit and we got some gas and coffee. He handed me the
keys. His car handled a lot easier than my truck. I smiled. "I've never
driven anything besides my truck."

"If you can handle that truck, you can handle anything."

"I'm sorry about last night," I said. "It's just that sometimes I have
things running around inside me, these feelings. I don't always know
what to do with them. That probably doesn't make any sense."

"It sounds normal, Ari."

"I don't think I'm so normal."

"Feeling things is normal."

"Except I'm angry. And I don't really know where all that anger
comes from."

"Maybe if we talked more."

"Well, which one of us is good with words, Dad?"

"You're good with words, Ari. You're just not good with words when you're around me."

I didn't say anything. But then I said, "Dad, I'm not good with words."

"You talk to your mother all the time."

"Yeah, but that's because it's a requirement."

He laughed. "I'm glad she makes us talk."

"We'd die in our own silence if she wasn't around."

"Well, we're talking now, aren't we?"

I glanced over and saw him smiling. "Yeah, we're talking."

He rolled down the window. "Your mother doesn't let me smoke in the car. Do you mind?"

"No, I don't mind."

That smell—cigarette—it always made me think of him. He smoked his cigarette. I drove. I didn't mind the silence and the desert and the cloudless sky.

What did words matter to a desert?

My mind drifted. I thought of Legs and Dante. I wondered what Dante saw when he looked at me. I wondered why I didn't look at the sketches he gave me. Not ever. I thought of Gina and Susie and wondered why I never called them. They bugged me, but that was their way of being nice to me. I knew they liked me. And I liked them back. Why couldn't a guy be friends with girls? What was so wrong with that? I thought about my brother and wondered if he'd been close to my aunt. I wondered why such a nice lady had divorced her family. I wondered why I'd spent a summer with her when I was only four.

"What are you thinking?" I heard my father's voice. He hardly ever asked that question.

"I was thinking about Aunt Ophelia."

"What were you thinking?"

"Why did you send me to spend the summer with her?"

He didn't answer. He rolled down the window and the heat of the desert came pouring into the air-conditioned car. I knew he was going to smoke another cigarette.

"Tell me," I said.

"It was just around the time of your brother's trial," he said.

That was the first time he'd ever said anything to me about my brother. I didn't say anything. I wanted him to keep talking.

"Your mother and I were having a very difficult time. We all were. Your sisters too. We didn't want you to—" He stopped. "I think you know what I'm trying to say." He had a very serious look on his face. More serious than usual. "Your brother loved you, Ari. He did. And he didn't want you to be around. He didn't want you to think of him that way."

"So you sent me away."

"Yeah. We did."

"It didn't solve a damn thing, Dad. I think of him all the time."

"I'm sorry, Ari. I just—I'm really sorry."

"Why can't we just—"

"Ari, it's more complicated than you think."

"In what way?"

"Your mother had a breakdown." I could hear him smoking his cigarette.

"What?"

"You were at your Aunt Ophelia's for more than a summer. You were there for nine months."

"Mom? I can't—it's just—Mom? Mom really had—" I wanted to ask my dad for a cigarette.

"She's so strong, your mother. But, I don't know, life isn't logical, Ari. It was like your brother had died. And your mother became a different person. I hardly recognized her. When they sentenced him, she just fell apart. She was inconsolable. You have no idea how much she loved your brother. And I didn't know what to do. And sometimes, even now, I look at her and I want to ask, 'Is it over? Is it?' When she came back to me, Ari, she seemed so fragile. And as the weeks and months went by, she became her old self again. She got strong again and—"

I listened to my dad cry. I pulled the car over to the side of the road. "I'm sorry," I whispered. "I didn't know. I didn't know, Dad."

He nodded. He got out of the car. He stood out in the heat. I knew he was trying to organize himself. Like a messy room that needed to be cleaned up. I left him alone for a while. But then, I decided I wanted to be with him. I decided that maybe we left each other alone too much. Leaving each other alone was killing us.

"Dad, sometimes I hated you and mom for pretending he was dead."

"I know. I'm sorry, Ari. I'm sorry, I'm sorry, I'm sorry."

Thirteen

BY THE TIME WE REACHED TUCSON, MY AUNT OPHELIA was dead.

There was standing-room-only at her funeral mass. It was obvious that she had been deeply loved. By everyone except her family. We were the only ones there. My mom, my sisters, me, and my dad.

People I didn't know walked up to me. "Ari?" they would ask.

"Yes, I'm Ari."

"Your aunt adored you."

I was so ashamed. For having kept her on the margins of my memory. I was so ashamed.

Fourteen

MY SISTERS WENT BACK HOME AFTER THE FUNERAL.

My mom and dad and I stayed on. My mom and dad closed up my aunt's house. My mom knew exactly what to do, and it was almost impossible for me to imagine her residing on the borders of sanity.

"You keep watching me," she said one night as we watched a summer storm coming in from the west.

"Do I?"

"You've been quiet."

"Quiet's pretty normal for me."

"Why didn't they come?" I asked. "My uncles and aunts? Why didn't they come?"

"They didn't approve of your aunt."

"Why not?"

"She lived with another woman. For many years."

"Franny," I said. "She lived with Franny."

"You remember?"

"Yes. A little. Not much. She was nice. She had green eyes. She liked to sing."

"They were lovers, Ari."

I nodded. "Okay," I said.

"Does that bother you?"

"No."

I kept playing with the food on my plate. I looked up at my father. He didn't wait for me to ask my question.

"I loved Ophelia," he said. "She was kind and she was decent."

"It didn't matter to you that she lived with Franny?"

"To some people it mattered," he said. "Your uncles and aunts, Ari, they just couldn't."

"But it didn't matter to you?"

My father had a strange look on his face, as if he was trying to hold back his anger. I think I knew that his anger was aimed at my mother's family, and I also think he knew that his anger was useless. "If it had mattered to us, do you think we'd have let you come and stay with her?" He looked at my mother.

My mother nodded at him. "When we get back home," she said. "I'd like to show you some pictures of your brother. Would that be okay?"

She reached over and wiped my tears. I couldn't speak.

"We don't always make the right decisions, Ari. We do the best we can."

I nodded, but there weren't any words and the silent tears just kept running down my face like there was a river inside me.

"I think we hurt you."

I closed my eyes and made the tears stop. And then I said, "I think I'm crying because I'm happy."

286

Fifteen

I CALLED DANTE AND TOLD HIM THAT WE'D BE BACK in a couple of days. I didn't tell him anything about my aunt. Except that she'd left me her house.

"What?" he said.

"Yeah."

"Wow."

"'Wow' is right."

"Is it a big house?"

"Yeah. It's a great house."

"What are you going to do with the house?"

"Well, apparently there's a friend of my aunt's who wants to buy it."

"What are you going to do with all that money?"

"I don't know. I haven't thought about it."

"Why do you suppose she left you the house?"

"I have no idea."

"Well, you can quit your job at the Charcoaler."

Dante. He could always make me laugh.

"So what have you been up to?"

"Working at the drugstore. And I'm sort of hanging out with this guy," he said.

"Yeah?" I said.

"Yeah."

I wanted to ask his name but I didn't.

He changed the subject. I knew when Dante was changing the subject. "My mom and dad are in love with Legs."

Sixteen

ON THE FOURTH OF JULY, WE WERE STILL IN TUCSON.

We went to watch the fireworks.

My dad let me a have a beer with him. My mother tried to pretend she didn't approve. But if she hadn't approved, she would have put a stop to it.

"It's not your first beer, is it, Ari?"

I wasn't going to lie to her.

"Mom, I told you when I broke the rules, I was going to do it behind your back."

"Yes," she said. "That's what you said. You weren't driving, were you?"

"No."

"You promise?"

"I promise."

I drank the beer slowly and watched the fireworks. I felt like a small boy. I loved fireworks, the explosions in the sky, the way the crowd sometimes uuhhhed and aahhed and oohhhed.

"Ophelia always said Franny was the Fourth of July."

"That's really a great thing to say," I said. "So what happened to her?"

"She died of cancer."

"When?"

"About six years ago, I guess."

"Did you come to the funeral?"

"Yes."

"You didn't bring me."

"No."

"She used to send me Christmas gifts."

"We should have told you."

Seventeen

I THINK MY MOTHER AND FATHER HAD DECIDED THAT there were too many secrets in the world. Before we left my aunt's house, she put two boxes in the trunk of the car. "What's that?" I asked.

"The letters I wrote to her."

"What are you going to do with them?"

"I'm going to give them to you."

"Really?"

I wondered if my smile was as big as hers. Maybe as big. But not as beautiful.

Eighteen

ON THE DRIVE BACK TO EL PASO FROM TUCSON, I SAT in the backseat. I could see that my mom and dad were holding hands. Sometimes they would glance at each other. I looked out at the desert. I thought of the night Dante and I had smoked pot and run around naked in the rain.

"What are you going to do the rest of the summer?"

"I don't know. Work at the Charcoaler. Hang out with Dante. Work out. Read. Stuff like that."

"You don't have to work," my father said. "You have the rest of your life to do that."

"I don't mind working. And anyway, what would I do? I don't like to watch TV. I'm out of touch with my own generation. And I have you and mom to thank for that."

"Well, you can watch all the television you like from here on in."

"Too late."

They both laughed.

"It's not funny. I'm the uncoolest almost-seventeen-year-old in the universe. And it's all your fault."

"Everything is our fault."

"Yes, everything is your fault."

My mom turned around just to make sure I was smiling.

"Maybe you and Dante should take a trip together. Maybe go camping or something."

"I don't think so," I said.

"You should think about it," my mom said. "It's summer."

It's summer, I thought. I kept thinking of what Mrs. Quintana had said: *Remember the rain.*

"There's a storm up ahead," my father said. "And we're about to run into it."

I looked out the window at the black clouds ahead of us. I opened the back window and smelled the rain. You could smell the rain in the desert even before a drop fell. I closed my eyes. I held my hand out and felt the first drop. It was like a kiss. The sky was kissing me. It was a nice thought. It was something Dante would have thought. I felt another drop and then another. A kiss. A kiss. And then another kiss. I thought about the dreams I'd been having—all of them about kissing. But I never knew who I was kissing. I couldn't see. And then, just like that, we were in the middle of a downpour. I rolled up the window and I was suddenly cold. My arm was wet, the shoulder of my T-shirt soaked.

My father pulled the car over. "Can't drive in this," he said.

There was nothing but darkness and sheets of rain and the awe of our silence.

My mom held my father's hand.

Storms always made me feel so small.

Even though summers were mostly made of sun and heat,

summers for me were about the storms that came and went. And left me feeling alone.

Did all boys feel alone?

The summer sun was not meant for boys like me. Boys like me belonged to the rain.

All the Secrets of the Universe

Through all of youth I was looking for you
without knowing what I was looking for
—W. S. Merwin

One

IT RAINED OFF AND ON THE WHOLE TRIP BACK TO El Paso. I dozed off to sleep. I'd wake every time we hit a heavy downpour.

There was something very serene about that trip back home.

Outside of the car, there was an awful storm. Inside of the car, it was warm. I didn't feel threatened by the angry, unpredictable weather. Somehow, I felt safe and protected.

One of the times I fell asleep, I started dreaming. I think I could dream on command. I dreamed my father and my brother and I were all having a cigarette. We were in the backyard. My mother and Dante were at the door. Watching.

I couldn't decide if the dream was a good dream or a bad dream. Maybe a good dream because when I woke I wasn't sad. Maybe that's how you measured whether a dream was good or bad. By the way it made you feel.

"Are you thinking of the accident?" I heard my mother's soft voice.

"Why?"

"Does the rain ever remind you of the accident?"

"Sometimes."

"Do you and Dante talk about it?"

"No."

"Why?"

"We just don't."

"Oh," she said. "I thought you two talked about everything."

"No," I said. "We're just like everyone else in the world." I knew it wasn't true. We weren't like everyone else in the world.

When we drove up to the house, it was pouring. Thunder and lightning and wind, the worst storm of the summer season. My dad and I got soaked taking the suitcases back into the house. My mom turned on the lights and put on some tea as my father and I changed into dry clothes.

"Legs hates thunder," I said. "It hurts her ears."

"I'm sure she's sleeping right next to Dante."

"Yeah, guess so." I said.

"Miss her?"

"Yeah." I pictured Legs lying at Dante's feet, whimpering at the sound of the thunder. I pictured Dante kissing her, telling her everything was all right. Dante who loved kissing dogs, who loved kissing his parents, who loved kissing boys, who even loved kissing girls. Maybe kissing was part of the human condition. Maybe I wasn't human. Maybe I wasn't part of the natural order of things. But Dante enjoyed kissing. And I suspected he liked masturbating too. I thought masturbating was embarrassing. I didn't even know why. It just was. It was like having sex with yourself. Having sex with yourself was really weird. Autoeroticism. I'd looked it up in a book

298

in the library. God, I felt stupid just thinking about these things. Some guys talked about sex all the time. I heard them at school. Why were they so happy when they talked about sex? It made me feel miserable. Inadequate. There was that word again. And why was I thinking about these things in the middle of a rainstorm, sitting at the kitchen table with my mother and father? I tried to bring my thoughts back into the kitchen. Where I was. Where I lived. I hated the thing of living in my head.

My mother and father were talking and I sat there, trying to listen to their conversation but not really listening at all, just thinking about things. My mind just wandering around. And then my thoughts fell on my brother. They always fell there. It was like my favorite parking spot in the desert. I just sort of drove there all the time. I wondered what it would have been like if my brother had been around. Maybe he could have taught me stuff about being a guy and what guys should feel and what they should do and how they should act. Maybe I would be happy. But maybe my life would be the same. Maybe my life would be even worse. Not that I had a bad life. I knew that. I had a mom and dad and they cared, and I had a dog and a best friend named Dante. But there was something swimming around inside me that always made me feel bad.

I wondered if all boys had that darkness inside them. Yes. Maybe even Dante.

I felt my mother's eyes on me. She was studying me. Again.

I smiled at her.

"I'd ask you to tell me what you're thinking, but I don't think you'd tell me."

I shrugged. I pointed at my father. "Too much like him, I guess."

That made my father laugh. He looked tired but at that moment, as we sat at the kitchen table, there was something young about him. And I thought that maybe he was changing into someone else.

Everyone was always becoming someone else.

Sometimes, when you were older, you became someone younger. And me, I felt old. How can a guy who's about to turn seventeen feel old?

It was still raining when I went to sleep. The thunder was far away and the soft sound of it was more like a distant whisper.

I slept. I dreamed. It was that dream again, that dream that I was kissing someone.

When I woke, I wanted to touch myself. "Shaking hands with your best friend." That was Dante's euphemism. He always smiled when he said that.

I took a cold shower instead.

Two

FOR SOME REASON I HAD A FUNNY FEELING IN THE PIT of my stomach. Not just the dream thing, the kissing thing, the body thing, and the cold shower. Not just that. There was something else that didn't feel right.

I walked over to Dante's house to get Legs. I was dressed for a run in the cool morning. I loved the dampness of the desert after all the rains.

I knocked at the front door.

It was early, but not too early. I knew Dante was probably still asleep, but his parents would be awake. And I wanted Legs.

Mr. Quintana answered the door. Legs rushed out and jumped up at me. I let her lick my face, which is not something I let her do very often. "Legs, Legs, Legs! I missed you." I kept petting her and petting her, but when I looked up, I noticed that Mr. Quintana looked—he looked, I don't know—there was something in his face.

I knew something was wrong. I looked at him. I didn't even ask the question.

"Dante," he said.

"What?"

"He's in the hospital."

"What? What happened? Is he okay?

"He's pretty beat up. His mother stayed with him overnight."

"What happened?"

"Would you like a cup of coffee, Ari?"

Legs and I followed him into the kitchen. I watched as Mr. Quintana poured me a cup of coffee. He handed me the cup and we sat across from each other. Legs placed her head on Mr. Quintana's lap. He kept running his hand over her head. We sat there in the quiet, me watching him. I waited for him to talk. Finally, he said, "How close are you and Dante?"

"I don't understand the question," I said.

He bit his lip. "How well do you know my son?"

"He's my best friend."

"I know that, Ari. But how well do you know him?"

He sounded impatient. I was playing dumb. I knew exactly what he was asking. I felt my heart beating against my chest. "Did he tell you?"

Mr. Quintana shook his head.

"So you know," I said.

He didn't say anything.

I knew I had to say something. He looked lost and afraid and sad and tired and I hated that, because he was such a kind and good man. I knew I had to say something to him. But I didn't know what. "Okay," I said.

"Okay? What, Ari?"

"When you left for Chicago, Dante told me that someday he

wanted to marry another boy." I looked around the room. "Or at least kiss another boy. Well, actually, I think he said that in a letter. Or maybe he said some of that after he got back."

He nodded. He stared into his cup of coffee.

"I think I knew," he said.

"How?"

"The way he looks at you sometimes."

"Oh." I looked down at the floor.

"But why didn't he tell me, Ari?"

"He didn't want to disappoint you. He said—" I stopped and then looked away from him. But then I made myself stare back into his black, hopeful eyes. And even though I felt I was betraying Dante, I knew I had to talk him. I had to tell him. "Mr. Quintana—"

"Call me Sam."

I looked at him. "Sam," I said.

He nodded.

"He's crazy about you. I guess you know that."

"If he's so crazy about me, then why didn't he tell me?"

"Talking to dads isn't that easy. Even you, Sam."

He sipped on his coffee nervously.

"He was so happy that you were going to have another baby. And not just because he was going to be a big brother. And he said, 'He has to be a boy and he has to like girls.' That's what he said. So that you could have grandchildren. So that you could be happy."

"I don't care about grandchildren. I care about Dante."

I hated watching the tears falling down Sam's face.

"I love Dante," he whispered. "I love that kid."

"He's lucky," I said.

He smiled at me. "They beat him," he whispered. "They beat my Dante all to hell. They cracked some ribs, they punched his face. He has bruises everywhere. They did that to my son."

It was a strange thing to want to hold an adult man in your arms. But that's what I wanted to do.

We finished our coffee.

I didn't ask any more questions.

Three

I DIDN'T KNOW WHAT TO TELL MY MOM AND DAD. NOT that I knew anything. I knew that someone, maybe several some-ones, had beat Dante so badly that he'd wound up in a hospital. I knew that it had something to do with another boy. I knew that Dante was at Providence Memorial Hospital. That's all I knew.

I came home with Legs, who went berserk when I brought her home. Dogs didn't censor themselves. Maybe animals were smarter than people. The dog was so happy. My mom and dad too. It felt good to know that they loved the dog, that they let themselves do that. And somehow it seemed that the dog helped us be a better family.

Maybe dogs were one of the secrets of the universe.

"Dante's in the hospital," I said.

My mother was studying me. So was my father. They both wore a question mark on their faces.

"Someone jumped him. He's hurt. He's in the hospital."

"No," she said. "Our Dante?" I wondered why she'd said, "Our Dante."

"Was it a gang thing?" my father whispered.

"No."

"It happened in some alley," I said.

"In the neighborhood?"

"Yes. I think so."

They were waiting for me to tell them more. But I couldn't. "I think I'll go," I said.

I didn't remember leaving the house.

I didn't remember driving to the hospital.

Next thing I knew I was standing in front of Dante, looking at his puffed up, punished face. He was unrecognizable. I couldn't even see the color of his eyes. I remember taking his hand and whispering his name. He could hardly talk. He could hardly see, his eyes nearly swollen shut.

"Dante."

"Ari?"

"I'm here," I said.

"Ari?" he whispered.

"I should have been here," I said. "I hate them. I hate them." I *did* hate them. I hated them for what they'd done to his face, for what they'd done to his parents. *I should have been here. I should have been here.*

I felt his mother's hand on my shoulder.

I sat with his mother and father. Just sat. "He'll be okay, won't he?"

Mrs. Quintana nodded. "Yes. But—" She looked at me. "Will you always be his friend?"

"Always."

306

"No matter what?"

"No matter what."

"He needs a friend. Everybody needs a friend."

"I need a friend too," I said. I had never said that before.

There was nothing to do at the hospital. Just sit and look at each other. None of us seemed like we were in the mood to talk.

As I was leaving, his parents walked out with me. We stood outside the hospital. Mrs. Quintana looked at me. "You should know what happened."

"You don't have to tell me."

"I think I do," she said. "There was an old woman. She saw what happened. She told the police." I knew she wasn't going to cry. "Dante and another boy were kissing in an alley. Some boys were walking by and saw them. And—" She tried to smile. "Well, you saw what they did to him."

"I hate them," I said.

"Sam told me you know about Dante."

"There are worse things in the world than a boy who likes to kiss other boys."

"Yes, there are," she said. "Much worse. Do you mind if I say something?"

I smiled at her and shrugged.

"I think Dante's in love with you."

Dante was right about her. She *did* know everything. "Yes," I said. "Well, maybe not. I think he likes that other guy."

Sam looked at right me. "Maybe the other guy's just a stand in."

"For me, you mean?"

He smiled awkwardly. "I mean, sorry. I shouldn't have said that."

"It's okay," I said.

"This is hard," he said. "I'm—hell, I'm just feeling a little lost right now."

I smiled at him. "You know what the worst thing about adults is?"

"No."

"They're not always adults. But that's what I like about them."

He took me in his arms and held me. Then let me go.

Mrs. Quintana watched us. "Do you know who he is?"

"Who?"

"The other boy?"

"I have an idea."

"And you don't care?"

"What am I supposed to do?" I knew my voice was cracking. But I refused to cry. What was there to cry about? "I don't know what to do." I looked at Mrs. Quintana and I looked at Sam. "Dante's my friend." I wanted to tell them that I'd never had a friend, not ever, not a real one. Until Dante. I wanted to tell them that I never knew that people like Dante existed in the world, people who looked at the stars, and knew the mysteries of water, and knew enough to know that birds belonged to the heavens and weren't meant to be shot down from their graceful flights by mean and stupid boys. I wanted to tell them that he had changed my life and that I would never be the same, not ever. And that somehow it felt like it was Dante who had saved my life and not the other way around. I wanted to tell them that he was the first human being aside from my mother who had ever made me want to talk about the things that scared me. I

308

wanted to tell them so many things and yet I didn't have the words. So I just stupidly repeated myself. "Dante's my friend."

She looked at me, almost smiling. But she was too sad to smile. "Sam and I were right about you. You *are* the sweetest boy in the world."

"Next to Dante," I said.

"Next to Dante," she said.

They walked me to my truck. And then a thought entered into my head. "What happened to the other guy?"

"He ran," Sam said.

"And Dante didn't."

"No."

That's when Mrs. Quintana broke down and cried. "Why didn't he run, Ari? Why didn't he just run?"

"Because he's Dante," I said.

Four

I DIDN'T KNOW THAT I WAS GOING TO DO THE THINGS I did. It wasn't like I had a plan. It wasn't like I was really thinking. Sometimes, you do things and you do them not because you're thinking but because you're feeling. Because you're feeling too much. And you can't always control the things you do when you're feeling too much. Maybe the difference between being a boy and being a man is that boys couldn't control the awful things they sometimes felt. And men could. That afternoon, I was just a boy. Not even close to being a man.

I was a boy. A boy who went crazy. Crazy, crazy.

I got in my truck and drove straight to the drugstore where Dante worked. I ran through the conversation we'd had. I remembered the guy's name. Daniel. I walked into the drugstore and he was there. Daniel. I saw his name tag. *Daniel G.* The guy Dante said he wanted to kiss. He was at the counter. "I'm Ari," I said.

He looked at me, a look of panic on his face.

"I'm Dante's friend," I said.

"I know," he said.

"I think you should take a break."

"I don't—"

I didn't wait for his lame excuses. "I'm going to go outside and wait for you. I'm going to wait for exactly five minutes. And if you're not out there in five minutes, then I'm going to walk back inside this drugstore and kick your fucking ass in front of the whole world. And if you don't think I'll do it, you better look into my eyes and study them."

I walked out the front door. And waited. It didn't take five minutes before he was standing there.

"Let's walk," I said.

"I can't be gone long," he said.

He followed me.

We walked.

"Dante's in the hospital."

"Oh."

"Oh?"

"You haven't gone to visit." He didn't say anything. I wanted to beat the holy shit out him right then and there. "Don't you have anything to say, you asshole?"

"What do you want me to say?"

"You bastard. Don't you feel anything?"

I could see he was trembling. Not that I cared. "Who were they?"

"What are you talking about?"

"Don't screw with me, asshole."

"You're not going to tell anyone."

I grabbed him by the collar and then let him go. "Dante's lying in a hospital and the only thing you're worried about is who I'm going to tell. Who am I going to tell, asshole? Just tell me who they were."

"I don't know."

"Bullshit. *You tell me now* and I won't kick your ass from here to the South Pole."

"I didn't know all of them."

"How many?"

"Four guys."

"All I need is one name. *Just one.*"

"Julian. He was one of them."

"Julian Enriquez?"

"Him."

"Who else?"

"Joe Moncada."

"Who else?"

"I didn't know the other two."

"And you just left Dante there?"

"He wouldn't run."

"And you didn't stay with him?"

"No. I mean, what good would it have done?"

"So you didn't care?"

"I do care."

"But you didn't go back, did you? You didn't go back to see if he was all right, did you?"

"No." He looked scared.

I shoved him against the wall of a building. And walked away.

Five

I KNEW WHERE JULIAN ENRIQUEZ LIVED. I'D PLAYED baseball with him and his brothers when I was in grade school. We'd never really liked each other. Not that we were enemies or anything like that. I drove around for a little while, then found myself parking my truck in front of his house. I walked up to his front door and knocked. His little sister answered the door. "Hi, Ari," she said.

I smiled at her. She was pretty. "Hi, Lulu," I said. My voice was calm and almost friendly. "Where's Julian?"

"He's at work."

"Where does he work?"

"Benny's Body Shop."

"What time does he get off?" I said.

"He usually gets home after five sometime."

"Thanks," I said.

She smiled at me. "Should I tell him you came by?"

"Sure," I said.

Benny's Body Shop. Mr. Rodriguez, one of my dad's friends, owned it. They'd gone to school together. I knew exactly where it was. I went driving around all afternoon, just waiting for five o'clock to come around. When it was almost time, I parked around the corner from the body shop. I didn't want Mr. Rodriguez to see me. He'd ask questions. He'd tell my dad. I didn't want questions.

I got out of my truck and walked across the street from the body shop. I wanted to make sure I'd see Julian when he walked out of the garage. When I spotted him, I waved him over.

He walked across the street.

"What's up, Ari?"

"Not much," I said. I pointed to my truck. "Just driving around."

"That your truck?"

"Yup."

"Nice wheels, *vato*."

"Want to get a good look?"

We walked up to my truck and he ran his hand over the chrome fenders. He knelt down and studied the chrome rims. I pictured him kicking Dante as he lay on the ground. I pictured me beating the crap out of him right then and there.

"Want to take a ride?"

"Got some stuff going on. Maybe you can come by later and we can take a spin."

I grabbed him by the neck and pulled him up. "Get in," I said

"What the hell crawled up your ass, Ari?"

"Get in," I said. I threw him against the truck.

"*Chingao, ese.* What the shit's wrong with you, man?"

He took a swing at me. That was all I needed. I just went to it. His nose was bleeding. That didn't stop me. It didn't take long before he was on the ground. I was saying things to him, cussing at him. Everything was a blur and I just kept going at him.

Then I heard a voice and a pair of arms grabbing me and holding me back. The voice was yelling at me and the arms were strong and I couldn't swing anymore.

I stopped struggling.

And everything stopped. Everything stood still.

Mr. Rodriguez was staring at me. "What the hell's the matter with you, Ari? *Que te pasa?*"

I didn't have anything to say. I looked down at the ground.

"What's going on here, Ari? *A ver. Di me.*"

I couldn't talk.

I watched as Mr. Rodriguez knelt down and helped Julian get up off the ground. His nose was still bleeding.

"I'm gonna kill you, Ari," he whispered.

"You and whose army," I said.

Mr. Rodriguez glared at me. He turned toward Julian. "Are you okay?"

Julian nodded.

"Let's get you cleaned up."

I didn't move. Then I started to get in the truck.

Mr. Rodriguez shot me another look. "You're lucky I don't call the cops."

"Go ahead and call them. I don't give a damn. But before you call them, you better ask Julian what he's been up to."

I got in my truck and drove away.

315

Six

I DIDN'T NOTICE THE BLOOD ON MY KNUCKLES AND ON my shirt until I drove up to my house.

I just sat there.

I didn't have a plan. So I just sat. I would sit there forever—that was my plan.

I don't know how long I sat there. I started shaking. I knew I'd gone crazy but I couldn't explain it to myself. Maybe that's what happens when you go crazy. You just can't explain it. Not to yourself. Not to anyone. And the worst part about going crazy is that when you're not crazy anymore, you just don't know what to think of yourself.

My dad came out of the house and stood on the front porch. He looked at me. I didn't like the look on his face. "I need to talk to you," he said. He'd never said that to me before. Not ever. Not like that. His voice made me afraid.

I got out of the truck and sat on the front steps of the porch.

My dad sat next to me. "I just got a call from Mr. Rodriguez."

I didn't say anything.

"What's wrong with you, Ari?"

"I don't know," I said. "Nothing."

"Nothing?" I could hear the anger in my father's voice.

I stared at my bloody shirt. "I'm going to take a shower."

My dad followed me into the house. "Ari!"

My mom was in the hallway. I couldn't stand the way she was looking at me. I stopped and looked down at the floor. I couldn't stop the shaking. My whole body was trembling.

I stared at my hands. Nothing could stop the shaking.

My father grabbed my arm, not hard or mean but not soft either. He was strong, my father. He moved me toward the living room and sat me down on the couch. My mother sat next to me. He sat on his chair. I felt numb and wordless.

"Talk," my father said.

"I wanted to hurt him," I said.

"Ari?" My mother just looked at me. I hated that look of disbelief. Why couldn't she believe that I'd want to hurt someone?

I looked back at her. "I *did* want to hurt him."

"Your brother hurt someone once," she whispered. And then she started sobbing. And I couldn't stand it. I hated myself more than I had ever hated myself. I just watched her cry and finally I said, "Don't cry, Mom, please don't cry."

"Why, Ari? Why?"

"You broke that boy's nose, Ari. And the only reason you're not at a police station is because Elfigo Rodriguez is an old friend of your father's. We have to pay for that little hospital visit. *You* have to pay, Ari."

I didn't say anything. I knew what they were thinking. *First your brother and now you.*

"I'm sorry," I said. It sounded lame even to me. But part of me wasn't sorry. Part of me was glad I'd broken Julian's nose. I was only sorry that I'd hurt my mom.

"Sorry, Ari?" He had this look on his face. Like steel.

I could be like steel too. "I'm *not* my brother," I said. "I hate that you think that. I hate that I live in his f—" I stopped myself from using that word in front of my mother. "I hate that I live in his shadow. I hate it. I hate having to be a good boy just to please you."

Neither of them said anything.

"I don't know that I am sorry," I said.

My father stared back at me. "I'm selling your truck."

I nodded. "Fine. Sell it."

My mother had stopped crying. She had a strange look on her face. Not soft, not hard. Just strange. "I need you to tell me why, Ari."

I took a breath. "Okay," I said. "And you'll listen?"

"Why wouldn't we listen?" My dad's voice was firm.

I looked at my dad.

Then I looked at my mom.

Then I looked down at the floor. "They hurt Dante," I whispered. "You can't even tell what he looks like. You should see his face. They cracked some of his ribs. They left him lying in an alley. Like he was nothing. Like he was a piece of trash. Like he was shit. Like he was nothing. And if he would have died, they wouldn't have cared." I started to cry. "You want me to talk? I'll talk. You want me to tell you? I'll tell you. He was kissing another boy."

I don't know why, but I couldn't stop crying. And then I stopped and I knew I was really angry. More angry than I'd ever been in my life. "There were four of them. The other boy ran. But Dante didn't run. Because Dante's like that. He doesn't run."

I looked at my dad.

He didn't say a word.

My mother had moved closer to me. She couldn't stop combing my hair with her fingers.

"I'm so ashamed," I whispered. "I wanted to hurt them back."

"Ari?" My father's voice was soft. "Ari, Ari, Ari. You're fighting this war in the worst possible way."

"I don't know how to fight it, Dad."

"You should ask for help," he said.

"I don't know how to do that, either."

Seven

WHEN I GOT OUT OF THE SHOWER, MY FATHER WAS gone.

My mother was in the kitchen. The manila envelope with my brother's name was on the table. My mother was drinking a glass of wine.

I sat across from her. "I drink beer sometimes," I said.

She nodded.

"I'm not an angel, Mom. And I'm not a saint. I'm just Ari. I'm just screwed-up Ari."

"Don't you ever say that."

"It's true."

"No, it isn't." Her voice was fierce and strong and sure. "You're not screwed up at all. You're sweet and good and decent." She took a sip of her wine.

"I hurt Julian," I said.

"That wasn't a very smart thing to do."

"And not very nice."

She almost laughed. "No, not nice at all." She was running her hands over the envelope. "I'm sorry," she said. She opened up the envelope and took out a picture. "This is you. You and Bernardo."

She handed me the picture. I was a little boy and my brother was holding me in his arms. And he was smiling. He was handsome and smiling and I was laughing.

"You loved him so much," she said. "And I'm sorry. It's like I said, Ari, we don't always do the right things, you know? We don't always say the right things. Sometimes, it seems like it just hurts too much to look at something. So you don't. You just don't look. But it doesn't go away, Ari." She handed me the envelope. "It's all in there." She wasn't crying. "He killed someone, Ari. He killed someone with his bare fists." She almost smiled. But it was the saddest smile I'd ever seen. "I've never said that before," she whispered.

"Does it still hurt a lot?"

"A lot, Ari. Even after all these years."

"Will it always hurt?"

"Always."

"How do you stand it?"

"I don't know. We all have to bear things, Ari. All of us. Your father has to bear the war and what it did to him. You have to bear your own painful journey to becoming a man. And it is painful for you, isn't it, Ari?"

"Yes," I said.

"And I have to bear your brother, what he did, the shame of it, his absence."

"It's not your fault, Mom."

"I don't know. I think mothers always blame themselves. Fathers too, I think."

"Mom?"

I wanted to reach over and touch her. But I didn't. I just looked at her and tried to smile. "I didn't know I could love you this much."

And then her smile wasn't sad anymore.

"*Hijo de mi corazon*, I'll tell you a secret. You help me bear it. You help me bear all my losses. You, Ari."

"Don't say that, Mom. I'll only disappoint you."

"No, *amor*. Not ever."

"What I did today. I hurt you."

"No," she said. "I think I understand."

But the way she said it. It was like she understood something about me that she'd never quite understood before. I always felt that when she looked at me, she was trying to find me, trying to find out who I was. But it seemed at that moment that she saw me, that she knew me. But that confused me.

"Understand what, Mom?"

She pushed the envelope toward me. "Aren't you going to look through that?"

I nodded. "Yes. Not right now."

"Are you afraid?'

"No. Yes. I don't know." I ran my finger over my brother's name. We sat there, my mother and I, for what seemed a long time.

She sipped on her glass of wine and I looked at pictures of my brother.

My brother when he was a baby, my brother in my father's arms, my brother with my sisters.

My brother sitting on the front steps of the house.

My brother, a little boy, saluting my father in uniform.

My brother, my brother.

My mother watched me. It was true. *I had never loved her more.*

"WHERE DID DAD GO?"

"He went to see Sam."

"Why?'

"He just wanted to talk to him."

"About what?"

"About what happened. They're friends, you know, your father and Sam."

"That's interesting," I said. "Dad's older."

She smiled. "So what?"

"Yeah, so what."

Nine

"CAN I FRAME THIS ONE AND PUT IT IN MY ROOM?" IT was a picture of my brother saluting my father.

"Yes," she said, "I love that one."

"Did he cry? When Dad left for Vietnam?"

"For days. He was inconsolable."

"Were you afraid Dad wouldn't come back?"

"I didn't think about it. I made myself not think about it." She laughed. "I'm good at that."

"Me too," I said. "And all this time I thought I got that trait from Dad."

We laughed. "Can we put that picture in the living room? Would you mind, Ari?"

That was the day that my brother was in our house again. In a strange and inexplicable way, my brother had come home.

It wasn't my mother who answered my hungry questions. It was my father. My mother would listen sometimes as my father and I talked about Bernardo. But she would never say a word.

I loved her for her silence.

Or maybe I just understood it.

And loved my father too, for the careful way he spoke. I came to understand that my father was a careful man. To be careful with people and with words was a rare and beautiful thing.

Ten

I VISITED DANTE EVERY DAY. HE WAS IN THE HOSPITAL for about four days. They had to make sure he was okay because he'd had a concussion.

His ribs hurt.

The doctor said the cracked ribs would take a while to heal. But they weren't broken. That would have been worse. The bruises would heal on their own. At least the ones on the outside.

No swimming. He couldn't do much, really. He could lie around. But Dante liked lying around. That was the good thing.

He was different. Sadder.

The day he came home from the hospital, he cried. I held him. I thought he would never stop.

I knew that a part of him would never be the same.

They cracked more than his ribs.

Eleven

"ARE YOU OKAY, ARI?" MRS. QUINTANA WAS STUDYING me just like my mother studied me. I sat across from Dante's parents at their kitchen table. Dante was asleep. Sometimes when his ribs were bothering him, he took a pill. They made him drowsy.

"Yeah, I'm fine."

"Are you sure?"

"You think I need a therapist?"

"There's nothing wrong with going to see a therapist, Ari."

"Spoken like a therapist," I said.

Mrs. Quintana shook her head. "You didn't used to be smart aleck until you started hanging around with my son."

I laughed. "I'm fine," I said. "Why wouldn't I be fine?"

The Quintanas glanced at each other.

"Is that a parent thing?"

"What?"

"Those looks moms and dads like to give each other."

Sam laughed. "Yeah, I guess so."

I knew that my father and he had talked. I knew that he knew what I'd done. I knew they both knew.

"You know who the boys are, don't you, Ari?" Mrs. Quintana was back to her strict self. Not that I minded.

"I know who two of them are."

"And the other two?"

I thought I'd make a joke. "I bet I could make them talk."

Mrs. Quintana laughed. That surprised me.

"Ari," she said. "You're a crazy boy."

"Yeah, I guess I am."

"It's all about loyalty," she said.

"Yeah, I guess so."

"But, Ari, you could have gotten yourself in a lot of trouble."

"It was wrong. I know it was wrong. I just did it. I can't explain it. They're never going to do anything to those boys, are they?"

"Maybe not."

"Yeah," I said, "like the cops are really working this case."

"I don't care about those other boys, Ari." Sam was looking straight into my eyes. "I care about Dante. And I care about you."

"I'm fine," I said.

"You're sure?"

"I'm sure."

"And you're not going to go after those other boys?"

"The thought crossed my mind."

Mrs. Quintana didn't laugh that time.

"I promise."

"You're better than that," she said.

I wanted so much to believe her.

"But I'm not going to pay for Julian's broken nose."

327

"Have you told your father?"

"Not yet. But I'm just going to tell him that if those bast—" I stopped. I didn't finish the word I'd started. There were other words I wanted to use. "If those *guys* don't have to pay for Dante's hospital stay, then I don't have to pay for Julian's little ER visit. If Dad wants to take the truck away, then it's okay with me."

Mrs. Quintana was wearing a smirk. She didn't smirk much. "Let me know what your father says."

"And another thing. Julian can call the cops if he wants." I was wearing a smirk of my own. "You think that's going to happen?"

"You're pretty streetwise, aren't you, Ari?" I liked the look Sam had on his face.

"I know my way around."

Twelve

MY DAD DIDN'T ARGUE WITH ME ABOUT NOT PAYING for Julian's hospital bill. He looked at me and said, "I guess you've just decided to settle out of court." He just kept nodding pensively. "Sam talked to the old lady. She could never recognize those boys. Not in a million years."

Julian's dad came over and had a talk with my dad. He didn't look very happy when he left.

My dad didn't take away my truck.

Thirteen

IT SEEMED THAT DANTE AND I DIDN'T HAVE MUCH TO say to each other.

I borrowed books of poems from his father and read to him. Sometimes, he would say, "Read that one again." And so I would. I don't know what was wrong between us in those last days of summer. In some ways I had never felt closer to him. In other ways I had never felt further away.

Neither one of us went back to work. I don't know. I guess, after what had happened, it all seemed so pointless.

I made a bad joke one day. "Why does summer always have to end with one of us all beat to hell?"

Neither one of us laughed at the joke.

I didn't take Legs to see him because she liked to jump on him and she could hurt him. Dante missed her. But he knew I was right not to take her over.

One morning, I went to Dante's house and showed him all the pictures of my brother. I told him the story as I understood it, from the newspaper clippings, from the questions my father answered.

"So you want to hear the whole thing?" I said.

"Tell me," he said.

We were both tired of poetry, tired of not talking.

"Okay. My brother was fifteen years old. He was angry. From everything I understand about him, he was always angry. I especially got that from my sisters. I guess he was mean or, just, I don't know, he was just born angry. So one night he's roaming around the streets of downtown, looking for trouble. That's what my father said. He said: 'Bernardo was always looking for trouble.' He picked up a prostitute."

"Where'd he get the money?"

"I don't know. What kind of a question is that?"

"When you were fifteen, did you have money for a prostitute?"

"When I was fifteen? You say it like it was a long time ago. Hell, I barely had money for a candy bar."

"That's my point."

I looked at him. "Can I finish?"

"Sorry."

"The prostitute turns out be a guy."

"What?"

"He was a transvestite."

"Wow."

"Yeah. My brother goes ballistic."

"How ballistic?"

"He killed the guy with his fists."

Dante didn't know what to say. "God," he said.

"Yeah. God."

A long time went by before either one of us said anything.

331

Finally, I looked at Dante. "Did you know what a transvestite was?"

"Yeah. Of course I did."

"Of course you did."

"You didn't know what a transvestite was?"

"How would I know?"

"You're so innocent, Ari, you know that?"

"Not so innocent," I said.

"The story gets sadder," I said.

"How can the story get sadder?"

"He killed someone else."

Dante didn't say anything. He waited for me to finish. "He was in a juvenile detention center. I guess one day, he took out his fists again. My mom is right. Things don't just go away because we want them to."

"I'm sorry, Ari."

"Yeah, well, there's nothing we can do, is there? But it's good, Dante. I mean, it's not good for my brother. I don't know if anything's ever going to be good with him. But it's good it's all out there, you know. In the open." I looked at him. "Maybe someday I'll know him. Maybe someday."

He was watching me. "You look like you're going to cry."

"I'm not. It's just too sad, Dante. And you know what? I'm like him, I think."

"Why? Because you broke Julian Enriquez's nose?"

"You know?"

"Yeah."

332

"Why didn't you tell me you knew?"

"Why didn't *you* tell *me*, Ari?"

"I'm not proud of myself, Dante."

"Why'd you do it?"

"I don't know. He hurt you. I wanted to hurt him back. I did a stupid kind of math in my head." I looked at him. "Your black eyes are almost gone."

"Almost," he said.

"How are the ribs?"

"Better. Some nights it's hard to sleep. So I take a pain pill. I hate them."

"You'd make a bad drug addict."

"Maybe not. I really liked pot. I really did."

"Maybe your mother should interview you for that book she's writing."

"Well, she already gave me hell."

"How'd she find out?"

"I keep telling you. She's like God. She knows everything."

I tried not to laugh but I couldn't help it. Dante laughed too. But it hurt him to laugh. With his cracked ribs.

"You're not," he said. "You're not like your brother at all."

"I don't know, Dante. Sometimes I think I'll never understand myself. I'm not like you. You know exactly who you are."

"Not always," he said. "Can I ask you a question?"

"Sure."

"Does it bother you, that I was kissing Daniel?"

"I think Daniel's a piece of shit."

333

"He's not. He's nice. He's good-looking."

"He's good-looking? How shallow is that? He's a piece of shit, Dante. He just left you there."

"You sound like you care more than I do."

"Well, you should care."

"You wouldn't have done that, would you?"

"No."

"I'm glad you broke Julian's nose."

We both laughed.

"Daniel doesn't care about you."

"He was scared."

"So what? We're all scared."

"You're not, Ari. You're not scared of anything."

"That's not true. But I wouldn't have let them do that to you."

"Maybe you just like to fight, Ari."

"Maybe."

Dante looked at me. He just kept looking at me.

"You're staring," I said.

"Can I tell you a secret, Ari?"

"Can I stop you?"

"You don't like knowing my secrets."

"Sometimes your secrets scare me."

Dante laughed. "I wasn't really kissing Daniel. In my head, I was kissing you."

I shrugged. "You got to get yourself a new head, Dante."

He looked a little sad. "Yeah. Guess so."

Fourteen

I WOKE UP EARLY. THE SUN WASN'T OUT YET. THE SECOND week of August. Summer was ending. At least the part of summer that had to do with no school.

Senior year. And then life. Maybe that's the way it worked. High school was just a prologue to the real novel. Everybody got to write you—but when you graduated, you got to write yourself. At graduation you got to collect your teacher's pens and your parents' pens and you got your own pen. And you could do all the writing. Yeah. Wouldn't that be sweet?

I sat up on my bed and ran my fingers over the scars on my legs. Scars. A sign that you had been hurt. A sign that you had healed.

Had I been hurt?

Had I healed?

Maybe we just lived between hurting and healing. Like my father. I think that's where he lived. In that in-between space. In that ecotone. My mother, too, maybe. She'd locked my brother somewhere deep inside of her. And now she was trying to let him out.

I kept running my finger up and down my scars.

Legs lay there with me. Watching. *What do you see, Legs? What do you see? Where did you live before you came to me? Did someone hurt you, too?*

Another summer was ending.

What would happen to me after I graduated? College? More learning. Maybe I would move to another city, to another place. Maybe summers would be different in another place.

Fifteen

"WHAT DO YOU LOVE, ARI? WHAT DO YOU REALLY LOVE?"

"I love the desert. God, I love the desert."

"It's so lonely."

"Is it?"

Dante didn't understand. I *was* unknowable.

Sixteen

I DECIDED TO GO SWIMMING. I GOT THERE RIGHT WHEN the pool opened so I could swim some laps in peace before it got crowded. The lifeguards were there, talking about girls. I ignored them. They ignored me.

I swam and swam until my legs and lungs hurt. Then took a break. Then swam and swam some more. I felt the water on my skin. I thought of the day I met Dante. "You want me to teach you how to swim?" I thought of his squeaky voice and how he'd outgrown his allergies, how his voice had changed and deepened. Mine, too. I thought of what my mom had said. "You talk like a man." It was easier to talk like a man than to be one.

When I got out of the pool, I noticed a girl staring at me. She smiled.

I smiled back. "Hi." I waved.

"Hi." She waved back. "You go to Austin?"

"Yeah."

I think she wanted to keep talking. But I didn't know what to say next.

"What year?"

"Senior."

"I'm a sophomore."

"You look older," I said.

She smiled. "I'm mature."

"I'm not," I said. That made her laugh. "Bye," I said.

"Bye," she said.

Mature. Man. What exactly did those words mean anyway?

I walked to Dante's house and knocked at the door. Sam answered.

"Hi," I said.

Sam looked relaxed and happy. "Hi, Ari. Where's Legs?"

"Home." I pulled at the damp towel I'd flung over my shoulder. "I went swimming."

"Dante will be jealous."

"How's he doing?"

"Good. Getting better. You haven't been over in a while. We've missed you." He led me into the house. "He's in his room." He hesitated a moment. "He has company."

"Oh," I said. "I can come back."

"Don't worry about it. Go on up."

"I don't want to bother him."

"Don't be crazy."

"I can come back. It's not a big deal. I was just coming back from swimming—"

"It's just Daniel," he said.

"Daniel?"

I think he noticed the look on my face. "You don't like him very much, do you?"

"He sort of left Dante hanging," I said.

"Don't be so hard on people, Ari."

That really made me mad, that he said that. "Tell Dante I came by," I said.

Seventeen

"MY DAD SAID YOU WERE UPSET?"

"I wasn't upset." The front door was open and Legs was barking at a dog passing by. "Just a minute," I said. "Legs! Knock it off."

I took the phone into the kitchen and sat down at the table. "Okay," I said. "Look, I wasn't upset."

"I think my dad would know."

"Okay," I said. "What the shit difference does it make?"

"See. You *are* upset."

"I just wasn't in the mood to see your friend Daniel."

"What's he ever done to you?"

"Nothing. I just don't like the guy."

"Why can't we all be friends?"

"The bastard left you there to die, Dante."

"We talked about it. It's okay."

"Okay then. Good."

"You're acting crazy."

"Dante, you're so full of shit sometimes, you know that?"

"Look," he said. "We're going to some party tonight. I'd like it if you came."

"I'll let you know," I said. I hung up the phone.

I went down to the basement and lifted some weights for a couple of hours. I lifted and lifted until every part of my body was in pain.

Pain wasn't so bad.

I took a shower. I lay down on my bed and just lay there. I must have fallen asleep. When I woke, Legs had her head on my stomach. I kept petting her. I heard my mom's voice in the room. "Are you hungry?"

"Nah," I said. "Not really."

"You sure?"

"Yeah. What time is it?"

"Six thirty."

"Wow. Guess I was tired."

She smiled at me. "Maybe it was all that exercise?"

"Guess so."

"Something wrong?"

"No."

"You sure?"

"Just tired."

"You've been hitting those weights a little hard, don't you think?

"No."

"When you're upset, you do weights."

"Is that another one of your theories, Mom?"

"It's more than a theory, Ari."

Eighteen

"DANTE CALLED."

I didn't say anything.

"Are you going to call him back?"

"Sure."

"You know you've been moping around the house for the past four or five days. Moping and lifting weights."

Moping. I thought of what Gina always said about me, "Melancholy Boy."

"I haven't been moping. And I haven't just been lifting weights. I've been reading. And I've been thinking about Bernardo."

"Really?"

"Yeah."

"What have you been thinking?"

"I think I want to start writing to him."

"He returned all my letters."

"Really? Maybe he won't return mine."

"Maybe not," she said. "It's a worth a try. Why not?"

"Did you stop writing?"

"Yes, I did, Ari. It hurt too much."

"That makes sense," I said.

"Just don't be too disappointed, Ari, okay? Don't expect too much. Your father went to see him once."

"What happened?"

"Your brother refused to see him."

"Does he hate you and Dad?"

"No. I don't think so. I think he's angry at himself. And I think he's ashamed."

"He should get over it." I don't know why, but I punched the wall.

My mother stared at me.

"I'm sorry," I said. "I don't know why I did that."

"Ari?"

"What?"

There was something in her face. That serious, concerned look. She wasn't angry, she wasn't wearing that stern look that she sometimes wore when she was playing mother. "What's wrong, Ari?"

"You say that like you have another theory about me."

"You bet your ass I do," she said. But her voice was so nice and kind and sweet. She got up from the kitchen table and poured herself a glass of wine. She took out two beers and put one of them in front of me. She put the other at the center of the table. "Your father's reading. I think I'll go get him."

"What's going on, Mom?"

"Family meeting."

"Family meeting? What's that?"

"It's a new thing," she said. "From here on in, we're going to have a lot more of them."

344

"You're scaring me, Mom."

"Good." She walked out of the kitchen. I stared at the beer in front of me. I touched the cold glass. I didn't know if I was supposed to drink from it or just stare at it. Maybe it was all a trick. My mom and dad walked into the kitchen. They both sat down across from me. My father opened his beer. Then he opened mine. He took a sip.

"Are you ganging up on me?"

"Relax," my father said. He took another drink from his beer. My mother sipped on her wine. "Don't you want to have a beer with your mom and dad?"

"Not really," I said. "It's against the rules."

"New rules," my mother said.

"A beer with your old man isn't going to kill you. It's not as if you haven't had one before. What's the big deal?"

"This is really weird," I said. I took a drink from the beer. "Happy now?"

My father had a really serious look on his face. "Did I ever you tell you about any of my skirmishes while I was in Vietnam?"

"Oh, yeah," I said. "I was just thinking about all those war stories you tell me about."

My father reached over and took my hand in his. "I deserved that one." He kept squeezing my hand. Then he let go.

"We were in the north. North of Da Nang."

"Is that where you were, Da Nang?"

"That was my home away from home." He smiled at me crookedly. "We were on a reconnaissance mission. Things were pretty quiet for a few days. It was monsoon season. God, I hated those endless rains. We were just ahead of a convoy. The area had been cleared. We were there to make sure the coast was clear. Then all hell broke loose. There were bullets all over the place. Grenades going off. We were pretty much ambushed. It wasn't the first time. But this time was different.

"There was shooting from all sides. The best thing to do was just fall back. Beckett called for a chopper to get us out. There was this guy. A really good guy. God, he was so young. Nineteen years old. God, he was just a boy." My father shook his head. "His name was Louie. Cajun guy from Lafayette." There were tears running down my father's face. He sipped on his beer. "We weren't supposed to leave a man down. That was the rule. You don't leave a man down. You don't leave a man to die." I could see the look on my mother's face, her absolute refusal to cry. "I remember running toward the chopper, Louie was right behind me, bullets flying everywhere. I thought I was a dead man. And then Louie went down. He yelled my name. I wanted to go back. I don't remember exactly, but the last thing I remember was Beckett pulling me onto the chopper. I didn't even know I'd been shot. We left him there. Louie. We left him." I watched my father lean into his own arms and sob. There was something about the sound of a man in pain that resembled the sound of a wounded animal. My heart was breaking. All this time, I'd wanted my father to tell me something about the war and now I couldn't stand to see the rawness of his pain, how new it was after so many years, how that pain was alive and thriving just beneath the surface.

"I don't know if I believed in the war or not, Ari. I don't think I did. I think about it a lot. But I signed up. And I don't know what I felt about this country. I *do* know that the only country I had were the men that fought side by side. They were my country, Ari. Them. Louie and Beckett and Garcia and Al and Gio—they were my country. I'm not proud of everything I did in that war. I wasn't always a good soldier. I wasn't always a good man. War did something to us. To me. To all of us. But the men we left behind. Those are the ones who are in my dreams."

I drank my beer. My father drank from his. My mother drank from her glass of wine. We were all silent for what seemed a long time.

"I hear him sometimes," my father said. "Louie. I hear him calling my name. I didn't go back."

"You would've been killed too," I whispered.

"Maybe. But I didn't do my job."

"Dad, don't. Please—" I felt my mother reaching across the table, combing my hair with her hands and wiping my tears. "You don't have to talk about this, Dad. You don't."

"Maybe I do. Maybe it's time to stop the dreams." He leaned on my mother. "Don't you think it's time, Lilly?"

My mother didn't say a word.

My father smiled at me. "A few minutes ago your mother walked into the living room and took the book I was reading out of my hands. And she said: 'Talk to him. Talk to him, Jaime.' She put on that fascist voice of hers she has."

My mother laughed softly.

"Ari, it's time you stopped running."

I looked at my dad. "From what?"

"Don't you know?"

"What?"

"If you keep running, it will kill you."

"What, Dad?"

"You and Dante."

"Me and Dante?" I looked at my mother. Then looked at my father.

"Dante's in love with you," he said. "That's obvious enough. He doesn't hide that from himself."

"I can't help what he feels, Dad."

"No. No, you can't."

"And besides, Dad, I think he's gotten way over that. He's into that guy, Daniel."

My father nodded. "Ari, the problem isn't just that Dante's in love with you. The real problem—for you, anyway—is that you're in love with him."

I didn't say anything. I just kept looking at my mother's face. And then my father's face.

I didn't know what to say. "I'm not sure, I mean, I don't think that's true. I mean, I just don't think so. I mean—"

"Ari, I know what I see. You saved his life. Why do you suppose you did that? Why do you suppose that, in an instant, without even thinking, you dove across the street and shoved Dante out of the way of a moving car? You think that just happened? I think you couldn't stand the thought of losing him. You just couldn't. Why would you risk your own life to save Dante if you didn't love him?"

348

"Because he's my friend."

"And why would you go and beat the holy crap out of a guy who hurt him? Why would you do that? All of your instincts, Ari, all of them, tell me something. You love that boy."

I kept staring down at the table.

"I think you love him more than you can bear."

"Dad? Dad, no. No. I can't. I can't. Why are you saying these things?"

"Because I can't stand watching all that loneliness that lives inside you. Because I love you, Ari." My mother and father watched me cry. I thought maybe I was going to cry forever. But I didn't. When I stopped, I took a big drink from my beer. "Dad, I think I liked it better when you didn't talk."

My mother laughed. I loved her laugh. And then my father was laughing. And then I was laughing.

"What am I going to do? I'm so ashamed."

"Ashamed of what?" my mother said. "Of loving Dante?"

"I'm a guy. He's a guy. It's not the way things are supposed to be. Mom—"

"I know," she said. "Ophelia taught me some things, you know? All those letters. I've learned some things. And your father's right. You can't run. Not from Dante."

"I hate myself."

"Don't, *amor. Te adoro.* I've already lost a son. I'm not going to lose another. You're not alone, Ari. I know it feels that way. But you're not."

"How can you love me so much?"

"How could I not love you? You're the most beautiful boy in the world."

"I'm not."

"You are. *You are.*"

"What am I going to do?"

My father's voice was soft. "Dante didn't run. I keep picturing him taking all those blows. But he didn't run."

"Okay," I said. For once in my life, I understood my father perfectly.

And *he* understood *me*.

Nineteen

"DANTE?"

"I've been calling you every day for the past five days."

"I have the flu."

"Bad joke. Screw you, Ari."

"Why are you so mad?"

"Why are *you* so mad?"

"I'm not mad anymore."

"So maybe it's my turn to be mad."

"Okay, that's fair. How's Daniel?"

"You're a piece of crap, Ari."

"No. Daniel's a piece of crap."

"He doesn't like you."

"I don't like him either. So, is he like your new best friend?"

"Not even close."

"You guys been kissing?"

"What's it to you?"

"Just asking."

"I don't want to kiss him. He's nothing."

"So what happened?"

"He's a self-involved, conceited, piece of shit. And he's not even smart. And my mother doesn't like him."

"What does Sam think of him?"

"Dad doesn't count. He likes everybody."

That really made me laugh.

"Don't laugh. Why were you mad?"

"We can talk about it," I said.

"Yeah, like you're so good at that."

"Give me a break, Dante."

"Okay."

"Okay. So what are you doing tonight?"

"Our parents are going bowling."

"They are?"

"They talk a lot."

"They do?"

"Don't you know anything?"

"I guess I'm a little aloof sometimes."

"A little?"

"I'm trying here, Dante."

"Say you're sorry. I don't like people who don't know how to say they're sorry."

"Okay. I'm sorry."

"Okay." I could tell he was smiling. "They want us to go along."

"Bowling?"

Twenty

DANTE WAS SITTING ON THE FRONT PORCH, WAITING. He bounced down the steps and hopped in the truck. "Bowling sounds really boring."

"Have you ever gone?"

"Of course I have. I'm not good at it."

"Do you have to be good at everything?"

"Yes."

"Get over it. Maybe we'll have fun."

"Since when do you want to hang out with your parents?"

"They're okay," I said. "They're good. Something you said."

"What?"

"You said you'd never run away from home because you were crazy about your parents. I thought it was a really weird thing to say. I mean, not normal. I mean, I thought parents were aliens, I guess."

"They're not. They're just people."

"Yeah. You know, I think I've changed my mind about my mom and dad."

"You mean you're crazy about them."

"Yeah. I guess so." I started the truck. "I'm a pretty shitty bowler too. Just so you know."

"I bet we're better than our mothers."

"We sure as hell better be."

We laughed. And laughed. And laughed.

When we got to the bowling alley, Dante looked at me and said, "I told my mom and dad that I never, ever wanted to kiss another guy for the rest of my life."

"You told them that?"

"Yeah."

"What did they say?"

"My dad rolled his eyes."

"What did your mom say?"

"Not much. She said she knew a really good therapist. 'He'll help you come to terms,' she said. And then she said, 'Unless you want to talk to me instead.'" He looked at me. We busted out laughing.

"Your mom," I said. "I like her."

"She's tough as hell," he said. "But soft, too."

"Yeah," I said. "I noticed that."

"Our parents are really weird," he said.

"Because they love us? That's not so weird."

"It's how they love us that's weird."

"Beautiful," I said.

Dante looked at me. "You're different."

"How?"

"I don't know. You're acting different."

"Weird?"

"Yeah, weird. But in a good way."

"Good," I said, "I've always wanted to be weird in a good way."

I think our parents were really surprised to see that we'd actually showed up. Our fathers were drinking beer. Our mothers were drinking 7UP. Their scores were lousy. Sam smiled at us. "I didn't think you guys would actually show up."

"We were bored," I said.

"I liked you better when you weren't such a smart aleck."

"Sorry," I said.

It was fun. We had fun. It turned out I was the best bowler. I bowled over 120. And my third game I bowled 135. Terrible, really, when you think about it. But the rest of the crew really sucked. Especially my mom and Mrs. Quintana. They talked a lot. And laughed a lot. Dante and I kept looking at each other and laughing.

Twenty-One

WHEN DANTE AND I LEFT THE BOWLING ALLEY, I DROVE the truck toward the desert.

"Where are we going?"

"My favorite hangout."

Dante was quiet. "It's late."

"You tired?"

"Sort of."

"It's just ten o'clock. Get up early, do you?"

"Wiseass."

"Unless you want to just go home."

"No."

"Okay."

Dante didn't put in any music. He thumbed through my box full of cassette tapes, but couldn't settle on anything. I didn't mind the quiet.

We just drove into the desert. Me and Dante. Not saying anything.

I parked in my usual spot.

"I love it here," I said. I could hear the beating of my own heart.

Dante didn't say anything.

I touched the tennis shoes he'd sent me that were hanging from my rearview mirror. "I love these things," I said.

"You love a lot of things, don't you?'

"You sound mad. I thought you weren't mad anymore."

"I think *I am* mad."

"I'm sorry. I said I was sorry."

"I can't do this, Ari," he said.

"Can't do what?"

"This whole friend thing. I can't do it."

"Why not?"

"I have to explain it to you?"

I didn't say anything.

He got out of the truck and slammed the door. I followed after him. "Hey," I said. I touched his shoulder.

He pushed me away. "I don't like it when you touch me."

We stood there for long time. Neither one of us said anything. I felt small and insignificant and inadequate. I hated feeling that way. I was going to stop feeling that way. *I was going to stop.* "Dante?"

"What?" I could hear the anger in his voice.

"Don't be mad."

"I don't know what to do, Ari."

"Remember that time you kissed me?"

"Yeah."

"Remember I said it didn't work for me?"

"Why are you bringing this up? I remember. I remember. Dammit to hell, Ari, did you think I'd forgotten?"

"I've never seen you this mad."

"I don't want to talk about that, Ari. It just makes me feel bad."

"What did I say when you kissed me?"

"You said it didn't work for you."

"I lied."

He looked at me.

"Don't play with me, Ari."

"I'm not."

I took him by the shoulders. I looked at him. And he looked at me. "You said I wasn't scared of anything. That's not true. *You*. That's what I'm afraid of. I'm afraid of you, Dante." I took a deep breath. "Try it again," I said. "Kiss me."

"No," he said.

"Kiss me."

"No." And then he smiled. "*You* kiss *me*."

I placed my hand on the back of his neck. I pulled him toward me. And kissed him. I kissed him. And I kissed him. And I kissed him. And I kissed him. And he kept kissing me back.

We laughed and we talked and looked up at the stars.

"I wished it was raining," he said.

"I don't need the rain," I said. "I need you."

He traced his name on my back. I traced my name on his.

All this time.

This was what was wrong with me. All this time I had been trying to figure out the secrets of the universe, the secrets of my own body, of my own heart. All of the answers had always been so close and yet I had always fought them without even knowing it. From the minute I'd met Dante, I had fallen in love with him. I just didn't let myself know it, think it, feel it. My father was right. And it was true what my mother said. We all fight our own private wars.

As Dante and I lay on our backs in the bed of my pickup and gazed out at the summer stars, I was free. Imagine that. Aristotle Mendoza, a free man. I wasn't afraid anymore. I thought of that look on my mother's face when I'd told her I was ashamed. I thought of that look of love and compassion that she wore as she looked at me. "Ashamed? Of loving Dante?"

I took Dante's hand and held it.

How could I have ever been ashamed of loving Dante Quintana?

In *Aristotle and Dante Discover the Secrets of the Universe*, two boys in a border town fell in love. Now, they must discover what it means to stay in love in the highly anticipated sequel, *Aristotle and Dante Dive into the Waters of the World*.

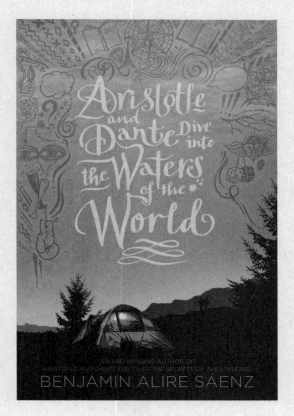

Turn the page for a sneak peek.

And here he was, Dante, with his head resting on my chest. In the stillness of the dawn, there was only the sound of Dante's breathing. It was as though the universe had stopped whatever it was doing just to look down on two boys who had discovered its secrets.

As I felt the beating of Dante's heart against the palm of my hand, I wished that I could somehow reach into my chest and rip out my own heart and show Dante everything that it held.

And then there was this: Love didn't just have something to do with my heart—it had something to do with my body. And my body had never felt so alive. And then I *knew*, I finally knew about this thing called desire.

I hated to wake him. But this moment had to end. We couldn't live in the back of my pickup forever. It was late, and already it was another day, and we had to get home, and our parents would be worried. I kissed the top of his head. "Dante? Dante? Wake up."

"I don't ever want to wake up," he whispered.

"We have to go home."

"I'm already home. I'm with you."

That made me smile. Such a Dante thing to say.

'C'mon, let's get going. It looks like rain. And your mother's going to kill us."

Dante laughed. "She won't kill us. We'll just get one of her looks."

I pulled him up and we both stood there, looking up at the sky. He took my hand. "Will you always love me?"

"Yes."

"And did you love me from the very beginning, the way that I loved you?"

"Yes, I think so. I think I did. It's harder for me, Dante. You have to understand that. It will always be harder for me."

"Not everything is that complicated, Ari."

"Not everything is as simple as you think it is."

He was about to say something, so I just kissed him. To shut him up, I think. But also because I liked kissing him.

He smiled. "You finally figured out a way to win an argument with me."

"Yup," I said.

"It'll work for a while," he said.

"We don't always have to agree," I said.

"That's true."

"I'm glad you're not like me, Dante. If you were like me, I wouldn't love you."

"Did you say you love me?" He was laughing.

"Cut it out."

"Cut what out?" he said. And then he kissed me. "You taste like the rain," he said.

"I love the rain more than anything."

"I know. I want to be the rain."

"You *are* the rain, Dante." And I wanted to say *You're the rain and you're the desert and you're the eraser that's making the word "loneliness" disappear*. But it was too much to say and I would always be the guy that would say too little and Dante was the kind of guy who would always say too much.

We didn't say anything on the drive back home.

Dante was quiet. Maybe too quiet. He, who was always so full of words, who knew what to say and how to say it without being afraid. And then the thought came to me that maybe Dante had always been afraid—just like me. It was as if we had both walked into a room together and we didn't know what to do in that room. Or maybe, or maybe, or maybe. I just couldn't stop thinking about things. I wondered if there would ever come a time when I would stop thinking about things.

And then I heard Dante's voice: "I wish I were a girl."

I just looked at Dante. "What? Wanting to be a girl is serious business. You really wish you were a girl?"

"No. I mean, I like being a guy. I mean, I like having a penis."

"I like having one too."

And then he said, "But, at least, if I were a girl, then we could get married and, you know—"

"That's not ever gonna happen."

"I know, Ari."

"Don't be sad."

"I won't be."

But I knew he would be.

And then I put on the radio and Dante started singing with Eric

Clapton and he whispered that "My Father's Eyes" was maybe his new favorite song. "Waiting for my prince to come," he whispered. And he smiled.

And he asked me, "Why don't you ever sing?"

"Singing means that you're happy."

"You're not happy?"

"Maybe only when I'm with you."

I loved when I said something that made Dante smile.

When we pulled up in front of his house, the sun was on the verge of showing its face to the new day. And that's just how it felt—like a new day. But I was thinking that maybe I would never again know—or be sure of—what the new day would bring. And I didn't want Dante to know that there was any fear living inside me at all because he might think that I didn't love him.

I would never show him that I was afraid. That's what I told myself. But I knew I couldn't keep that promise.

"I want to kiss you," he said.

"I know."

He closed his eyes. "Let's pretend we're kissing."

I smiled—then laughed as he closed his eyes.

"You're laughing at me."

"No, I'm not. I'm kissing you."

He smiled and looked at me. His eyes were filled with such hope. He jumped out of the truck and shut the door. He stuck his head through the open window. "I see a longing in you, Aristotle Mendoza."

"A longing?"

"Yes. A yearning."

"A yearning?

He laughed. "Those words live in you. Look them up."

I watched him as he bounded up the steps. He moved with the grace of the swimmer that he was. There was no weight or worry in his step.

He turned around and waved, wearing that smile of his. I wondered if his smile would be enough.

God, let his smile be enough.

I don't think I'd ever felt this tired. I fell on my bed—but sleep didn't feel like paying me a visit.

Legs jumped up beside me and licked my face. She nudged closer when she heard the storm outside. I wondered what Legs made up in her head about thunder or if dogs even thought about things like that. But me, I was happy for the thunder. This year, such beautiful storms, the most beautiful storms I'd ever known. I must have nodded off to sleep because, when I woke, it was pouring outside.

I decided to have a cup of coffee. My mom was sitting at the kitchen table, cup of coffee in one hand, a letter in the other.

"Hi," I whispered.

"Hi," she said, that same smile on her face.

"You got in late."

"Or early—if you think about it."

"For a mother, early is late."

"Were you worried?

"It's in my nature to worry."

"So you're like Mrs. Quintana."

"It might surprise you to know that we have a lot of things in common."

"Yeah," I said, "you both think your sons are the most beautiful boys in the world. You don't get out much, do you, Mom?"

She reached over and combed my hair with her fingers. And then she had that look that was waiting for an explanation.

"Dante and I fell asleep in the back of my pickup. We didn't . . ." I stopped, and then I just shrugged. "We didn't do anything."

She nodded. "This is hard, isn't it?"

"Yes," I said. "Is it supposed to be hard, Mom?"

She nodded. "Love is easy and it's hard. It was that way with me and your father. I wanted him to touch me so much. And I was so afraid."

I nodded. "But at least—"

"At least I was a girl and he was a boy."

"Yeah." She just looked at me in that same kind of way that she had always looked at me. And I wondered if I could ever look at anybody like that, a look that held all the good things that existed in the known universe.

"Why, Mom? Why do I have to be this way? Maybe I'll change and then like girls like I'm supposed to like them? I mean, maybe what me and Dante feel—it's like a phase. I mean, I only feel this way about Dante. So what if I don't really like boys—I only like Dante because he's Dante."

She almost smiled. "Don't kid yourself, Ari. You can't think your way out of this one."

"How can you be so casual about this, Mom?"

"Casual? I'm anything but. I went through a lot of struggles with myself about your aunt Ophelia. But I loved her. I loved her more than I'd ever loved anyone outside of you and your sisters and your father." She paused. "And your brother."

"My brother, too?"

"Just because I don't talk about him doesn't mean that I don't think about him. My love for him is silent. There are a thousand things living in that silence."

I was going to have to give that some thought. I was beginning to see the world in a different way just by listening to her. To listen to her voice was to listen to her love.

"I guess you could say that this isn't my first time at bat." She had that fierce and stubborn look on her face. "You're my son. And your father and I have decided that silence is not an option. Look at what the silence regarding your brother has done to us—not just to you, but to all of us. We're not going to repeat that mistake."

"Does that mean I have to talk about everything?"

I could see the tears welling up in her eyes and hear the softness in her voice as she said, "Not everything. But I don't want you to feel that you're living in exile. There's a world out there that's going to make you feel like that you don't belong in this country—or any other country, for that matter. But in this house, Ari, there is only belonging. You belong to us. And we belong to you."

"But isn't it wrong to be gay? Everybody seems to think so."

"Not everybody. That's a cheap and mean morality. Your aunt Ophelia took the words *I don't belong* and wrote them on her heart. It took her a long time to take those words and throw them out of her body. She threw out those words one letter as a time. She wanted to know why. She wanted to change—but she couldn't. She met a man. He loved her. Who wouldn't love a woman like Ophelia? But she couldn't do it, Ari. She wound up hurting him because she could never love him like she loved Franny. Her life was something of a secret. And that's sad, Ari. Your aunt Ophelia was a beautiful person. She taught me so much about what really matters."

"What am I gonna do, Mom?"

"Do you know what a cartographer is?"

"Of course I do. Dante taught me that word. It's someone who creates maps. I mean, they don't create what's there, they just map it out and, well, show people what's there."

"That's it, then," she said. "You and Dante are going to map out a new world."

"And we're going to get a lot of things wrong and we're going to have to keep it all a secret, aren't we?"

"I'm sorry that the world is what it is. But you'll learn how to survive—and you'll have to create a space where you're safe and learn to trust the right people. And you will find happiness. Even now, Ari, I see that Dante makes you happy. And that makes me happy—because I hate to see you be miserable. And you and Dante have us and Soledad and Sam. You have four people on your baseball team."

"Well, we need nine."

She laughed.

I wanted so much to lean into her and cry. Not because I was ashamed. But because I knew I was going to be a terrible cartographer.

And then I heard myself whisper, "Mom, why didn't anybody tell me that love hurts so much?"

"If I had told you, would it have changed anything?"

There wasn't much left of the summer. There seemed to be a few rainy days still to come before they went away and left us in our usual drought. While I was lifting weights in the basement, I wondered about picking up some kind of hobby. Maybe something to make me a better person or that would just get me out of my head. I wasn't good at anything, not really. Not like Dante, who was good at everything. I realized I didn't have any hobbies. My hobby was thinking about Dante. My hobby was feeling my whole body tremble when I thought of him.

Maybe my real hobby would be having to keep my whole life a secret. Was that a hobby? Millions of boys in the world would want to kill me, *would* kill me if they knew what lived inside me. Knowing how to fight—that was no hobby. It was a gift I just might need to survive.

I took a shower and decided to make a list of things I wanted to do:

- ~~Learn to play the guitar~~

I crossed out *Learn to play the guitar* because I knew I would never be good at it. I wasn't cut out to be Andrés Segovia. Or Jimi Hendrix. So I just got on with my list.

- Apply for college
- Read more
- Listen to more music

- Go on a trip (maybe at least go camping—with Dante?)
- Write in a journal every day (try anyway)
- Write a poem (stupid)
- ~~Make love to Dante~~

I crossed that out. But I couldn't cross it out of my mind. You couldn't cross out desire when it lived in your body.

I got to thinking about Dante and how he must have been so afraid when those assholes jumped him and left him there on the ground, bleeding. What if he had died? They wouldn't have given a damn. And I wasn't there to protect him. I should have been there. I couldn't forgive myself for not being there.

RIVETED

BY *simon* teen ♥

BELIEVE IN YOUR SHELF

Visit RivetedLit.com & connect with us on social to:

- **DISCOVER** NEW YA READS
- **READ** BOOKS FOR FREE
- **DISCUSS** YOUR FAVORITES
- **SHARE** YOUR IDEAS
- **ENTER SWEEPSTAKES** FOR THE CHANCE TO WIN BOOKS

Follow @SimonTeen on

to stay up to date with all things Riveted!